A Dance of Sugarplums and Power Plays

A Nutcracker Retelling

Jess Christine

Ebook ISBN:979-8-9904385-6-9

Paperback ISBN: 979-8-9904385-7-6

Cover designed by Kimberly Sable | KBG Designs

Editing by Tina Otero

Formatting by Kalie Gerwig | Good Girl Author Services

Chapter Images by Kimberly Sable | KBG Designs

Map Illustration by Francesca Weber

Playlist

Please click the link or scan the QR Code below for the link to the Spotify Playlist created for *A Dance of Sugarplums and Power Plays.*

Dear Reader

This may sound a bit cliché, but I've always loved the Christmas season. There's magic this time of year that can be found if you look hard enough, and I think it's so important to continue to believe that it's there—even on the days it feels just out of reach. From the twinkling lights and holiday romances read by the fire to the promise of snow, this season has always been my favorite.

One of my most treasured traditions is watching *The Nutcracker.* Before our daughter was born, my husband surprised me with tickets to see it at The Fox Theater in Atlanta. He bought me a new dress, took me to dinner, and then to the show. It was a perfect evening and one I still hold close to my heart. The dancers were mesmerizing, the music filled me with warmth, and for a few hours, it truly felt as though we were witnessing Christmas magic come to life.

Now, years later, we have the joy of watching our daughter perform *The Nutcracker* each holiday season with her dance studio. Seeing her on stage, doing something she loves, is its own kind of magic.

My goal was to write something that felt like drinking a cup of hot chocolate by a Christmas tree and roaring fire, all the while getting railed by a pierced and tattooed hockey player with a dirty mouth and a soft spot for the girl he loves.

So pour yourself a favorite holiday drink, curl up by the Christmas tree, and get ready to meet Everett Nuttall—he's waiting for you!

A Dance of Sugarplums and Power Plays is the first interconnected standalone novel in the Fairytale Season series. This story has been years in the making and has evolved in ways I never could've imagined when I first jotted the idea down in my phone. I'm really proud of the final version and excited to share it with you. Please note, while this is a Christmas story, it is intended for persons eighteen years or older and does contain mature language and explicit open door/ sexual content.

Contents

DICKTIONARY

For those readers who want to skip the smut or go straight to it, do with this list what you will.

Sugarplum Park
Stella's
The Book Rack
Dew Drops & Daisies
THE MUSIC BOX
GUM DROP SUGAR SHOP

Pirouettes and Plies
Citrine BREWS
COFFEE & TEA
Drosselmeyer's DOLLS
the Chocolate Bar
sweets

PROLOGUE
EVERETT

FOUR AND A HALF YEARS AGO - JUNE

"Is that all you got?" Claire bites out as I wrap my fist in her long, raven hair. Rocking my hips forward, I take in the sight before me. She's hot as hell when she gives me shit and lets me fuck her like this—bent over her kitchen counter.

She gasps as my other hand connects with the soft skin of her ass in a slap. "Don't be a brat," I say, immediately soothing the spot that's now a little red.

My hand trails over her hip, pulling her back into me and deepening my thrusts. She lets out a moan, and tension coils at the base of my spine. "I need more," she says, a little annoyed.

"Tell me what you want, Sugar."

At the word *sugar,* she pops off my dick and spins around so we're facing each other.

"I said no nicknames and I meant it," she scolds, tilting her head upward, pressing her lips together and pushing a finger into my chest.

When we started this six months ago, we both made promises.

No nicknames.

No sleepovers.

No strings attached.

"But you're sexy when I make you mad," I say, stepping toward her so our bodies are touching. My condom-wrapped dick presses into her abdomen, aching with need. "You gonna stand there mad at me, *Sugar*, or are you gonna let me finish fucking the bad day you had right out of you? I don't have all night." My lips curl into a smirk.

She rolls her eyes, but despite her irritation, her breath still hitches when my arm wraps around her waist. Picking her up, I sit her on the faux granite surface, and she cuts her eyes, causing me to chuckle.

Bending down slightly, my lips find the pulse point on her neck, and I kiss her gently, causing her peach skin to erupt with goose-bumps. "Would hate to ruin our last night together…" I trail my tongue from her shoulder to her ear. Dropping my voice to a whisper, I finish, "because I made you *mad*."

"God," she huffs out. "You really are so incredibly…" Her voice trails off when I rake my teeth over her earlobe. One of my fingers finds her slick center. Dragging a finger upward, I stop to tease her clit.

"What was that, Claire? I'm so incredibly…what?"

"Irritating," she stammers, despite trying her best to pretend like my touch doesn't affect her.

"I thought I told you to stop being a brat," I say, pushing one finger in and then adding another.

Her breath catches as I curl them deep inside her, and she does her best to maintain her composure, but she's soaked, letting me know just how much I'm turning her on.

"So what if I am. It's not like you'll do anything about it," she quips, her words wavering slightly and her blue eyes finding mine with a daring stare.

I remove my fingers from between her thighs in a quick motion.

"Why'd you stop?" she chides.

"Brats don't get rewarded," I say, raking my hands over her hips. Gripping her ass, I yank her to the edge of the counter.

Leaning back slightly on her hands, she hooks one of her legs around my back, pulling me closer.

"Have I ever told you how much I like that you're a ballerina?" My left hand trails down her other leg until it gets to her ankle. "How hot it is when I can bend you any way I like?" I lift it, placing it over my shoulder.

Her hand reaches forward and grasps my length, lining me up. "Stop playing around and fuck me, Ev."

"I thought you said no nicknames." I quirk my eyebrow upward. "Does that mean you're done being a brat?"

She shakes her head slowly. "Never."

"Good," I say, wrapping one of my hands around the column of her throat and pushing my hips forward. Her pussy tightens around the head of my dick and the silver stud that adorns it as I stretch her slowly. The sensation is maddening. "Is this what you want, Claire? Want my hand around your throat and my cock between your thighs?"

"Fuck...yes," she says, our breaths becoming heavy as I continue to push forward, tilting my hips so that the smooth balls of my piercing hit her most sensitive spot just right.

Her head lolls back, and the look on her face is euphoric. Pupils blown and cheeks flushed. Her onyx hair cascading down her back.

"Fuck."

Thrust.

"Look."

Thrust.

"At."

Thrust.

"You."

My grip tightens ever so slightly around her neck.

"Yes," she breathes out.

"You like that?"

"God, yes."

Pulling out slightly, I ram my hips forward, and she yells out my name. Again and again, we continue to move against each other, one of my hands firmly on her hip and the other still gripping the column of her throat.

"That's it; *use me*, Sugar. Take everything you need."

Her heel digs into me as she tugs me closer, taking me deeper. "Fuck," she breathes out. We continue to move in tandem. Her chest rises and falls as her eyes find where we connect, and she watches as I fuck her.

"Let go," I say. "I want to feel you choke my cock." I pull her into me, rotating my hips again to get the perfect angle. Yelling out my name, her pussy tightens around my dick as she falls, and I unload into the condom.

We pause for a moment, catching our breaths. My hand moves

from her neck and pushes a strand of fallen hair behind her ear. Her throat bobs up and down as our eyes meet.

Neither of us speaks for a long moment, lost in each other's stare. Leaning down, I try to kiss her, but she moves before I can, and disappointment settles into my chest.

"Well, that was hot," she says, nonchalantly, removing her leg from my shoulder and popping off the counter. I watch as she moves toward her bathroom, swiping my dress shirt from the floor. She pulls it on as she walks, untucking her black waves from below the collar so they fall down her back.

"That's mine," I say.

The bathroom door shuts in response, and I'm reminded that I'm leaving tomorrow, officially ending our arrangement. I throw the condom into the trash and move around the small studio apartment, looking for the rest of my clothes.

Pulling on my pants, I look up to find her walking back towards me. The top few buttons of my shirt remain unbuttoned, and it completely swallows her tiny frame.

"For someone who claims not to like me most days, you sure like stealing my clothes," I say, chuckling.

"Don't be so dramatic." She laughs. Walking over to her dresser, she digs in her drawer until she pulls out my old, worn New York Crowns T-shirt and tosses it in my direction.

"I'm leaving tomorrow. You sure you want the button down over the comfy sleep shirt. You can only keep one. I need something to wear in Texas."

She inhales and exhales an annoyed breath, beginning to unbutton the shirt.

"You know, if you wanted to see my tits one more time, you could've just asked." She smirks, slowly pulling it from her shoulders, revealing her bare body and tossing it at my head. "Give me the T-shirt."

"Ask nicely." The corner of my mouth tips upward.

"You're insufferable." She scoffs. "Can I please have the T-shirt, asshole?" She extends her arm outward and gestures impatiently.

"Always such a brat." I throw the shirt towards her, and she catches it before pulling it over her head. "You know, now that I've been traded, you're gonna have to get yourself a Stallions shirt."

"I'm pretty loyal to New York, and I don't see that changing any time soon," she says. "What time do you leave tomorrow?"

"Early."

"Hmm," she hums, running her hand through her hair.

"Don't tell me after months of not liking me, you're gonna miss me."

"Ha! Your dick? Yes. But you? Not a chance." She shakes her head. "Call me if you're ever back in New York," she says, walking towards her door.

"Kicking me out already?"

Her eyes flit to the clock on the microwave. "Everett, this was fun, but I don't do goodbyes well, and you're leaving tomorrow, and we'll probably never see each other again."

Something foreign tugs at my heart, and for a split second I consider staying. Maybe taking her to dinner and giving our one very bad date a do-over, so we can say goodbye properly, but I know that would complicate our little arrangement, and that's not what we are. We were always supposed to be temporary. A blip— one star in the midst of an expansive night sky. Burning fast and bright, until it dimmed completely and we moved on from each other.

"You know Charlotte is going to be back soon," she continues, opening the door.

"Hiding me from your roommate?"

"No." She shakes her head. "It's just getting late, and she and I will have to be up early tomorrow for rehearsals."

"Yeah, okay," I agree. "You're right. If you're ever in Texas…"

"Yeah," she says, a small smile ghosting across her lips. "Then, I'll call."

It's an empty promise, and we both know it. There's another pause, and I pull her into a hug and kiss her forehead. "Bye, Sugar."

"Bye, Ev."

Pulling away, I turn and walk down the hall, doing my best not to look back at the girl I'm leaving behind because, despite my original thoughts about her, I think I might actually miss having her in my life. But we both said we wouldn't fall, and I've always been a man of my word.

ACT 1:
New York

CHAPTER 1: CHRISTMAS?

CLAIRE

"You wanted to see me before I left?" I ask, tapping on the glass window of our creative director, Dimitri's, door.

"Oh, yes. Come in. Come in." He closes his laptop and peers up from behind his desk. His dark hair is laced with strands of gray and is parted to one side. He's dressed in a black turtleneck that contrasts against his pale skin, and his wire-framed glasses sit low on his long, thin nose. "I thought you'd left. It's pretty late to still be here, even for you." He checks his watch and then looks back up at me.

"Well, you know what they say—practice makes perfect," I answer, shrugging and moving into his small, dimly lit office. Papers are scattered all over the top of the desk, and costume sketches for our spring performance of *Sleeping Beauty* are taped to the wall. My eyes land on the sketch of the Lilac Fairy's costume, and hope blooms in my chest that one day, if I stay focused, I'll get to wear it.

"I've noticed how hard you've been working," he muses. "And I've been very impressed by your work ethic since you were promoted."

"Thank you," I say, playing with the initial charm dangling from the chain around my neck. "I have really big goals. And my hope is that if I continue to put in the work, then I'll reach them."

"Like the Sugar Plum Fairy?"

His question catches me off guard. It's no secret that I wanted that part and was devastated when I didn't get it, but this is the first time he's acknowledging my disappointment.

"Well, yes, but I'm enjoying the role of understudy, and of course performing as the Snow Queen is an honor." The lie slips out easily, and I try to mask my face with a smile. At twenty-nine, I should've earned a better role by now, and it's a little embarrassing to have been given understudy to a dancer three years younger than me.

He hums to himself and spins one of the many gold and silver rings that decorate his long fingers.

"Are you a hockey fan?" he asks, eyeing the custom purple and black puffer jacket I'm wearing. The New York Rat Kings emblem is stitched across the chest, and the number seven sits below the name Ulrich across the back.

"Sort of. My boyfriend plays for the Rats, and tonight is one of the only home games that I can make."

The feelings I was trying to dance away all day in the studio return. I internally scold myself for not ending rehearsal earlier, but I know something deep inside me is avoiding this game because I know who else will be there. Some might call it serendipity or kismet, that the one game I'm able to attend this season just so happens to be the game that Everett Nuttall will also be playing in, but it feels more like some type of joke. Like the powers that be are sitting on their thrones and laughing at this predicament I'm finding myself in tonight.

It's been a long time since he and I were in the same place, and while, realistically, the odds of him seeing me tonight are slim, I know I will certainly see him. My stomach flips at the thought, and then guilt follows because that's not something that should make me excited. I should be excited to see the man whose number I'm wearing. The man who will be sleeping in my bed when it's all over. But there has always been something about Everett. Even when I thought I hated him, I couldn't stay away.

"I see; well I won't keep you very long. You're a very talented dancer, Claire, and it's why it was an easy decision to make you the Snow Queen and Marie's understudy for the Sugar Plum Fairy."

I push down the embarrassment, forcing another smile in response to the half-compliment.

"Thank you." There's another long pause, and I check the clock hanging on his wall. It's five forty-five. Andi is going to kill me for making her wait in the cold, and Raph is going to be so pissed if I miss the start of his game. "Is there anything else—" I begin, suddenly feeling the urge to get out of here before I make anyone angry with me.

"Yes," he begins. "The reason I asked to see you today was because this morning I spoke with Marie about her ankle." My heart rate begins to climb as he speaks, anticipation rising in my throat. "As you may know, two nights ago, she finished her performance despite taking a nasty fall during rehearsal the day before, and it seems it's not getting better. According to her doctor, she needs to let it heal, or her career may end altogether."

I swallow down the excitement threatening to burst from my mouth. "Does that mean?"

"Yes, we need you to take over her role of the Sugar Plum Fairy for the foreseeable future," he says, plainly, as if he isn't making five-year-old me's dreams come true.

"Oh, my god. This is fantastic! I mean, not for Marie. Shit, I'm not saying it's great that she's hurt, but I've just wanted this role for as long as I can remember."

He fidgets with his rings as I attempt to rein myself in.

"Thank you. Thank you, Dimitri. I won't let you down. I've been dreaming of this my entire life. I promise you won't be disappointed."

"As you know, Marie was part of our A cast, which means she was my Sugar Plum for the Christmas performance."

"Christmas?"

Holy Fucking Shit. That's right. I get to dance as *the* Sugar Plum in *the* Christmas performance. Years of hard work and dedication, finally paying off. This feels like a dream.

"Yes, which, as I'm sure you know, is our most important performance of the season. Can I trust that you'll be ready?"

"Yes, of course. I'll be ready." My head spins with everything I need to do in order to prepare for this role. With what it could finally mean for my career. The weight of the opportunity settles deep in my bones. This is huge. This could be it for me. "Thank you."

He nods. "I'll let Harper know she will be taking over the Snow Queen for you, and I'll see you tomorrow for rehearsal."

I offer him a smile, then turn to head out of his office, feeling overwhelmed with excitement and nerves.

"Oh, and Claire?"

"Yes?" I pause, looking over my shoulder.

"If this goes well, then the part of the Lilac Fairy might be in your future." I hold back a squeal.

"Thank you. Seriously, thank you so much. I won't let you down," I promise, turning on my heels and hurrying down the hall until I know I'm out of his earshot.

Pulling out my phone from my purse, I click on my mom's contact and place it to my ear. "Come on, come on, pick up."

"Hold on, honey. It's Claire," she answers the phone, talking to my dad in the background. "Hi, sweetheart. Everything okay?"

"Yeah. Everything's great, actually. I have really good news," I whisper as I walk past a studio with an open door. There are a few dancers inside, but they're the last people who would care to hear my good news. "How would you and Dad feel about spending Christmas Eve in the city this year?"

"Hun, get in here. Claire Bear has news."

There's a shuffling on the other end of the phone, and I try to contain the excitement pulsing through my body.

"Alright, you're on speaker, and your dad can hear," she says.

"Hi, Bear."

"Hey, Dad."

"So, what's the good news, and why does it mean we'll have to venture into the city?" my mom asks.

"Well, you're talking to the new cast A Sugar Plum Fairy for The City Ballet," I gush, tears welling in my eyes as the words fall from my mouth. My mom shrieks so loud that I have to move the phone away from my ear.

"Incredible," my dad boasts. "Just incredible. I knew you could do it, kiddo."

"My next performance will be the Christmas show. Dimitri said if I do well, then he'd consider me for the Lilac Fairy in the spring, which would be insane."

"We're so proud of you," my mom chimes in, her voice cracking a little as she speaks.

"I was thinking I could put tickets aside for you two and Andi for the show, and then we could spend the holiday together here. It's a matinee, so we'd still have time for dad to cook dinner."

"And Raphael, right?" my mom questions, her voice returning to normal cadence. "If we're coming all the way to the city, we need to meet this new man of yours. I know your father has been dying to meet *the* Raphael Ulrich. Isn't that right, honey?"

"Definitely. We wouldn't miss your performance for the world, and we'd love to meet Raphael." my dad adds around a bite of some type of food.

"Okay," I say, my excitement turning to hesitation. "I know Raph has been meaning to come to a show. His hockey schedule makes it difficult, but I'll see if he can swing it."

"Sounds like the perfect way to spend Christmas," my mom says, clapping her hands together. "We're so proud of you, my sweet girl. You've worked so very hard, and this is very deserved."

"Thank you," I say, attempting to push the idea of convincing Raph to make time to meet my family aside. "I'm on my way to meet Andi, so she doesn't know yet."

"Mum's the word," my dad says. "We'll talk to you soon."

"We love you," my mom says.

"I love you both too."

Chapter 2: Fuck Me

The bitter cold hits me in the face the second I swing the doors open. It's not just cold. It's bone chilling, multiple layers of outerwear, need a hot beverage cold. It's the type of cold that immediately makes your cheeks sting and your nose run. A shiver snakes down my spine, and I pull my black beanie around my ears, smoothing my long waves so they fall on either side of my shoulders. The heels of my boots click against the concrete as I move quickly across the sidewalk.

It's amazing how you can feel like pure sunshine on the inside and still be at risk of freezing to death because of the weather.

The arena is less than thirty minutes away on foot, but I'm late and cold. Exhaustion covers my every move as I attempt to sort out the emotions flooding my head. Maybe I should go home and watch the game from the comfort of my couch, get some rest, and prepare for the week. This would also solve the problem of seeing Everett, but I don't know how I would even begin to explain to Raph why I wasn't there. He doesn't exactly take my career seriously, and I don't have it in me to deal with him moping around because I don't support him.

I make it to the curb and throw my hand in the air to signal for a cab. Pulling the jacket I'm wearing tight against me, I try to seal in the last bit of warmth I can, but it's no use. It was a gift from Raph, and while I'm sure it cost him a small fortune to have someone make his jersey into a stylish puffer jacket for me, it's not the most practical piece of outerwear in my closet, and the frigid air is creeping in through the seams and settling deep in my bones. I really should've layered better.

My phone vibrates, but I ignore it. Whoever it is can wait until I'm somewhere warm. A cab zips through traffic, then pulls up next to the curb. Swinging the door open, I climb inside.

"Where to?" the driver asks.

"Madison Square Garden."

The car begins to move as I settle into my seat, grabbing my phone out of my pocket. Two missed calls from my sister, Andi, flash across the screen.

> I'm on my way. Sorry, I've got huge news and I got caught up at the studio!

ANDI:

> News?!? Spill!

> No, it needs to be shared in person!

ANDI:

> Ugh, you and your surprises…hurry up! I'm about to turn into the human version of an icicle.

I do my best to quiet my head, trying to focus on the good news I was just given instead of the idea that my past and present will literally be colliding three feet in front of me tonight. Snow begins to fall, and as I rest my head against the glass, I watch as it accumulates against the cold surface.

There is something about the snow that I've always loved. It seems to slow the city down and wrap it in magic, turning it into a picturesque postcard. Waking up to untouched blankets of white is one of my favorite things, especially this time of year. With the holidays right around the corner, a December snow seems to add to the enchantment and nostalgia of the Christmas season.

"It's snowing," the driver says.

"I see that."

"I'm Stella, by the way" she says, turning to face me when she comes to a stop at a traffic light.

Her round face glows from the surrounding brake lights. She's a middle-aged woman with pink curls that jut out below a hand-knitted hat. The pale skin on either side of her violet eyes creases when she smiles.

"Claire."

"It's nice to meet you," she says, turning back to face the road ahead. She's wearing a thick brown coat, and when she taps her fingers against the steering wheel, I notice worn, knitted, fingerless pink gloves on each of her hands. A pink moon shaped crystal is knotted into twine hanging from her rearview mirror with a small gold star charm at the base.

"You know, some believe the snow can make anything happen. Maybe it'll bring you some luck tonight." There's a wistful tone to her speech.

"Maybe." I shrug, my shoulders relaxing. "I know I could use it."

"Just believe and it'll happen," she says, turning to wink at me over her shoulder.

She lets out an unnerving laugh and then turns back to face the street ahead. I don't know what it is about cab drivers in this city, but they're always so strange.

The next ten minutes are spent in silence with my head up against the window. The snow is really starting to come down. Large flakes hit the glass and stick to the sidewalk.

My phone chimes, and I swipe up to find another text from my sister.

ANDI:

Hello???

ANDI:

Do I need to send out a search party? Where are you and why didn't you text me back?

Sooo dramatic...I'll be there soon. Traffic is awful.

ANDI:

Please hurry. I'm going to be pissed if we miss watching them warm up. My whole feed is hockey players stretching, and I want to see it in person.

What happened to swearing off all athletes? LMAO! Weren't you just saying yesterday that you were done sleeping with Isaac?

ANDI:

Just because I have no desire to end up with an athlete doesn't mean I can't look at an athlete who has a nice ass!

ANDI:

Also, Isaac and I are done.

Sure you are!

ANDI:

I think. I don't know. He did text me earlier.

Ha! Mom and Dad would be so proud of your remarkable ability to make bad decisions.

ANDI:

Ugh. I know. Please don't tell Mom. You know she hates him.

ANDI:

Speaking of making bad decisions…how are you feeling about Everett being at the game?

ANDI:

Godddd I saw him on TV the other day and HOLY SHIT I think he got hotter since you were fucking him.

Everett is in the past. I don't care that he'll be there. You know I'm with Raph.

ANDI:

Raph's a nice guy. I think you'd like him if you got to know him.

ANDI:

He's a notorious playboy. Do you know how many pictures with random chicks there are online?

I let out a loud groan and sink further into the backseat of the cab. Raph is fine. He's gone a lot with hockey, and I'm busy with dance. We have our separate lives, and it feels like it's working, but we've only been together for a few months. Sometimes I wonder what it would feel like to have a partner. Someone who I could support but would also support me in return. What it would feel like to hear *I love you* and be able to say it back.

Swiping out of my sister's texts, I click on the internet icon and type the name of the man who has been on my mind since I agreed to come to the game—Everett Nuttall—into the search bar. I'm not sure why I'm doing this to myself. Maybe it's curiosity, or maybe it's something else.

Link after link pops up on the screen, and because I can't help myself, I click on photos.

Among the mix of action shots, there is a photo of Everett at a post-game press conference. His dark hair is longer than it was the last time I saw him and sticks out under a backwards ballcap. His jawline is shadowed by dark stubble, and above his lip sits a mustache that I definitely don't hate. He's wearing a black T-shirt that accentuates his arms. A panty-melting grin covers his face. It's clear the four and a half years we've been apart did him good. He's practically aging backwards.

Fuck me.

My mind betrays me with thoughts of how he worked my body all those years ago, always knowing exactly what I needed and never afraid to take what he wanted. Sex with Everett was the hottest I've ever had. There was nothing vanilla about it. Pierced and huge, his dick used to take me to places I didn't know existed, but then he left, and sadly all men aren't as talented as he was in that department.

"Fuck, what I wouldn't give to sleep with him just one more time." The words come out mumbled, but *out* nonetheless.

"What was that?" Stella says.

My face heats, and I massage my temples. I should be thinking about sleeping with the guy I'm currently seeing, not the guy who was never more than a mood booster on a shitty day. Locking my phone, I stuff it back into my purse, groaning again.

"Sorry, um, nothing. It's nothing."

"Didn't sound like nothing," she muses.

I blow out a long breath. I'm not actually going to tell this stranger what I'm thinking. I can't believe I actually said that out loud.

"It was nothing. I'm just tired."

She hums and begins to dig in a small fabric bag sitting on the passenger seat. "Here," she says, handing me a smooth, ocean blue stone.

"What's this?"

"Consider it my Christmas gift to you. I think it matches your eyes."

"Thank you," I say, rubbing the smooth surface between my finger tips. My shoulders begin to relax, and an ease settles over me. "But why are you giving me a gift? You don't even know me. Also how do you know it matches my—"

"It's something I like to do this time of year," she explains, smiling warmly.

I study the stone for a few moments, trailing my fingers along the imperfections, and my head begins to clear.

"So," she says, glancing into the rearview mirror. "You were going to tell me what you were grumbling about back there."

"Oh, right. Um, it's just the guy I'm dating plays for the Rat Kings, and the guy I used to hook-up with just got traded back to the Crowns, and they're playing each other tonight. So, for the first time in a long time, I'll be in the same place as him, and he had to go get hotter since I've seen him, which seems really unfair because now I'm dating Raph who is also hot and mostly fine, but something is missing..."

"And you think you might find what's missing with the guy you used to sleep with?"

"Honestly, I've wondered what would happen if we had another chance, but I'm with Raph, and I'm sure Everett, my ex-fling, is with someone new. He and I never really got along outside of the bedroom anyway, but people change." I laugh to myself, and my phone chimes. Placing the stone in my purse, I realize everything I just told her. "Ha! Ignore me. I don't know why I'm telling you all of this. I don't even know you."

"I have that effect on people." She turns and winks again.

What the hell? Why did I just spill my guts to this woman? That's not like me at all. Shaking my head, my eyes flutter shut, and I breathe in deeply.

CHAPTER 3:
KEEPING TABS
EVERETT

The energy in Madison Square Garden is electric as I skate around the ice while warming up for tonight's home game. A sea of purple and red fills the stands as fans make their way into the arena to watch New York's oldest rivalry—The Crowns vs. The Rat Kings.

It feels good to be wearing red and gold. To be home.

The first season back with the team that started my professional hockey career—the team I grew up rooting for—feels like a dream. While I wouldn't change the years I spent in Texas, there's something irreplaceable about skating on your home ice.

I breathe in deeply, the cold air energizing me and burning my lungs. Gliding across the rink, I move the puck with perfect control, shooting it forward and into the back of the net.

"Let's hope we see a lot of that tonight," Theo Carter, our starting right-winger, says, skating around me and pounding his glove against my shoulder. "I fucking hate those guys." He tilts his head toward our opponents.

"What are the chances Ulrich plays fair?" I ask, finding my old teammate and defenseman for the Rat Kings stretching on the other side of the rink. A smug grin is plastered across his face as he completes a set of frog stretches and stares down a pink-haired girl on the other side of the glass. Her gaze shifts from him to me, and a chill moves through the arena like a rush of wind causing the hairs on my neck to stand and my skin to erupt with goosebumps. *Weird.*

"Not a chance in fucking hell," he says, chuckling.

"Did you feel that?" I ask.

"Feel what?"

"It got colder in here for a minute, didn't it? It felt almost like wind."

Theo laughs. "No, it didn't. You getting sick, Nuttall?"

"No, I'm fine." I glance back towards the pink-haired girl, but she's gone. Quickly searching the stands, I expect to see her moving up the stairs, but she's nowhere to be found.

Turning to continue my warmup, I attempt to shake off the strange feeling, but freeze when I spot the photo on one of the large screens hanging above the rink. Pictured is a group of ballerinas advertising *The Nutcracker* at Lincoln Center. They're dressed in white corsets with long tulle skirts. Snow falls all around them, and they're holding what looks like snowballs. My eyes lock on the girl in the center. She isn't just any ballerina. She's Claire Silverman. Her onyx hair is pulled into a tight bun and is adorned with a white and silver crown. The ribbons of her pointe shoes wrap around her ankles, causing me to swallow hard.

My mind is instantly overwhelmed with visions of her soft pink lips and fair skin. Her body and mine tangled in her bed. Her delicate frame bent over her kitchen counter and my fist in her raven hair. My head between her thighs. What started as the worst blind date she claimed she'd ever been on turned into casual hook-ups fueled by her ability to bring me to my knees with her quick-witted mouth and our attraction to one another, until we both went our separate ways.

I'd be lying if I said that I hadn't been pining for her like a lovesick asshole for all these years.

I absolutely have, and I hate myself for it.

After I walked away, the what-ifs nagged at me constantly, and on occasion, the regret of not telling her how I was feeling kept me awake at night, but she was so clear about what she wanted back then. And that wasn't me. So, regardless of all the feelings I was having—*am still having*—I let my ego get in the way every time I considered doing something about it.

When I moved back to the city, I seriously considered reaching out to her, but instead searched for her name on my socials. Black hair wrapped up into a tight bun, blush painted on her cheeks, and those same soft pink lips that for a short time I knew so well. She looked beautiful, and pride radiated off her in every photo, much like the picture I'm looking at right now.

She did it. She was a principal dancer on New York's biggest stage, and I smiled to myself knowing our hard work paid off and we had both reached our goals. Despite the pull to send her a message, I didn't. Instead, I tucked my phone back into my pocket because if she didn't want me four years ago, there was absolutely no way in hell she'd want me now.

The screen changes to an advertisement for a concert a few months away. Lost in my thoughts, I don't realize how close to the red line I've drifted until I feel someone hit me hard against my shoulder, causing a shooting pain to radiate down my arm. Turning, I find Raphael Ulrich standing to my right.

"Can I help you?" I ask, rolling my shoulder and trying to mask the discomfort that I've been feeling for months now. Pain that I've been pretending doesn't exist, but this asshole just reminded me of with one hit.

"Claire sure is pretty, isn't she?"

"What?" I grit out.

"Oh, don't think I didn't notice you staring at her photo." He chuckles. "I had planned on taking it easy on you tonight, old man, but now it seems you need to learn your lesson. She's not yours anymore. She's mine."

What the fuck?

As far as I knew, she didn't like hockey players, and he was dating a model.

"Thought you were with some blonde?"

"Keeping tabs on me, are we?" He snickers.

"You see, that's the thing about being me. You can have more than one woman and they all feel so lucky to be dating me, they don't notice when I'm with the other one." His whole chest moves when he laughs.

My blood begins to boil. He's seeing multiple women and none of them have any idea. Claire has no idea.

"Don't look so surprised," he taunts, hitting my shoulder again. "I'll keep Claire warm tonight; don't worry."

His tone causes the grip on my stick to tighten. I move even closer to the red line, and the energy shifts. In my periphery, I can see blurs of red and purple skating to meet us.

If I had it my way, I'd pummel his ass into the ice, but I know better than to do something that stupid, and I'm not entirely sure my shoulder would make it through a fight, so I take a step back, trying to calm down.

"You were always so easy to rile up." He begins to skate away and then stops. Turning to face me, he yells, "I better not catch you looking at her tonight in the stands." A smirk paints his face below his visor, and he cocks his head toward some empty seats on the other side of the glass before another laugh rumbles his shoulders.

"You good?" Elijah Roberts, a defenseman, asks.

"Yeah," I say, my mind still trying to process Raph's words.

Claire is going to be here tonight, she's dating him, and he's cheating on her. What a piece of shit..

"What was that about?" Elijah questions.

"Who knows," I lie, and we move with our teammates toward the bench.

You don't win games when you're distracted by the past, and tonight we need to win. This is our first game against the Rats this season, and last season they led us 2-1. I'll be damned if I let that happen again now that I'm back on the team. And I'll especially be damned if it's because Raphael Ulrich got under my skin.

CHAPTER 4:
MISS MONDAY
CLAIRE

"Finally," Andi grits out as I approach the front of the arena.

"You know you could've gone in without me," I say, wrapping her in a hug. Pulling away, I take in what she's wearing. Her blonde hair is curled, and a white beanie, covered with snow, is pulled over her ears. A red hockey jersey peeks out from under her thick black coat. She's styled it with black leather leggings and trendy sneakers. "You wore a Crowns jersey? You know Raph plays for the Rats."

"Precisely why I wore red." She smirks and looks down at her outfit. "I do like that jacket though. Where did you get it?"

"It was a gift. Raph said he wanted to see me in his number, so he had it made for me. It's cute but not very warm." A shiver runs down my spine as the wind rips through me and the snow tickles my cheeks.

"Okay, tell me your news," she says as we begin to walk toward the front of the arena.

"Marie, the girl who I was understudying for, hurt her ankle, and that means that I'll be performing as the cast A Sugar Plum Fairy!"

"You're kidding?" she asks, stopping and grabbing my arm.

"Nope, and that's not even the best part. I get to dance it in the Christmas show."

Andi's eyes fill with tears, and she wraps me in a hug. "This is so fucking cool. You're going to kill it."

"Thanks. I feel bad that she's hurt, but I'm really excited.

Dimitri said if it goes well then another big role might be in my future."

"Do Mom and Dad know?"

"Yep." I nod. "I called them the minute I left his office. They're going to come to the city for Christmas and see the show. I thought we could all spend it together here."

"I love that idea." She hugs me again, and we continue to move toward the long security line that's formed outside the arena's doors.

"Is this new boyfriend of yours going to join us for Christmas?"

"I'm not sure. I haven't talked to him yet with the game being tonight. Mom was all over me about meeting him."

"Well you're his girlfriend, right? So, I'm sure he'll be just as excited as we are."

"Yeah," I mutter, causing her to glance at me sharply.

"Shouldn't he be able to get us in through a special entrance?" Andi asks, pushing herself up on her toes, trying to get a better view of how long the line actually is.

"What do you mean?"

"I mean he got us the tickets, and the other WAGS aren't coming through the general admission doors." Andi crosses her arms over her chest as we get into the security line behind two men wearing gold Crowns on their heads.

"It's fine. We're not exclusive, exclusive. I don't think I'm technically considered a WAG yet. Plus I'm excited to sit with you close to the ice." My heart rate starts to quicken as I attempt to explain myself, but the look on my sister's face says everything I wish it didn't.

"You're not exclusive, exclusive? What the fuck does that even mean?"

I shrug. "I just meant we're just seeing where things go. He just got out of a relationship, so we are taking it easy. We're both in really busy seasons of our lives."

She inhales deeply as we step forward. "Are you sure he's only sleeping with you?"

My stomach sinks. "I mean, we've talked about it, and he said that he…well he said that I'm his special girl…"

"Oh, my god, Claire! His special girl? What the fuck does *that* mean?" She throws her hands into the air as she talks. "How many special girls does he have? Am I talking to Miss Tuesday?"

"Miss Tuesday?"

"I'm sorry, today is Monday. Are you Monday's special girl? Should I call you Miss Monday? My mistake."

"That's not what he meant."

"You don't know that!" she says. "God, he has a reputation. Do you think Miss Friday and Miss Wednesday have dark hair too, or do you think they're blonde?"

"You're hilarious."

"I mean no judgment if you want to fuck him, but he's the Rats' star player and has a reputation of being a total dick. Wasn't he dating that model for a little while. Gah, what was her name? Monica or something?"

"He's not really like that off the ice, and yes he was dating Monica Meyer, but they broke up."

"Well he's making you walk through the general admission line, so I'm not so sure he's not a total asshole, but I've never met him."

My stomach turns at her words.

"I don't know," I try. "I actually met one of the other players' girlfriends the other night—Lily. She's dating the goalie."

"That's promising, I guess."

"What do you mean?"

"Just that you're meeting his friends is a good thing, so maybe I'm wrong."

The uneasy feeling in my stomach worsens as I think back to the night I met Lily.

"What's that look?" my sister questions.

"Nothing."

"What happened with this Lily girl?"

"Nothing. She said I could text her and she'd get me back after the game, so I'll get to be with all the WAGS then. I actually really like her, and we've been texting on and off since we met. Feels like maybe we could be friends."

"Don't you dare lie to me," she warns.

"I'm not."

"Are too. Claire Elise Silverman, tell me what happened before I make a scene." She crosses her arms, scowling at me dramatically like she's our mother and not my little sister.

"Fine. Raph and I were at dinner the other night and they walked into the same restaurant. I don't know, the whole interaction was weird, and then Lily insisted they join us at our table, and Raph got super uncomfortable."

"How so?"

"I don't know how to explain it, but they ended up joining us anyway, and she seemed really nice. I think he was just upset they interrupted. We don't get to spend a lot of time together with our schedules."

Her brow raises as she looks at me with judgy eyes.

"What?"

She shrugs.

"No, tell me what you're thinking."

"You know I just want what's best for you. You deserve someone who doesn't get weird about you meeting his friends and will treat you like a goddamn queen."

A fan ahead of us wearing a rat head stumbles backwards, bumping into Andi and stepping on her foot.

"For fuck's sake," she says, shoving him off of her.

"And you don't think he treats me like that?"

"No. Queens don't have to walk into stadiums with hundreds of drunk fans. They get special treatment. You're the fucking Sugar Plum Fairy for Christ's sake!" Her voice rises as she talks, and the man wearing the rat head looks over his shoulder.

So much for not causing a scene.

"Can you lower your voice? People are staring."

"I'm not wrong, and you know it." She looks down at her phone, and a smile breaks across her face.

"You're one to talk. Is that Isaac?"

"It is. He wants me to come over after the game."

I shake my head and laugh. "Goodness, we're a mess."

"No. You're a mess. I'm fully aware that Isaac and I are a bad idea."

"Please come this way," a security attendant says, moving the retractable belt barrier so that the line begins to move in a different direction with us in the front. We follow him toward a metal detector.

"Place your bag on the table and step through with your hands up," he shouts, motioning Andi and me forward. We quickly move through the security checkpoint and collect our belongings.

Scanning our tickets, we walk through the doors of Madison Square Garden. The electric energy hits us as soon as we walk into the arena. Loud music and shouts from the rowdy crowd carry throughout the expansive space and drown out the thoughts spinning around my head. There is a noticeable chill in the air, but compared to the temperature outside, it's comfortable, and I can feel my hands beginning to defrost.

Near the doors, workers are set up next to two life-sized cutouts of two Crowns players. The man on the right I don't recognize, but the one on the left is Everett.

"Fuck, even the cardboard version of him is hot," Andi says, running up to the cutout and posing next to it for a selfie. "Maybe you should ditch the rat and give him a chance." She gestures toward the cutout with her thumb and then begins typing on her phone.

"Okay, for one, I told you I'm with Raph. For two, I barely have time to sleep with one guy let alone two, and for three, for all I know Everett's married with a baby. It's not like I keep tabs on him."

Except I do, and according to his socials and the news, he's definitely not married with a baby.

"Oh, no…" She laughs. "I meant the cardboard cutout, not the real person, but I'm glad to know you're wondering if Everett is single."

"You're lucky that we're blood, or I would kill you."

"Trading cards?" one of the workers asks, interrupting us.

"Oh, um," I stammer, taking in her appearance and name. Her pink hair is styled in two french braids, and a name tag that reads *Stella* is pinned to her shirt, causing me to freeze. Star tattoos trail up her right arm and disappear under the sleeve of her work-issued polo. Around her neck is a gold chain holding a moon-shaped pink crystal. "No, thank you. We're cheering on the Rats tonight."

"Come on." Stella smiles, holding out a silver packet of cards. "You're in luck. There's only one set left. Looks like it was meant to be." The skin around her eyes creases, despite her young age, and her violet eyes seem to sparkle as she looks at me, daring me to take the card pack.

Reaching my hand out, I take it from her at the same time a group of obnoxious Rats fans barrel in chanting something. One of the men, not paying attention, pushes me into the Everett cutout, causing it to topple over and my purse to fly out of my hand. Lipstick, my wallet, my phone, a bottle of ibuprofen, and my keys spread across the floor.

"Shit," he yells, stumbling past us without stopping and kicking my keys further away.

"What a dick! Are you alright?" Andi asks, assessing me for any sign that he may have hurt me, but he didn't.

"I'm fine. Just help me grab all of this stuff before something gets lost." We both bend down and frantically begin collecting my belongings. The crowd is huge, and people are coming and going in every direction. It feels incredibly overwhelming as I try to dodge being stepped on and account for all of my things.

"You know this wouldn't have happened if Raph had gotten us in with the rest of the WAGS," my sister shouts, making her way towards my keys.

"Point made," I bite out, grabbing a tube of lipstick from the floor.

"Here you go," I hear a feminine voice say behind me. Still crouched down, I look over my shoulder to find the young Stella holding my purse.

"Thank you," I say, grabbing my bag and placing my things inside.

"You dropped these too," young Stella says, handing me the pack of trading cards.

She moves to pick up the cutout of Everett. "Let me help you with that," I offer.

We work together to stand it up. I must've damaged it when I was pushed into it because the right arm is now cracked near the shoulder.

"I'm so sorry," I say, running my hand over the damage. "If I need to pay for this I can. Can I give you my number or something?"

"Oh, don't worry about it," she says, smiling again. "These things are easily fixed. Enjoy the game."

"Are you sure?"

She nods and turns away, continuing to greet entering spectators.

Linking arms with my sister, I attempt to shake the sense that I've met this Stella before, but that seems impossible.

Right?

Right.

We maze through the crowd, only stopping to grab a bag of peanut M&Ms and a beer for Andi and popcorn and a water for me.

"Wow, these are great," my sister chimes, moving past a few fans already seated in our row.

They are great seats. Center ice. Right behind the glass. The perfect view of the game and *every player.* Both teams are lined up, waiting for the National Anthem to be performed, and I breathe out a small sigh of relief that I made it before the start of the game. My eyes survey the players in red first, and I immediately find Everett.

For a split second, my heart stops and my breath catches. He has the same hair and beard from the photo. I remember him being tall, but in his skates he's even taller. His bulky uniform and pads leave a lot to the imagination, but I know I wouldn't have to think too hard to picture what he looks like under all of it—perfectly sculpted body, slutty thigh tattoo that made me weak, and a small trail of hair leading straight to his…

"Where's Raph?" my sister asks, interrupting the thoughts I know I shouldn't be having.

"He's number seven," I say, gesturing absently toward the line of players wearing purple and black.

Raph is just shy of six feet—a fact he absolutely hates. He has light skin, dark hair and eyes, and I don't think I've ever seen him with a beard. He's handsome, but sometimes it feels like that's all he is.

"And what's Everett's number?"

"Eleven."

Andi begins to laugh, popping a few peanut M&Ms into her mouth. "Tonight's going to be interesting isn't it?"

"Just because I know his number doesn't mean anything."

"Sure it doesn't," she deadpans, shaking her head. "Oh, look it's you!" My sister points to a large screen where a photo from the "Waltz Of The Snowflakes" scene is displayed advertising *The Nutcracker.*

"I didn't know they had an ad here," I say.

"So, now that you've been moved up to Sugar Plum, are you going to have to do both roles?"

"No. My understudy will take over for me, and I'll take over for Marie."

"That's so exciting! How are you feeling about the switch?"

"Nervous, but really excited. I've wanted this role since I can remember, so the fact that I finally got it, and I get to perform it in the Christmas show, feels unreal. I just hope I do it justice."

"You will." She smiles and pops a couple more pieces of candy into her mouth.

The announcer comes over the loud speaker and introduces the performer who will be singing the National Anthem tonight, and cheers roll through the arena. We stand, and my feet ache as the singer belts out each line of the song, holding a few of the notes longer than she should.

I really should've opted for a more sensible shoe.

When it's over, the crowd erupts and a hype video with loud music begins to play from the jumbotron. Everyone around us stays standing, but I fall back into my seat and my sister does the same.

"So, what trading cards did you get?" Andi asks, sipping her beer. Crossing her legs, she leans back in the chair, eyeing the card packet I'm still holding.

"Oh, I almost forgot," I begin as I tear it open. "That interaction was so weird. My cab driver on the way here had the same pink hair, violet eyes, and was also named Stella. What are the chances I meet two people with that description on the same night?"

"Impossible. I think you're exhausted from long dancing days, and your mind is playing tricks on you. Her eyes were definitely blue, and I don't think her name was Stella."

Pulling three cards from the packet, I flip the first one over.

Andi covers her mouth so that the sip of beer she just took doesn't spray all over the glass in front of us.

"You got Everett. I'm dead." The photo on the card is a picture of younger Everett, back when I knew him and he played for the Crowns the first time.

What are the fucking chances?

Taking a deep breath, I flip over the next trading card. Everett again, but this time he's wearing his Texas jersey.

Is this a joke?

"Wait, I thought the whole point of these cards was that you got Crowns players. Why did you get a Texas Stallions player?"

"It's Everett," I say softly. "That's why he and I stopped hooking up, remember? He got traded to Texas."

"Oh, my god!" Her pitch rises. "Who's on the third one?"

Flipping it over, I already know who it's going to be before I see the picture. It's the man I couldn't peel my eyes away from the moment we got to our seats. Everett Nuttall. Number eleven. Forward and captain for the New York Crowns.

"Seriously?" She gasps. "What are the odds that you would get your former fuck buddy on all three cards? We should play the lottery or something tonight. I mean, that's insane."

"I told you there was something weird about the Stella girl. Maybe she's a witch."

Andi leans forward, placing the back of her hand on my forehead and then each of my cheeks. "Do you feel okay? You aren't warm, but you sound crazy. A witch?"

"How else would you explain me getting three Everett Nuttall cards?"

"I think it's just a coincidence and you're letting your imagination get the best of you." She laughs, sitting back in her chair again. "I told you the card girl wasn't named Stella. Her eyes were blue, not purple. Are you sure you aren't feeling sick?"

"I'm fine." Tucking the three cards into my purse, I turn to face the rink. My eyes shift back and forth between Raph and Everett as the players skate around the ice and line up for the game to begin. The crowd roars as Everett and the Rat Kings' forward meet at center ice. The referee blows his whistle and drops the puck. Everett wins the draw, pulling the puck back towards another red jersey.

The players glide over the ice, moving the puck between them and dodging the other team. Everett regains possession and manages to knock the puck toward another player before Raph comes out of nowhere, barreling them both into the glass in front of us.

In front of me.

"That was boarding!" the man next to me yells, throwing his fists against the glass, but the referee seems oblivious to what just happened. More shouts echo through the stadium as fans become angry that no call was made.

My eyes stay locked on the men in front of me. Raph turns and throws me a wink before shoving Everett back into the boards and skating towards the play. Everett pauses for a split second. His hazel eyes find mine. My lips part slightly, and I bring my hand up in a small wave, and then he's gone. Skating like mad and fighting to win.

"I imagine that means Raph knows about you and Everett's history?" Andi asks, grimacing.

"Yeah," I say, dropping my hand. "They played together on the Crowns for a season before Everett left."

Raph knows exactly what he's doing, and my stomach turns at the realization that while I've been worried about what would happen if Everett and I saw each other, I should've been worrying about Raph interacting with him instead.

Chapter 5: This Isn't Going Away

Tension ripples through the arena as my stare meets hers. Her pink lips part, and her eyes widen. I wasn't expecting to see her in person tonight. My eyes rake down her body, and I realize she's wearing his number on her jacket.

It shouldn't matter. Our history is barely history, but something about her wearing the number seven makes me feral. I feel drawn to her, and now that we've seen each other again, I don't know if I'll be able to stay away.

"Nuttall," my teammate yells, pulling my attention back into the game.

My shoulder took the brunt of Ulrich's hit, and pain ripples down my right arm. Turning, I do my best to push through it, but I can't. The puck slides across the ice, and as I wind up to fire it on goal, another shooting pain radiates from my shoulder, causing me to wince and the puck to go sliding with little force toward the Rats' goalie who redirects it toward a player in purple.

Fuck. This isn't going away.

Skating toward the bench, I yell, alerting Kai McCormick, another forward, that I'm coming out and he needs to be ready. As I approach, he jumps over the boards and I step off. Motioning for Dr. Hamilton, I sit on the bench, and he walks to meet me.

"My shoulder's fucked," I say.

"You think you can go back out, or you want me to take you back and give you something for it?"

"That hit by Ulrich did something. I'm feeling a shooting pain when I move it. It's why I missed that shot."

"Take him now. We need him out there," Rob Zillman, our head coach, orders.

The crowd erupts, and I turn to see that the Rats now lead 1-0. *Fuck.*

Removing my helmet, I follow the team doctor to the locker room.

"You can't keep this up," he says as we move down the tunnel.

"I'll be fine," I bite out.

"Yeah, but your shoulder won't be."

He's telling me what I already know. My shoulder has always given me trouble, but after a gnarly hit in our second game this season, it's been giving me more problems than usual. One more wrong hit and my career will be over. Fuck, the way it's currently feeling, it may already be, but I'm not ready. At thirty-three, I know I don't have much more time left out on the ice, but in no way did I think this would be my last season.

We walk into the medical room, and I sit on one of the tables, removing my jersey and shoulder pads. Dr. Hamilton assesses my shoulder, muttering to himself when he attempts to move it and I wince at the pain.

"For fuck's sake, Nuttall," he says. "I'll give you a shot of Toradol, but we're gonna have to do something more about this."

"Yeah," I grumble. There's only so much ice, tape, and the shots will do. It needs to be formally assessed, and I need more than a temporary bandage. My leg bounces up and down as I watch the clock. He needs to fucking hurry so I can get back out there.

He prepares my shoulder for the injection and then administers the shot.

"Should kick in after ten minutes," he says, starting to clean up the supplies as I re-dress for the game. "Let's take it easy the rest of the first, and you can go back in at the start of the second."

"I think I'm good," I say, rotating my shoulder. The pain is still present, but I can already feel the miracle drug working.

He shakes his head. "You're insane."

Making my way back to the bench, there are three minutes left in the first period. We're still down 1-0, and I don't want to go into intermission behind. I take a seat with the rest of my team, biding my time until it's my turn to get back out there.

Kai makes his way down the ice toward the goal, our two wingers trailing close behind. He looks gassed, and guilt crawls up my throat at the thought that my teammates have had to make up for me being gone. As the defense closes in on him, he attempts to shoot the puck, but it bounces off the right post and the Rats regain possession.

Shouting his name from the bench, I alert him that I'm back. He gestures in my direction, and I ready myself for the ice.

A Rats defenseman skates off, and Ulrich rejoins the game. He passes our bench and throws me a wink and a smirk.

Kai makes it to me a second later, and I jump over the boards, rejoining the game as well.

There's only a minute and half left of the period, but that's more than enough time to even the score.

Theo passes me the puck, and I charge toward the Rats' end of the ice. Ulrich moves to rub me out against the board, but I pass back to Theo and manage to sidestep the asshole before he can finish his check.

Theo flicks the puck back across the middle of the ice to me, and when I wind up to shoot, I'm relieved to find the meds are working, the sharp pain that once radiated down my arm gone. I one-time to pass, narrowly missing the goalie's outstretched glove and into the back of the net.

"Fuck yeah!" I shout, my teammates circling around me in celebration. Turning, I find Claire again. She's standing among the erupting fans with her eyes locked on me. A subtle look of approval paints her face, and I have to remind myself to focus on the game.

We've evened up the score, but now we need to win.

Chapter 6: I Guess We're Fucking Doing This

Everett

I t's the third period, and the Rats are leading us 2-1. My heart pounds against my chest as I hustle up the ice. Theo skates down the left wing and into the Rats' defensive zone with the puck, and I trail behind, trying to stay open and ready for his pass.

We need another goal. Fuck, we need two goals because I want to see the look on Raph's smug face when we win.

I move in towards the goal from the point just as Theo whips a pass onto my stick from the corner. I hesitate, trying to freeze the goalie. The stadium goes silent as I focus on the goal. My stick curls as I wire a wrist shot at the net just as the butt of a stick jabs into my ribs, throwing me off my balance.

"Whoops," Ulrich says, laughing and returning his stick to the ice.

"What did you say?" I ask, moving forward and bumping my chest up against his. My blood runs hot, and it's taking everything in me not to drop the gloves with this guy. Fucking prick made me hit the post.

"Didn't see you there," he sneers.

I skate forward again, pushing him backward. Tension has been building the entire game, and I want to snap. "You need to fucking cool it, Ulrich," I warn. The hit against the boards at the start of the game was just the beginning. He's throwing questionable hits left and right, and the referees aren't doing anything to hold him accountable.

"Or what?"

Theo skates to meet us and pushes me back. I try to ignore the throbbing in my ribcage. They don't feel broken, but he sure as hell bruised them.

"That was a fucking penalty," I yell, skating towards the referee.

"Watch it," the ref warns.

Unfuckingbelievable.

I check the time on the clock. I need to change out, but I want to score. I want to win too badly, so I ignore what my body is telling me and continue to play.

Digging the puck out of a scrum in the corner, Theo wheels towards the slot, but he's quickly targeted by a Rats defenseman. He fights to keep control of the puck but is shoved off it, and the puck is sent up the ice to the Rats' left winger.

Theo charges the puck again, but Elijah is able to strip the puck carrier in the neutral zone. He turns back up ice and hits me with a pass near center ice.

In my periphery, I see Theo streaking down the wing, so I fire a backhand pass to him just before he reaches the Rats' blueline. He catches the defender flat-footed and is in all alone with their goalie.

He shoots and scores, causing the arena to erupt in loud cheers.

Hell yeah, 2-2.

Skating to the bench, Theo and I jump off, followed by Elijah.

The game moves fast, and I watch as the Rats next shot on goal is blocked, and Kai recovers the puck. Two Rats' blueliners swarm him before he's able to get past center ice.

Fuck.

"You coming out tonight?" Theo asks, pulling my attention from the game.

"Huh?"

"Are you coming out with the team?"

"Focus," I bark, returning my gaze to the ice.

Theo is a good player and friend, but he's young. I try to cut him some slack because I remember what it was like to be new to the league—the parties, the women, the attention. It was easy to get wrapped up in all the fun and lose sight of the job I was hired to do, but his head should be in the game and not on whatever plan he and the rest of the team has concocted for after. Getting distracted is going to cause us to lose, and we need to win.

"Come on Nuttall, don't be such an old man." He laughs. "Elijah got us the hookup at that new rooftop bar he was talking about at practice last week. It's going to be sick, dude."

"I'm good."

I know I sound old as fuck, but I don't care. Tonight, I want to win, and then I want to go home. A loud roof-top bar, my drunk teammates, and women I barely know begging for me to take them home sounds like my personal nightmare, especially when I can't have a drink thanks to the shot that was injected into my arm.

"Suit yourself," he says, standing. He follows Elijah, jumping over the boards as two of our players step off.

Adrenaline surges through my veins as I watch the clock, and my leg moves up and down as I anticipate the upcoming line change.

With nine minutes left in the game, I watch as Ulrich flies off the bench toward Theo. With all of his force, he elbows Theo in the head, causing him to fall to the ice.

"What the fuck?" I yell, moving to re-enter, but one of my teammates stops me, shoving me back down.

Elijah charges Ulrich, his glove making contact with his jaw before Raph can react. The crowd gets louder, egging them on as they meet each other blow for blow. The energy is palpable, and I want in.

Two linesmen skate toward the action, sounding their whistles and breaking up the two players. Everyone disperses, and my teammates help Theo to stand. He has that look in his eyes of a person who hit his head too hard. The look of someone who isn't registering everything that's going on. No doubt about it, he has a concussion.

Ulrich watches with a shit-eating grin on his face as Theo skates toward the bench. What a fucking dick.

The referee makes his way to center ice and calls a major for fighting and a minor for elbowing on Ulrich. Elijah gets a major as well.

Our coach attempts to argue the call, but it's useless.

Ulrich skates toward the penalty box laughing to himself, and our surrounding fans boo him. He moves his arms up and down, welcoming the attention and egging them on.

Prick.

Down a player, the Rats line up to face off against us, and I join my line on the ice.

The whistle sounds, and the puck hits the ice in front of me. The other center and I wrestle for it, but I ultimately win out, moving down the ice toward the opposing goal and crossing it to our left winger.

It's amazing how much better my shoulder feels since the injection. I don't have to anticipate the pain at all as I move, and I can focus clearly on my one goal—winning. We need one more, and I want to be the one to score it.

Moving as a unit, our left winger charges the goal with the puck as a Rats defenseman swarms around us and fights for possession.

He fires the puck towards me. Shooting, I miss wide. The puck rebounds off the post and is caught by our right winger, who tries to get a clear shot but is blocked by a purple jersey. I move behind the net to an open spot as I watch him fight to keep possession. The crowd roars around me as he manages to maintain the puck and feed it back to me. Moving quickly, I skate toward the top of the circle, toe drag, and flick the puck top shelf before the goalie can react.

The crowd erupts in cheers, and my teammates skate toward me in celebration.

3-2. Fuck yeah.

Making a lap around the ice, I pass by Ulrich, sitting in the penalty box, and throw him a wink. The jumbotron flashes video of fans all around the stadium chanting my name. The camera zooms in on Claire. Her whole face is lit up with a smile, and she's cheering as loud as the Crowns fans around her. She brings her hands up into a double high five, and the girl next to her follows her lead, playfully screaming in her face as their hands join.

My heart swells in my chest. Looking over toward Ulrich, I chuckle as I watch his eyes shift from the big screen to where she stands.

His face turns red, and his eyes go dark. He's gripping his stick so tightly it looks as though he could snap it. Without warning, he stands and leaves the box early, gunning straight for me.

Fuck.

I anticipate the blow before it happens. One of his hands finds the neck of my jersey while the other makes sharp contact with my chin.

I guess we're fucking doing this.

I attempt to shove him off of me, but he comes at me harder. His fist connects with my jaw again and knocks my helmet off.

My fist makes contact with the side of his face just as I hear a whistle blow. The crowd sounds insane, getting louder with every swing. The linesmen circle us trying to intervene. In my periphery, I can see that both sets of our teammates have joined in. Blurs of red and purple circle around us as everyone on the ice fights.

I strike the side of Raph's head, and we fall to the ice.

The weight of a linesman on top of me causes me to stop.

Chest heaving and adrenaline still coursing through me, the linemen separate us, and I watch as the remainder of the fight is broken up.

The referee skates to center ice, calls a major on every player involved, and ejects Raph from the game.

The crowd roars at the announcement, and all I can think is *finally*. Picking up my helmet, I move toward the penalty box with my teammates to sit out the next five minutes.

Glancing toward the stands, I find Claire standing, chewing on her thumb nail, nervously. Her eyes find me and then shift back to Ulrich, who's getting booed as he makes his way toward the tunnel.

Good riddance.

Chapter 7: Wags Only

Claire

"What a game," Andi says as we climb the stairs. "Seriously, I didn't think the Crowns were going to pull it off, but that final goal by your man..." She squeals with excitement. "Holy shit! What a shot! And then that fight between Everett and Raph...absolutely insane."

"Raph didn't score," I mumble.

"Ugh. You can't be serious right now." She shakes her head. "Don't tell me you're still considering him *your man*. He acted like a complete lunatic tonight."

My stomach turns as I think back over the game. Multiple dirty hits, and then instigating a final fight that got him ejected and every player on the ice put in the box. He was a total ass tonight, and part of me knows it had to do with me. I hope I'm wrong, but something deep in my gut tells me I'm not.

"You want to share a cab?" Andi asks when we get to the top of the stairs.

"Oh, um, no. I'm going to text Lily and go meet up with her while I wait on Raph."

My sister rolls her eyes. "Are you serious right now?"

"Yes."

"Do you want me to hang back with you?" she asks, reluctantly.

"No, I'll be fine. I'll call you tomorrow. Go see Isaac."

"How do you know that's where I'm going?"

"Oh, are you not going to get railed by the hot baseball player?"

"No, I am." She scrunches her nose before wrapping me in a hug. "Don't judge me. I love you."

"Never. I love you too."

I watch until she disappears into a crowd toward the front of the arena.

Pulling out my phone, I find Lily's contact and then make my way to meet up with her and the other girls.

"Claire!" Lily calls as I get to the entrance where all of the other women are waiting for the players. She is wearing baggy denim jeans, a tight white shirt, and a black leather bomber jacket. A Rat Kings trucker hat sits on top of her perfectly styled red waves.

A large security guard blocks the entrance, looking me up and down as I approach.

"Don't worry," she says with the confidence of a player's wife and not of a woman who has been dating the Rats' goalie for a few months. "She's one of us."

He nods and moves so I can pass by.

She wraps me in a hug. "I wish you had been with us during the game. Some of these women are total bitches," she whispers, giggling. "It would've been so nice to have another newbie with me."

I glance around the room and notice a group of women standing off to the side. The energy in the room is strange, and other than Lily, I don't feel welcome or that I belong.

Each of them is stunning, and they all look me up and down, making assumptions without even saying hello. I shift my purse higher on my arm, straightening my shoulders. Fidgeting with the jacket, I notice that no one here is wearing a jersey, so it's hard to tell which player they're with.

"Do you know how long the guys will be?" I ask.

"Who knows." Lily shrugs. "Could be an hour or longer. Come on; I'll introduce you." She grabs my hand and leads me to where the other women stand.

"Ladies, this is Claire," she begins, interrupting their conversation.

Their eyes shift to me, but no one makes an attempt to introduce themselves. Their stares feed all my deepest, darkest insecurities, and I'm pretty sure they could make even the most confident person feel small.

"Only wives and girlfriends of the team are supposed to be back here," a tall brunette says, turning towards Lily.

"Oh, she is. She's just new and doesn't get to make many games. Isn't that right, babe?" Lily chimes, nudging me with her elbow.

"Yeah, this is my first game this season," I say. "I'm a dancer for the City Ballet, and it keeps me really busy."

"And who do you belong to then," a blonde asks. Her eyes dart down to my jacket and then back up to my face.

"Um, well I don't belong to anyone," I say, my stomach turning at her words as I respond. "But I've been dating Raph Ulrich for a little over three months now."

"That's impossible," a woman with long blonde curls says, stepping forward. My mouth falls open as I take in who is standing before me—Monica Meyer. Raph's ex.

What in the hell is she doing here?

"What do you mean?" I ask, confused.

"Well, Raph and I have been together for almost a year," she says. "So, you must be lying." Her tone is sharp, and my heart sinks into my stomach.

"I'm not lying," I say, gesturing toward my coat. "Raph and I are dating."

"Impossible," she snaps.

"Security!" another woman calls. "This woman shouldn't be back here."

My eyes find Lily, but she's gone silent.

"Wait, I'm confused. I can prove that we're dating," I try again, pulling out my phone and swiping to a photo of me with him. The woman looks at it unphased, and so I bring up our text message chain and attempt to show them our texts, but there's no reaction from any of them.

"Maybe you should go, Claire," Lily says, moving to join the group. Monica locks arms with her and throws me a wicked grin.

Oh, my god. Everything makes sense at once. The tickets he

gave me, the general admission line, his reaction the other day when Lily showed up at the restaurant. His hesitation for me to come to a game, and his disinterest in meeting my family and friends. How little we actually see each other.

Andi was right. I'm just Miss Monday, and this woman in front of me is Miss Tuesday through Sunday.

Lily's kindness was a ruse to out me as the other fucking woman. They played me.

"Do you have something to say for yourself?" Lily asks. I look up, and all of the women in the room are sending daggers through me.

"I...I thought we were friends?"

"No, babe. I'm not friends with puck bunny whores." The other women snicker under their breath, and blush crawls up my neck.

"I'm so sorry," I stammer. "I really had no idea. He told me you broke up. If I had known I wouldn't have—"

"Wouldn't have what?" Monica asks. "Slept with my boyfriend?"

"Pathetic," one of the other women scoffs.

My heart rails against my ribcage, and the room begins to spin. Holding back tears, I flee, taking off my jacket and dropping it to the floor. I'm suddenly overcome with nausea. I don't know how I could have been so naive. How I didn't see all the signs as clearly as I can see them now.

Moving down a hall, I turn a corner and find a bathroom. Tears stream down my face. How did today go from all of my dreams coming true to this big of a shit show? Fumbling for my phone, I try my sister, but there's no answer. I try her again, but nothing.

Checking her location, I see she's at Isaac's apartment, so she's not going to be checking her phone for a while.

Staring at my reflection, my stomach rolls, and I put my phone back in my purse. Turning on the sink, I splash water on my face, attempting to clean off the mascara running down my cheeks and slow my breathing.

A flash of pink enters my periphery, catching my attention. I shift my gaze away from the mirror, finding a custodian with a short pink pixie cut beginning to clean the bathroom.

"It's late," she says.

"Oh, I know. Sorry. I'm on my way out." Reaching for a paper towel, I pat my face dry with the rough material and then walk it toward a trash can near where she stands.

She smiles, and her plum colored eyes make my breath catch.

"You okay?" she asks.

"Oh, yeah, I'll be fine."

"You strike me as someone who will," she muses, digging in her cleaning cart.

"What makes you say that?" I ask, tears welling in my eyes again because I'm not sure I will be.

It dawns on me that I'm not sad that Raph and I are over—even if he doesn't know it yet. I don't think I can get over the mortification of finding out the way I did. How, once again, I trusted someone who I thought could maybe be my friend and she let me down. And I don't know how I'm going to relive what happened when I inevitably have to talk to him to end things once and for all.

I wish I had just gone home after rehearsal. I wish I hadn't texted Lily. I wish I could find someone who wasn't a total douchebag and friends who didn't turn out to be bitches.

"I can just tell. Whatever happened, it'll work out." She smiles, and the skin surrounding her eyes crinkles just like the other pink-haired ladies I've met tonight.

"What's your name?" I blurt out.

"Excuse me?"

"Your name. I'm Claire. What's your name?"

"You should probably get out of here, Claire. The arena will be closing soon, and the snow is really coming down," she says kindly, avoiding my question.

"Right. Sorry. You just reminded me of someone. I thought maybe, but nevermind. It's silly."

She begins to sweep the floor, and I return to my reflection, quickly fixing my hair under my hat, attempting to hold my shoulders high.

"Be careful tonight," she warns as I pass by her. "You know what they say—the snow can make anything happen."

Her words cause me to pause for a split second.

"What did you say?"

"The snow," she repeats. "Some people believe that it can make anything happen."

That's the same thing Stella said in the cab, but she couldn't be, could she? No, that's impossible. She's not Stella. I need to get it together.

"Have a good night," I manage before walking away and shaking off all thoughts of pink hair. Making my way through the almost empty arena, I'm reminded I still need to break it off with Raphael. That I should call and tell him what I think about him. Fuck, I wish Andi would answer the phone. I could really use the moral support.

Chapter 8:
Last Question
Everett

When I started in the league, post-game interviews were something I looked forward to. Cocky and young, I enjoyed boasting about my performance during the game and flirting with the female reporters in the room. I liked having all the attention on me, but now, I dread being under the spotlight that way.

The older I've gotten, I've learned what to expect from the reporters sitting in the room, and while some of the questions are far too personal for my liking, the ones I really hate are the ones trying to corner me into saying something damning.

"Alright, so we're going to take five questions, and then you'll be done. Let's not mention the shoulder injury until we know more," Sally, our team's PR manager, lectures as we walk down the hallway.

"Five?" I groan.

"We can do four, but that's as low as I'll go. They're expecting to hear from you. You're the team captain after all."

"How about three?"

"Four," she snaps. "I don't have time for this little game."

She pushes the door open, and we walk into the well-lit press room. I find mostly familiar faces of reporters all waiting to talk to me, but I don't really want to talk. I want to go home and rest my body that took one too many hits tonight. Fortunately, my shoulder is still feeling good, but I know a few hours from now, the effects of the injection will wear off, and I'll be in pain again.

Following behind Sally, I take a seat at the table in the front of the room. Turning my hat backwards, I take a deep breath, readying myself for whatever they throw at me tonight.

"Dale Kisbee," Sally says, beginning the interview and calling on a man sitting in the front row.

"Hi, yes, thanks for taking the time to speak with us tonight, Everett," he begins.

I nod and offer him a smile.

"Tonight marks your first game against the Rats after returning to the Crowns this season. We know there's a longstanding rivalry between the two teams, but tonight seemed to be more intense than past games, specifically at the end. Did it feel that way out on the ice?"

I chuckle, thinking back to the game. "I'd say so," I begin. "The energy was definitely heightened tonight, and you know we go into games like this prepared for them to be a little more physical than others. I think it's just the nature of our teams' shared history. I was happy we pulled out the win."

A few hands shoot up, and Sally points to another man in the third row.

"Hello, Everett. Thank you for being here. Tonight you had a few run-ins with your old teammate, Raphael Ulrich. I was wondering if you could comment on how the referees handled some of the calls against him, specifically the hit that took Theo Carter from the game."

What a waste of a question. Maybe younger me would've taken the bait. Younger Everett would've given them the answer they wanted, and they would've eaten up every word. But, I'm not going to comment on bad calls against opposing players, especially after I walked away from that fight with only a major and no match penalty.

"I think the referees called what they saw. You know tensions were high, but that's part of the game."

"Two more," Sally says, moving the questions along. "Damian?"

"During the first period, you took a pretty nasty hit against the boards and then disappeared with the team doctor for a while before returning. Care to comment on what happened?"

I glance toward Sally, and she nods. "Yeah, sure. Doc wanted to make sure I was okay. Luckily, it was nothing serious, and I could return to the game."

The hands of a couple familiar reporters shoot up. Each one looking hungrier than the next for me to give more details about a possible injury, but I won't. Not tonight. Not until I fully understand what it means for my career.

"Alright, last question." Sally says, pointing to a female reporter sitting in the front row who I've never seen before. She looks to be in her mid-forties and is wearing a pink suit that matches the highlights in her long blonde hair.

"Hello, Everett. I'm here representing SDN. Great game tonight." She smiles. "There have been some rumors circulating that your return to the Crowns this season is signaling that you might be considering retirement soon. Is there any truth to these?"

Retirement rumors? Fucking perfect.

"As of now, I don't have plans to leave the league. I know that day will come eventually, as it does for every player, but I'm currently trying to focus on the present. Coming home to New York has been incredible, and I have every intent to finish out the season with this team. I plan to play as long as my body allows me to."

"Alright thank you every—" Sally begins, ending the interview as I start to stand.

"Actually, I do have a follow-up question," the reporter from SDN interjects, causing everyone in the room to turn to face her.

"I'm sorry. That's all Everett has time for tonight," Sally tries.

"It's a quick question," she argues. Her lavender eyes find mine, and I sink back into the chair.

"It's okay, Sally," I say. "I can take one more."

"Thank you," the pink-haired woman continues. "You said that you plan to play for as long as your body allows, so I guess that leaves me wondering if you're concerned about your current shoulder injury forcing you to retire."

Silence ripples through the small space, and when I look up, everyone's eyes are locked on me. Every reporter is poised with their recorders extended or their pens to paper waiting on my answer.

"Excuse me?" I ask, feigning confusion.

"Your shoulder," she repeats. "From my understanding, it's been giving you trouble since the second game this season. So, I'm curious if it'll be the reason you hang up your skates and I don't know…maybe settle down with someone special?"

My shoulder? Hang up my skates? Settle down? What is this woman getting at? There's currently no one special in my life, and the one person I ever even considered special enough to date seriously got away.

My eyes scan the crowd in front of me, and I know I need to answer her, but I can't form a coherent response.

"Who—" I begin, confused as to how she could know any of that. How anyone outside the team doctors could know.

"Thank you all for joining us," Sally says, abruptly interrupting me. She motions for me to stand. "That's all the time we have."

The room erupts with questions, and the bright lights of cameras flash as Sally ushers me out of the room. Following her to the door, my eyes find the pink haired reporter. She's wearing a smirk, and an uneasiness rolls through me. We hold each other's gazes until the door shuts behind me.

"What organization did she say she was with?" Sally asks, flustered.

"SDN," I say, thinking back to when she introduced herself.

"SDN?"

"That's what she said." I shrug. "You know I'm gonna have to address this."

She scans her phone and mumbles something under her breath.

"Go home and get some rest," she says. "We'll put out this fire tomorrow after you meet with the doctor and we have more information."

I hesitate before walking away, but my head is spinning with what-ifs and thoughts about retirement from the league. Whoever she was, she planted a seed in my head—and in the head of every major news organization that covers professional hockey.

Fuck.

My stomach turns at the thought. I'm not ready to quit. I don't need to quit—my shoulder is fine, and the meds are working. I can't let some reporter get under my skin. She doesn't know what she's talking about.

CHAPTER 9: IS IT REALLY YOU?

CLAIRE

I really should've kept the jacket until I got back to my apartment, and then I could've gotten rid of it properly instead of leaving it behind with those bitches and freezing my ass off.

Wanting to clear my head, I decided to walk home, but with every step, the bitter cold has sunk deeper into my bones, and now I'm just angry. Mad that I was too stupid to figure out that he was sleeping with me on the side. Furious that he lied so often, and I believed him every time. Enraged that I mistook Lily's kindness for friendship.

Fuck him and her and Monica and all her friends for making me feel like this.

I'm almost back to my place when I pass by Fritz's Hideaway. It's a dive bar down the street from my apartment that I've always seen but never entered. But tonight, something about it calls to me. Maybe it's the fact that I'm nearly hypothermic, or maybe I'm just not ready to go home alone. But, without giving it much thought, I pull the heavy wooden door open and walk inside.

It's a small establishment. Exposed brick and worn wooden floors give it a warm, welcoming atmosphere. There's a long bar on one side, and on the opposite wall is a row of retro pinball machines. The walls are decorated with an eclectic mix of video game and movie memorabilia. Two TVs are mounted on the back wall in front of two red couches. A group of men are gathered and playing some old-school video game.

Already feeling a little warmer, I brush off some of the snow stuck to my clothes and remove my hat. Smoothing my hair, I make my way over to the bar and sit on one of the leather barstools.

It's relatively quiet, but Rick Springfield's "Jessie's Girl" is playing just loud enough that you can enjoy it without getting a headache. Other than the small group in the back, there are two men sitting at one of the tables playing handheld video games. A woman and man are sitting at another table deep in a game of chess.

It's clear I'm out of my element, but there's something comfortable about being here.

"What can I get ya?" the bartender asks with a warm smile. He's an older man, with graying hair and wrinkled skin.

"Um, any chance you have coffee? I'm freezing."

"I do."

"I'll take one with some cream."

He nods and walks away.

Pulling out my phone, my finger lingers over Raph's contact, and I blow out a long breath. I don't want to relive the humiliation that I experienced back at the arena. I don't want to hear him try to explain himself. I just want this shit show to be over so I can move on and focus on me. Today was a good day until he ruined it.

Clicking on his name, I pull up our text thread. My whole body recoils as I read the last thing he sent me, causing me to drop my phone onto the bar top.

RAPH:

Don't make plans for after my game. I have a feeling I'll be hungry later 👅

Sitting there, I contemplate if I should text him. What a fucking douchebag, sending me that shit when he has a girlfriend.

This is why I don't usually mess with hockey players. This is why I steer clear of athletes—because this shit always happens. They're all cocky. They're all playboys. And they all think they can get away with absolutely asinine behavior.

The bartender returns with my drink, and I pick it up, taking a few sips. The hot, creamy coffee dances on my tongue, warming me up and giving me the confidence to do what I should've done before I left the arena.

Placing the mug down, I grab my phone. The tongue emoji

makes my stomach churn, and I do my best to ignore it as I type out my message.

> Ran into Monica after the game. Lose my number you piece of shit. We're over.

Harsh, but valid and completely deserved. I hit send and set it back on the bar top, feeling proud of myself for not giving him the chance to try to explain himself and risk falling for his bullshit. I don't care if he responds. I'd actually prefer it if he didn't.

Taking another sip of my drink, my shoulders relax for the first time since I saw Monica, and I do my best to focus on the good things that happened today—seeing my sister, my parents agreeing to come to the city for Christmas, and getting the part I've always wanted. I was given my dream role, in my dream ballet, and he's not going to tarnish this day for me.

I won't give him any more of my energy because he's not worth it.

A cold rush of air blows through the bar, causing me to shiver. Turning to see where it came from, the mug nearly slips from my hand.

Standing in the doorway is a tall man with broad shoulders. His brown hair sticks out under a backwards hat, and I watch as he unwinds the scarf around his neck, revealing his chiseled jaw that is covered with a short beard. I can't see his eyes from here, but I don't need to. I already know that they're the perfect mix of brown and green.

He shrugs off his black wool peacoat, and I take him in. Under his jacket, he's wearing a white hoodie and black sweatpants. He causally drapes his scarf and coat over his arm and then stomps his feet on the mat, kicking off the snow that has accumulated on his tennis shoes. Moving deeper into the bar, he looks over in my direction for the first time. Heat crawls up my neck when he catches me staring, and he lets out a low chuckle. His mouth breaks into a wide grin.

Lifting my hand into a small wave, I sip from the edge of my mug and watch as he moves directly for me.

The air between us is instantly charged and familiar. He's the last person I thought I'd see when I walked in here tonight, but I'm not mad about it. There is something reminiscent about me having a bad day and him showing up to help me forget about it. I feel instantly transported back in time.

"Hey, Sugar," he says, his eyes blinking, trying to take me in, and it's apparent we're both stunned to be looking at the other. I swallow hard, unsure of what to say. It's been a long time since I walked him to the door of my loft and said goodbye.

"Is it really you?" he asks, breaking the silence that hangs between us. His hand connects gently with my face, and his thumb grazes the apple of my cheek like he's checking to make sure I'm real. Electricity pulses through me under his touch before he realizes what he's doing and pulls away.

"I never liked that nickname," I say, lifting the corner of my mouth into a smirk.

"Never stopped me from using it before," he says, mirroring my facial expression.

I let out a small laugh. "You alone?" Peering behind him, I half expect a woman or a group of Crowns players to appear.

He nods. "Yeah. You? Or should I be worried Ulrich is about to walk out of the bathroom and kick my ass again?"

"He's not here," I grumble, taking a long sip of my coffee.

"No?" he questions, sliding on to the barstool next to me. The bartender walks over and places a beer in front of Everett.

"Thanks, Blake, but can I actually get a Coke instead. Not drinking tonight."

The bartender nods and turns to grab the soda, placing the beer to the side.

"Is he coming to join you?" Everett asks.

"Fuck, I hope not. I'm here trying to forget he exists."

A wide grin breaks across his face. The bartender returns with the drink, and Everett pulls out his wallet and flips it open. A small white piece of paper falls onto the bar when he slides out his card. In the center is a flower drawn with yellow and green crayon.

"For the Coke and whatever she's drinking. You can leave it open," he says, sliding his card toward the bartender.

"What's that?" I ask, pointing to a small piece of paper sitting on the bar top. He picks it up and studies it for a second.

"My nieces like to draw me pictures. This one is a tulip and is supposed to bring me good luck." His eyes become a little glossy, and his face falls slightly as he slips the tiny drawing back in his billfold and tucks it into his pocket.

"That's sweet that you keep it in your wallet."

I'm pretty sure I can hear my ovaries chanting, "Fuck him! Fuck him! Fuck him!" and who could blame them? He's sitting here in a backwards hat, black sweatpants, showing me his niece's art that he's saved in his wallet like some sort of perfect man, but I should know better. This is Everett. We didn't work before, so why would we work now?

"I don't get to see them often, and it makes me feel like I have them close by."

"Does that mean you've become a big softy since I last saw you?"

Grabbing his glass, he takes a sip and shakes his head. His throat bobs up and down as he swallows.

A distant memory of me telling him to call me if he was ever in town plays in my head, and my heart sinks at the idea that he didn't. Everett and I were hardly friends back then. We were good for one thing, and that was mind-blowing, toe-curling sex. My cheeks heat as I'm assaulted with a memory of us.

"Can I ask what happened?"

"Huh?"

"Between you and Ulrich," he clarifies.

"Oh! Let's see. We started dating a few months ago. He told me he and Monica, his ex, had broken up. I believed him, but then I found out after the game tonight, he lied."

"Damn," he says.

"Yeah, it was pretty mortifying getting blindsided by her and her pack of friends after the game."

"What did he say when you ended things?"

"Nothing yet. I texted him when I got here, and he hasn't responded."

"Are you okay?"

"At first I was hurt, but it only took the walk here to get over it and for the anger to settle in. I think I'm more upset about how I found out than about losing him."

"What do you mean?"

"You would think by now I wouldn't have to deal with mean girls. When I was young, I thought that, eventually, that behavior from other girls would stop. Like we would evolve or something, but apparently we haven't." I take another sip of my coffee. "I'm twenty-nine, and tonight I might as well have been fifteen, being embarrassed by the popular girl in the middle of the high school cafeteria."

He nods and sips his Coke.

"And I get it to some extent. She's hurt because her boyfriend cheated on her with me, and I wouldn't like me either. But..." I shake my head. "Calling me a whore and concocting a plan where someone pretended to be my friend just so they could mortify me was a new level of mean girl, and that's saying a lot because I've encountered plenty of Monicas in my life."

"You're not a whore."

"I know, and I don't know why I'm venting to you about this. I'm sure you don't care. Men don't have to deal with this shit."

"I care," he says. "And I think the fight at the end of the game tonight says otherwise. Men deal with that stuff in a different way."

"Right, men just punch one another and go about their day, while women are over here experiencing full on emotional warfare against one another. It's definitely the same thing."

He chuckles.

"Sorry he punched you," I offer.

"It wasn't the first fight I've been in, and it won't be my last." My eyes follow his hand as he rubs it along the hair covering his face, and a memory of him between my legs, peering up at me, assaults me from out of nowhere.

Shit, I need to get it together. It might feel like no time has passed, but it's been over four years. Raph and I just broke it off, but what I wouldn't give to let Everett help me forget all about him.

"You got a little bit of drool on your chin," he says, chuckling and pretending to wipe drool from his.

I grumble at his cockiness, diverting my gaze to one of the TVs hanging above the bar. It's a replay of his post-game interview.

Looking in Everett's direction, there's a noticeable change in his body language. His confidence seems to disappear as he zones in on the television.

We both sit in silence, watching. The clip of him cuts to a group of reporters sitting behind a table. We can't hear what they're saying, but the closed captioning on the bottom of the screen shows that one of the men is talking about a possible career ending shoulder injury.

"You mind changing the channel," he calls to the bartender, who looks up at the screen before nodding and switching it to some other sports channel. An image of Raph leaving the arena hand in hand with Monica flashes on the screen, and my heart sinks.

"Fuck," he breathes out. "Maybe just turn it off."

"How perfect." I look away, trying to hide the embarrassment that's creeping up my neck and covering my face.

The bartender lifts the remote, and the screen goes black. Sipping from his drink, he turns to face me again.

"I'm sorry," he says.

"Don't be. Want to talk about why you're here and not out celebrating the big win with your team?"

"Just needed to get my mind off things," he grumbles, taking another swig of his soda.

"Something to do with that shoulder injury they were talking about?"

He shrugs. "Maybe."

"Still grumpy, I see. I guess some things never change."

His jaw ticks, and the look on his face is the same one he gave me all those years ago when we played this little game. Warmth pools low in my belly, and my head floods with another memory of the two of us tangled together between my bed sheets. What it felt like when his tongue would…

He clears his throat, breaking my thoughts.

"You always liked when I was a little grumpy."

He's right. I did. I really fucking like it.

His hazel eyes rake over me, and I like the way it feels when he looks at me. I like it more than I know I should.

"You look beautiful," he says. His cheeks turn a soft shade of pink as he speaks.

"Seems like you're the one who's drooling," I swipe my thumb across my chin, repeating the same gesture he did. Our eyes lock on each other again, and for a moment, the rest of the bar melts away.

Never in a million years did I think I'd be close enough to touch him again, but here I am, sitting at a dive bar and wishing he'd pull me out of it, take me home, and make me forget the night I've had.

Chapter 10:
Quick Fingers

I swallow down a sip of my Coke as I take her in. Long onyx hair, delicate frame, black mini dress, and black thigh-high boots. I smile over my glass when I notice the jacket she was wearing in the arena is nowhere to be found.

Her blue eyes lock on mine, and she casually moves her ankle against the side of my calf, causing me to choke on the sip I just took.

"You good?" she asks, her mouth turning into a sultry smile.

"Fine," I cough out, clearing my throat.

"Everett, can I get you another one?" Blake asks.

"No, I'm good," I say, shaking my head. "Thanks, man."

"You hockey boys can't go anywhere without being noticed, can you?"

A laugh rumbles through my chest. She's not wrong. Most of the time, I'm bombarded by fans, women, and reporters. It's exhausting. Younger me craved that attention. I was desperate to be noticed everywhere I went, but now I prefer not to be bothered. It's my favorite thing about Fritz's. The only thing the regulars care about here is if their high score on one of the many game machines has been beaten.

It's why I walked in. I figured sitting at the bar for a little while, even if I can't drink with that shot, or playing some pinball was better than going home and being alone with my thoughts.

"Blake bartends most nights I'm here." I shrug, taking the last sip of my soda and placing the glass on the bar.

"Most nights?" Claire questions, moving her foot away. "Do you come here often then?" Her eyes move around the mostly empty bar. "Are you secretly really good at pinball or something?"

"You know I've always had quick fingers." I smirk.

She rolls her eyes and attempts to not be amused by my joke, but I know her better than that.

"Didn't realize the skills transferred so easily," she teases.

"Oh, they definitely do." I tap my fingers against the wood surface of the bar and watch her eyes narrow in on them as she gently bites her lip. She quickly redirects her gaze as her cheeks turn a rosey pink, causing me to wonder if she's thinking about how easily I could make her come undone with just one touch too. How I knew exactly how to use them to make her scream my name.

"So, um, is that why you come here?"

I chuckle. "To practice my quick fingers?"

Blush covers her face. "No. I meant to play pinball? You aren't drinking, so I thought maybe you came to play pinball."

"Oh, no. I'm not drinking because they gave me a shot of Toradol at the game for my shoulder." My left hand runs over the injection site.

"Then why are you here?"

"It's my favorite spot for when I need to clear my head. I know I'll be left alone. Most of the regulars know nothing about hockey."

"You? Wanting to be left alone? I don't believe that for a minute." She laughs.

"Is it that hard to believe I don't want to be in the spotlight?"

Another melodic laugh leaves her, and she plays with the curls of her hair, shaking her head. "It's just hard to believe that the man who was thirty minutes late to our first date because he was outside of the restaurant posing for photos wants to be left alone now."

"People change."

"Maybe so," she muses. Her gaze travels down to my cock and then back up to me. "Let's hope some things about you haven't."

Her mouth tips into a smirk. There's a daring glare in her baby blues, and my dick twitches below my sweatpants.

She's definitely thinking what I'm thinking.

Leaning forward, I invade her space and tuck a piece of her hair behind her ear. Her breath hitches as I continue to move in closer.

The scent of sweet vanilla perfume overwhelms my senses, and my cock grows harder. "I can assure you nothing has changed in that department, Sugar," I whisper into her ear. My fingers trail across the line of her jaw and then drop, causing her mouth to part slightly.

"I can see that," she says. "You're still as cocky as you ever were."

"And you don't like that?" I challenge.

"No, I think I do."

Her phone buzzes against the bar top, interrupting our moment, causing me to lean back onto my barstool, putting unwanted space between us.

I watch as she swipes up on the screen, and her face falls. "He can't actually be serious," she mutters under her breath. Locking the screen, she slams the phone back onto the wooden surface.

"Who was that?" I ask, hesitantly. I know I shouldn't pry into her personal life. That's never who we were to one another, but I also don't like that look on her face.

She hesitates for a moment, glancing towards me and then back to where the phone sits. "Raph," she says, running her hand through her hair. Her phone buzzes again and then again. "What a fucking dick."

"Is that him again?" I ask.

"I just want him to leave me alone so I can forget about him." Gone is the wild, flirty, confident girl who was just here. There's no fire in her eyes. She looks sad, and I hate it.

"Sugar, you deserve so much more than him."

She looks up at me with a glossy gaze, and I watch as she swallows down whatever feelings are flooding her head. This time, it's my breath that hitches as she leans forward, enclosing in on my space. The sweet smell of her perfume overwhelms me, and I find myself wanting to be the man who makes her forget how she's feeling. The man who makes her feel good tonight.

"Show me what I deserve," she says, her voice breathy with need. "Take me home and show me. Just like you used to do."

Without thinking, my hands move to caress either side of her face, and our mouths meet. Her lips part, letting me in.

Deep down, I know what this is. This is her using me to get back at the person who hurt her, and for a split second I consider stopping to protect my heart, but the taste of her tongue has my dick throbbing and my heart railing against my chest. The reason doesn't matter. I want to be the one who erases the bad night she's had, even if it's just for tonight. My hands trail down to her hips, pulling her from her barstool and causing her to straddle my leg.

She writhes against my thigh and moans into me as I shift my leg upward, creating the perfect friction against her clit. Her arms wrap around my neck, and she moves her hands through my hair, deepening our kiss.

I hear a throat clear behind me, and it dawns on me we're still sitting at the bar.

As much as my dick is begging me to sit her on top of the smooth wood surface, neither she nor I need the attention that would bring. Pulling away slightly, she lets out a small, disapproving gasp and locks her eyes on mine.

"Want to get out of here?" I ask, heart beating rapidly from our kiss.

"Please," she says, nodding. Her face is flushed, and her chest rises and falls as she attempts to catch her breath. I quickly take care of the tab, and we gather our belongings. Grabbing her hand, I lead her out of the bar and into the snow, not knowing if anything will come of this beyond tonight, but sure that whatever happens it will be worth it.

CHAPTER 11:
ANSWER IT
CLAIRE

Making out with random men in bars isn't like me, but it's Everett, and tonight I don't really feel like making all the right decisions when I could make the wrong ones.

The frosty air stings my cheeks and causes a shiver to run through me as we stumble out of Fritz's. The streetlights illuminate the falling snow. The traffic is unusually light for this time of night, but with the weather, I can't imagine many people wanting to be out and about.

"Fuck, it's cold," I say, letting go of his hand. I pull my hat over my ears and fold my arms across my chest, trying to hold in some of my body heat.

"Here," he says, wrapping his jacket around my shoulders. The heavy fabric of his coat engulfs me, immediately helping me to feel a little warmer.

"You don't want it?" I ask. "It's freezing out here."

He loosely wraps his scarf around his neck and tucks his hands into the pocket of his hoodie. "I'll be okay."

"So, where are we going?" I ask, desperate to get somewhere quickly so I can taste his kiss again and feel his hands on my body.

"My place is in the West Village, so it's a bit of a walk, but we could take a cab."

"I'm just six blocks this way." I gesture down the street.

He nods, and we begin to walk toward my apartment. The snow falls heavily, and he pulls me close. The night air is filled with the noises of the city. Glancing up, I find him looking at me, and tension ripples between us.

Grabbing my hand, he spins me out and then into his chest. His large hands find my face, and his mouth collides with mine. The kiss is urgent and needy, and I melt into him on the side of this snowy street as if no one can see us. A loud bang in the distance causes me to step back.

"Was that thunder?" I ask, peering up at the night sky and attempting to catch my breath.

"It sounded like it. Come on." Taking my hand, he begins to run down the sidewalk, dragging me behind him.

"Since when are you this spontaneous," I yell through a burst of laughter.

He pauses again, pulling me into him. His hands move through my hair and down my back as he kisses me once more.

"I told you people can change." An icy breeze blows through us, and we both take off again. Hand in hand, he pulls me along through the snow.

The Everett I used to know would've never run down the streets of New York in the middle of a snow storm with me. He was always so serious, so focused on his image. On his career.

"You're insane," I yell, continuing to weave down the street, barely missing a couple walking in the opposite direction.

"It's cold as shit," he hollers back. "But, I have an idea of how we can get warm."

"Ev, my shoes. They aren't made to run in the snow."

Without hesitation, he swings around and picks me up, cradling me in a bridal hold.

"Put me down!" I yell. "We're almost there."

"Good," he says, continuing to hold me in his arms as he moves across the blanket of white covering the path to the brownstone I call home.

"I can walk," I argue. "Your shoulder is hurt. You shouldn't be carrying me."

He stops moving and looks down. "Your shoes were slowing us down, and I'm desperate to make you feel good."

I swallow hard, and need courses through me again.

"So, are you going to continue to be a brat and fight me? Or are you good with me holding you?"

"If you insist," I say, shaking my head.

"Oh, I insist." He takes off, moving quickly down the sidewalk again. The smell of his cologne engulfing my senses as I nuzzle into his chest.

"Wait, you missed it," I yell as he bypasses my place and continues to head down the street. "It's the one with the blue door."

Stopping, he moves backward until I tell him to stop, and then he slowly lowers me to the ground, tracing the curve of my body with his hands.

"This is me," I say, nodding to the door at the top of the stairs.

"Can I come—" he begins, but he's interrupted by another loud crash in the distance, causing me to jump.

"Was that thunder again?" I ask, looking up at the night sky.

"I don't know. Thundersnow is pretty rare, but it's really coming down, so it could've been."

"Maybe we should—" I begin, but another boom echoes across the sky, and the street goes pitch black, leaving us in the dark.

"What the fuck?" I shout, stepping closer and wrapping my arms around his waist. There's not a working street or traffic light as far as we can see. A passing cab's headlights illuminate everything for a split second as it passes, but then we are returned to dark as it disappears down the road. We've had power outages before, but this is unbelievable. It's like someone flipped a switch and turned every light in the city off.

"Looks like the power's out," he says.

"Gathered that," I deadpan, looking around. "But why?"

"The snow storm? We better get inside." Pulling out his phone, he turns on the flashlight. We begin to carefully climb the stairs leading to the door of my place when another loud roll of thunder echoes through the darkness, making us both pause on the top step.

"Oh, my god," I say, taking in the sight before me. Swirls of pink dance across the sky above us, casting a soft, rose-colored glow on everything the light touches. It's like nothing I've ever seen before. It's ethereal and magical, and I can't look away.

"The northern lights?" Everett questions.

Cars passing by stop, and people join us on the street to take in the dancing lights.

"I've never seen anything so beautiful," I say, watching as the lights flow from a deep magenta to a soft blush, illuminating everything they touch.

"No?" he questions, his voice is a little raspy. "I have."

I turn to face him, fully expecting his eyes to be locked on the mesmerizing show in the sky, but instead, he's looking at me.

Just as I'm about to give him shit about the cheesy line, he takes my hands, and the world falls away as he stares deep into my eyes. His mouth finds mine again. This time, it's not desperate and needy, but instead it's soft and sweet. My knees buckle under the feel of his lips on mine, and he catches me, wrapping one of his arms around my lower back. His other hand finds the back of my head and pulls gently at the hair falling beneath my hat, tilting my head back and letting him take our kiss deeper. My hands explore his body, and the energy between us shifts again to something more heady. I want this man.

Fuck, I *need* this man.

Pulling away, I fumble for my key to unlock the door.

"Wait," he says. The lights move, casting a pink glow across his face and revealing a smirk. "You don't want to watch the lights a little bit longer."

"No," I say. "I want you."

He chuckles. Leaning forward, his mouth finds my ear. "Needy, are we?"

"Yes," I breathe out, turning the key and pushing the door open. We move inside quickly, and he follows me up the stairs to my second floor apartment. He pushes my back against the door, and his hands trail up my thigh, under my dress.

"Fuck, you're wet," he says, his fingers finding my center over my thin tights. I let out a laugh. Flipping around, I push the key into the door and then turn the knob to reveal my dark apartment. The pink lights cast a romantic glow throughout the space, and I swallow hard when I hear the door shut behind me. His hands find my hips and he spins me around, pushing me up against the wall in between a small entry table and the window. Taking a step back, his eyes rake over me. I drop my purse to the floor and then slowly remove the hat from my head and his coat from my shoulders, revealing the short black dress that hugs every curve of my body perfectly.

Grabbing the scarf that hangs around his neck, I pull him towards me. Our bodies collide, and his leg moves between my own, shifting upward and creating toe-curling pressure against my sensitive bud. I gasp at the feel of it as I grind against him, and his lips find mine again. His rough beard tickles against my face, and my hands move up his back.

Pausing our kiss for a moment, he chucks his scarf and hat across the room and then pulls his hoodie and shirt up and over his head, revealing his sculpted chest and abs. My hands trace the cut lines, and my fingers toy with the hem of his sweatpants.

Goosebumps erupt across my skin, and warmth pools low in my belly as he leans forward and his lips find the pulse point on my neck. He continues to trail his tongue up my throat, and I tilt my head, granting him more access to the sensitive skin there. At my feet, my phone begins to vibrate. I do my best not to let the ringing distract me from this moment, but Everett slows/ our kiss.

"Ignore it," I say, pulling him back into me and pushing my hips forward.

He chuckles against me. "Oh, I plan to," he says.

His mouth finds mine again, and I part my lips, letting him in. His hands work over my body, and I shift my hips forward, grinding against his thigh. His back muscles flex as I move my hands over them, pulling him closer, chasing my release.

My phone begins to ring again, but neither of us stops. When he picks me up, my legs wrap around his waist, and he pushes me against the wall. His hard length presses into me, and fuck, I want him inside me. My mouth. My pussy. At this point, I don't care. I just want him.

My phone begins to ring for a third time, and he breaks our kiss.

"Maybe you should answer it," he says, resting his forehead against mine.

"No," I say. "Whoever it is can wait until we're done."

"The power is out though. It could be someone trying to make sure you're okay."

He sets me down, and I let out a grumble just as the ringing stops.

Bending down, I grab my bag and dig out my phone. The vibrations begin for a fourth and very obnoxious time. Looking at the screen, I expect to see my sister's name or maybe my mom's, but instead I'm met with the words *Raph Ulrich.*

"He can't be serious," I say, silencing the ringer and forwarding him to voicemail.

"Is it Ulrich?"

"Yeah, so it's not important. Where were we?" My eyes find his, and my tongue wets my lips, eager to finish what we've started.

It begins to ring for a fifth time, causing me to shift my gaze back to my phone. Raph's name scrolls across the screen again. Blowing out a frustrated breath, I move my finger to ignore the call, but Everett stops me.

"Don't," he commands, his voice raspy. "Answer it. I have an idea."

Studying him for a second, I watch as he drops to his knees before me.

"Answer it, Sugar. Let me make you feel good while you tell him to fuck off." A sly smile erupts across his face. My heart begins to pound against my chest as I swipe my thumb across the screen, and he lifts one of my legs over his bare shoulder.

"Hello," I say, my voice wavering slightly.

"What the fuck, Claire." Raph's voice comes through the phone at the same time I watch Everett bunch up my dress and rip open my tights at the center, exposing my bare pussy underneath the thin black fabric. His eyes darken as he takes me in, and his tongue grazes his lower lip.

"Claire," Raph barks.

He's mad, and I do my best to focus on what he's saying, but I can't. I'm too distracted by the gorgeous man kneeling before me, staring at me like I'm his last fucking meal.

"Uh, yeah, I'm here. Sorry," I say.

Everett reaches up, taking the phone from my hand. Muting the call, he says, "Don't apologize. You don't deserve to be treated like this. You have nothing to be sorry for."

He's right. I don't have anything to be sorry for. Not for anything I did or anything I'm about to do. I lose focus of Raph's voice coming through the phone entirely. Everett turns his head and lays a kiss against my inner thighs, and then his gaze returns back to mine.

"Now, I'm going to unmute the phone and put it on speaker. I want you to use me, let me make you feel good, and when you're ready, I want you to tell him off. Show him what he fucked up and lost."

His voice is low and demanding, and I do my best to not internally combust, but with just his words, he's winding my core tighter and pushing me closer to the edge. Swallowing hard, I nod my head, silently agreeing.

"You think you can do that, Sugar?"

I let out a "Yes" that sounds more like a moan, and a wicked grin spreads across Everett's face. Raph continues to drone on about something, not even noticing I've gone silent, and Everett doesn't break eye contact as he runs his large hands over my delicate frame. It's otherworldly the effect he has on me, and despite the nagging feeling that this might be a very bad idea, it feels too good to tell him to stop.

CHAPTER 12: I KNEW YOU'D COME...

Claire looks wild. Her chest rises and falls as she stares down at me, eyes wide and dark. Her hair falls messily around her shoulders. At this moment, I have one goal—to let her use me until it's my name she's screaming and his she's forgotten.

I unmute the phone and place a finger across my lips, warning her to stay quiet. Tapping the speaker button, I set it on the entry table to her right.

"Are you even listening to me?" Raph bites out, frustrated.

"I'm busy. What do you want?" she asks, her voice more steady than before.

The pink lights are still dancing across the night sky outside and bleed through the blinds, casting a soft glow on her and the surrounding space.

Her pussy glistens with her arousal in the dim light, and my cock aches at the thought of how turned on she is. How badly she wants this—wants me.

My hands run over the smooth skin of her hips, ripping the fabric of her tights more and rolling them out of the way.

Her breath catches, and I give her a warning stare, returning my finger to my lip.

"Fuck, would you pay attention," Raph snaps, as I kiss her thigh right above the top of her boot. "I want to know why you texted me to lose your number. You can't be serious, baby. You know you're mine."

I pause, stopping myself from interjecting. If she needs me to step in I will, but I know she can do this. I place a few more kisses on her soft skin, inching my way closer to her center.

"I'm not yours," she says, doing her best to maintain her composure.

"You know that's not true," Raph tries.

I chuckle against her. What a fucking douchebag. Laying it on thick like he wasn't sleeping with multiple women.

In one long, languid stroke, I move my tongue up her slit, taking her into my mouth. Her body shudders under the feeling, and a moan escapes past her lips.

"What are you doing?" Raph questions.

My tongue toys with her clit for a few moments, and she goes silent. When I peer up, she's biting her hand, trying to not make a sound, and her eyes have fallen shut.

"Speak," he shouts, causing them to shoot open.

"I…um…it's none of your business." Her voice quivers as I continue to work between her legs. Her hands find my hair, and the heel of her boot digs into my back, pulling me closer.

"Whatever. I don't want to lose you, so can we just put this behind us and move on. I'll see you when I get home from Pittsburgh in a few days."

"No," she snaps. Her breaths are heavy.

"No?"

My mouth engulfs her, and I suck hard, causing her hips to buck.

"Yessss," she calls out, causing me to chuckle against her.

"Yes?" he questions. "I knew you'd come—"

"No!" she yells, realizing her mistake. "I meant no."

"No?"

My tongue continues to circle her bundle of nerves, and her body threatens to fold above me. In one movement, I position her other leg over my shoulder, grip her ass with both hands, and stand, lifting her with me. My mouth doesn't leave her pussy, and she lets out a squeal. The heels of her boots bite my skin, and my cock grows harder.

"What was that?"

"Nothing…I…um…oh god…" She moans as I continue to devour her, drinking her in. She tastes so fucking sweet, and based on the way her body is writhing against me, I can tell she's close.

"Are you fucking someone?" he shouts, just as my mouth finds her clit one more time. Her fingers knot in my hair, and she rocks her hips forward.

"Fuck…yes…don't stop…" she pants out. My hands dig into her perfect ass, and all it takes is a few more flicks of my tongue for her to come apart above me. Her body shakes as she falls, and Raph is screaming something through the phone, but I can't hear him. I'm too distracted by the sounds coming from her mouth and the way my name sounds on her lips. I carry her through her climax, and then when I'm sure she's completely unraveled, I carefully lower her to the floor, my mouth finding hers.

"Everett?" Raph screams. "You're fucking Nuttall?

Claire breaks our kiss and inhales deeply.

"Raph, I know it's really hard for you to accept that someone would want nothing to do with you, but just because your ego is fragile, doesn't mean I have to give you a second chance. If you haven't put it together, we're done." Her shoulders are held high, and despite still trying to catch her breath, she sounds so strong. My heart expands in my chest as I listen to her speak.

"I meant what I said," she continues. "Lose my number and leave me the fuck alone. I have no interest in being anyone's other woman, especially yours."

"You really are just some puck slut," he spits. "So desperate to fuck anyone with a stick, you don't care whose bed your climbing into. Good luck to Nuttall. I hope he's enjoying my sloppy seconds. I don't—"

"That's enough," I bark. "Don't speak to her like that."

"Fuck you," he shouts. The line goes silent, and when I look down at the phone, it's Claire's finger resting on the screen. She ended the call.

"You okay?" I ask.

"Yeah." Her fingers intertwine with mine, and she begins walking toward an open door, tugging me behind her.

The pink lights continue to glimmer around us, making the moment feel like a dream. We walk through the open door to her bedroom, and I take her in. She really is stunning.

The fact that this might only last for one night slams me in the chest. I've spent so long wishing we had another chance, but I have no idea where her head's at, and that's sobering.

Spinning around to meet me, her body presses up against mine, and my hands trail down her back to unzip her dress. She removes it, letting it pool on the floor. Her breasts are covered by a sheer lace bralette, and her tights are torn to pieces, hanging from her body above her boots.

Walking her backwards, she falls onto her mattress. Carefully, I unzip a boot, taking my time to remove it before moving to the other one. A soft smile covers her face as she watches me. She's leaned back on her elbows, and her eyes are full of need. Pulling her tattered tights off, I reveal her long, smooth legs.

"Those were my favorite pair of tights," she says, smirking.

"I think I like them better like this, " I say, chuckling and dropping them to the floor.

"Of course you do," she says, shaking her head.

My hands find the waistband of my pants, but Claire sits up and scoots closer to where I stand.

"Allow me," she says, her hands finding the band of my pants and briefs. She pulls them both down simultaneously, and my cock springs free.

Her eyes drop to my dick and land on the silver barbell that's pierced through the ridged edge of the head. Reaching out, she takes me into her hand and moves her palm down my shaft before stopping and running her thumb over the smooth metal balls on either side of the bar.

Her tongue juts out across her lower lip, and her gaze heats.

"Glad to see not everything has changed." She smirks, massaging her hand down my length again. My dick throbs under her soft touch.

"Do you have a condom?" she asks, letting go.

"Yeah." Bending down, I fumble to find my wallet in the pocket of my pants.

"Hurry," she teases.

"Don't be a brat," I say, finally locating the little foil packet and ripping it open.

"If I remember correctly, you used to like when I was a little bratty." Her lips curl upward, and she moves back on the bed, falling onto her elbows. I roll the condom down my shaft and crawl above her, pushing her legs further apart as I move.

"You look beautiful," I say, tracing my hand over the curve of her hip and up to her breasts. My fingers trail over the thin fabric covering her nipples. Rolling one between my finger and thumb, I pinch gently, causing her entire body to shudder.

"You don't look too bad yourself," she says, her hands exploring the cut lines of my chest and abs. My skin ignites under her touch, and I bend down, taking her mouth in mine. The tension between us snaps the minute our lips meet, and the kiss turns into a filthy mix of clashing teeth and twisting tongues.

Moaning, she pulls back. "Fuck me, Ev," she begs. "I don't want to wait."

"Gladly. How do you want me?"

She hesitates for a moment, and my cock pulses in anticipation with what she's going to say. It feels as if no time has passed, like we do this all the time.

"From behind," she says, rolling out from underneath me and positioning herself flat on her stomach with her head on her pillow.

Following her lead, I grip her hips firmly, pulling upward so that her ass is in the air. She gasps when I touch her, and a feral need overtakes me as I rake my hands over her soft skin, reveling in the view.

"Don't be gentle," she demands as I line myself up.

With one hand remaining firmly on her hip, I pull her back into me and let out a low groan as I slowly sink into her. Pushing forward, I gasp as her tight, perfect cunt strangles my cock.

"Fuck," she breathes out, drawing out the ending sound of the word. "You feel so fucking good."

This is nothing like it was four years ago. It's better, which I didn't think was possible. Sex with Claire was always good, but this —this is magic.

She pushes her hips into me as I pump forward.

"Is that all you got?" she asks, peering back at me over her shoulder. A smirk paints her face, and wild lust pulses through me.

This isn't the first time she's challenged me, but just like it did four years ago, it ignites something within me. My free hand knots in her hair, tugging a little harder than I should, and my hips continue to drive forward.

"More," she says. "Give me more."

I pull on her hair a little harder, causing her back to arch and her ass to grind against me. The moan that leaves her mouth threatens to end the fun we're having prematurely, so I slow down because I don't want this to end.

Letting go of her hair, I bend forward. Covering her body with mine, I pause my movements and try to regain control. She needs to come again.

Raking my teeth along her ear, I whisper, "You always looked so pretty when you let me fuck you like this."

Another moan falls past her lips, and she pushes back into me again, desperate for movement. One of my hands wraps under her waist. Finding her clit, I begin to toy with it.

"Please," she begs, attempting to writhe underneath me.

"I always liked how needy your cunt was when it came to me," I say. "How no matter what, you were desperate for me to fuck you. Desperate for me to play with you like this."

I quicken my circles, and she rocks back into me.

"Well, then give me what I want," she says, her voice breathy.

I sit up and run my free hand down her spine. Her skin erupts with goosebumps, and she throws her hips backward into me again.

Continuing to tease her sensitive nub, I push my hips forward, tilting them slightly so that I can create the pressure I know she craves.

Her hand finds mine. "Harder," she insists, replacing my hand with hers and beginning to play with herself. "Fuck me harder."

Her fingers move in precise circles, and I grip both of her hips, pulling her tightly against me.

Pressure builds as I watch her pleasure herself while I fuck her. Her face is buried in her pillow. Her dark waves are strung all around her.

"Yes, Everett," she yells, her voice muffled. "I'm so close."

In the past, I knew that there was no future between us, but as I watch her body move underneath me—watch her take me so well— I question if that still holds true today. The thought of being able to repeat this again, with her, pushes me closer to the edge, and I do my best to shake the thought.

Over and over, I thrust my hips forward, fighting the feelings I've had for four years. The sound of the creaking bed frame and the headboard knocking against the wall distracts me, but when my eyes rake over her and I see the look of euphoria painting her face in the dim light, thoughts of what could be come rushing back, threatening to catapult me over the finish line.

"Come with me, Sugar," I say, driving my hips forward, and that's all it takes.

Her pussy tightens around my shaft, and we ride out our orgasms together. Collapsing, we're both nothing but heavy breaths and moans. My body engulfs hers, and I nestle my face into the crook of her neck, breathing in her sugary scent. For a moment, I forget there's a chance she doesn't feel the same way as me. That whatever just happened was another blip, and as much as I liked it, she was just trying to forget the asshole who hurt her, but maybe there's a chance this time will be different.

Chapter 13: I'm Not a Psycho

Claire

Our bodies are still tangled, and I attempt to catch my breath. It's strange how you can go so long without seeing or touching a person, and it feels like no time has elapsed at all. Except it has. Something's different about him now. Not in the sex department. No. He still seems to know exactly what to do to make me come completely undone. How to cast a lustful haze over all of my decisions. And maybe that's what this is, but maybe not. His spontaneity tonight took me completely by surprise. The daring stares and chuckles against my skin were an entirely new side of him I've never seen before. I liked it, and I wonder if, given the chance, he'd continue to prove me wrong and let me know him completely. Or if I'm just hungover from his dick and not thinking clearly.

Honestly, it could be either one.

"You're crushing me," I tease, shoving him off.

Chuckling against my neck, his rough beard tickles my sensitive skin. "My bad," he says, rolling away and out of the bed. I watch as he crosses my room.

His strong body and tight ass stir something deep inside me, and I realize I'm in trouble. Big fucking trouble. Slamming my eyes shut, I hit my head against the pillow.

Do I regret what just happened? No.

Now that I've been reminded what sex with him is like, will I be able to stop? Probably not.

Has he really changed? Possibly.

Am I fucked? Definitely.

Exhaling, I sit up and attempt to tame my hair.

"Power's still out," he calls.

"Seriously?"

Climbing out of my bed, the waves of pink are still churning outside my bedroom window, and I fiddle with the lamp next to my bed, but it doesn't turn on.

"You didn't believe me?" he says, causing me to turn.

"The bathroom light was on the brink of going out the other day. I was just making sure," I explain, rounding my bed. He finds his underwear and pulls them on, snapping the waistband.

Tall, lean, muscular—he truly looks like he was created in a lab. Dark hair covers his chest and face. The lion tattoo that is an ode to his team was once the only thing to cover his left thigh, but it's now surrounded by large flowers and greenery, creating a sleeve that trails down his leg. The bulge of his pierced dick is perfectly outlined under his tight boxer briefs.

The images on the internet didn't lie. He's somehow more attractive than he was before he left, and I have to force myself to look away.

Yeah, I'm definitely fucked.

Walking out of my bedroom, I find my phone where we left it and blush at the thought of what took place against the wall in front of me.

How hot it was when Everett picked me up and ate me out with my legs locked around his shoulders. He felt so fucking strong underneath me, and I liked it. I liked it a lot—a little too much.

Fuck, I want to do that again.

Grabbing my phone, I swipe up, turning on my flashlight and walking back toward my bathroom. A stream of texts from Raph litter my screen, most of them qualifying as some sort of harassment. What a dick.

"You good?" Everett asks when I cross the threshold of my bedroom door.

"Oh yeah. Raph can't let it go that I dumped him. I think we bruised his neverending ego."

"What's he saying?" he asks, concern lacing his voice.

"It doesn't matter."

"It does matter," he says, stepping towards me, but I turn and head into the bathroom, shutting the door behind me.

It doesn't matter. I refuse to waste any of my energy worrying what he thinks of me. I have too much to unpack about the other parts of my day and night.

"You sure you're okay?" he asks from right outside the door.

"I'm fine," I shout, laughing. "I promise. Would you please let me pee in peace?"

"Oh, right…um…" The sound of his footsteps grows farther away, and my shoulders relax.

Massaging my temples, I grab my phone and tap through the steps of deleting Raph's texts and blocking the douchebag's number.

I stand and wash my hands.

One man dealt with, but now what do I do with the one still in my bedroom? Part of me wouldn't be surprised if I opened the door and found myself alone. He and I never spent the night with each other, so why would tonight be any different? Whatever feelings I'm having about this situation are present because he fucked all the sense from my head.

I fix my bralette over my tits and run my fingers through my hair. Exhaling, I open the door, bracing myself for an empty bedroom, but instead I'm met with a half-dressed Everett.

"Oh, you're still here," I say.

"Uh, yeah. I was just getting dressed."

"Oh, okay," disappointment settles in my chest.

He has no reason to stay, so why do I want him to?

Walking over to my dresser, I open the top drawer and pull out a thong. Looping my legs through the lace, I pull it up over my hips, and when I turn around, he's standing there, unmoved.

"You know you could stay over," I suggest, the words spilling from my mouth before I can stop them.

"Really?" There's an eagerness in his voice that makes me wonder if he's feeling the same as me. Like maybe he's wondering where this might go if we gave it a chance this time. Maybe he's curious too.

"I just meant with the snow storm and the blackout. It's probably a nightmare out there."

"Oh, right. The weather." His hands push into his pockets, and he rocks back on his heels. "You sure?"

Goddammit. Why did I say that?

"Yeah," I try a little more enthusiastically. I walk over and place my phone on the nightstand and crawl into bed. He starts to walk toward the door.

"Wait. Where are you going?" I ask, snuggling under the comforter and into my pillow.

"I figured you'd want me to crash on the couch. Plus, I don't want to wake you in the morning. I'm going to need to run by my place before meeting with the team doctor tomorrow for my shoulder."

"Oh, no, it's fine," I say, patting the bed next to me. "I was planning to get to the studio early before rehearsals officially start. We can share."

Tilting his head to the side, the corner of his mouth tips upward. "Okay."

Pulling off his sweatpants again, he drops them by the bed and joins me under the covers.

The mattress shifts under his weight, and he fluffs the pillows behind him. "Do you have another pillow?"

"Another pillow?"

"Yeah, I like to sleep with three."

Three pillows? Is this some primadonna star athlete shit?

"Three?"

"I mean, it's how I usually sleep, but if you don't have one it's fine," he says, adding a bit of mopiness for dramatic effect. "I'll manage."

"Top shelf in the closet, princess," I jest, giggling. "Can you grab it, or do you need me to fetch it for you?"

He chuckles loudly, throwing the covers off of him. "Is three that big of a deal?" he asks, padding across the room toward my closet.

"I barely need one, let alone three. It's a little extra."

"What does barely one mean?" He disappears into my closet. "It's dark as shit in here? Which side?"

"Top left. Behind the door." I pause. "I usually push the pillow I'm using out of the way and just sleep on the mattress."

"You don't sleep with a pillow?"

There's a crash, and I hear him curse under his breath.

"You good in there?" I yell, sitting up.

"Fine. Just knocked some shoes down."

There's another pause.

"I do sleep with one, just not the whole night."

"How did I not know this about you?" he asks, walking back into the room, holding a pillow.

"We never actually made it to the sleeping portion of the night."

"I guess not." He rolls his shoulder and shakes his arm. "Fuck."

"What's wrong?"

"I think the pain meds are finally wearing off. When I reached up to get the pillow, a sharp pain shot down my arm, and now I can't seem to shake it."

He tosses the pillow into the bed and then rubs the opposite hand over the injured joint as he walks the last few steps.

"Probably shouldn't have lifted me like you did earlier. I'm sorry."

"You gotta stop apologizing." He pauses before climbing on top of the mattress. "Do you have any ibuprofen?"

"In my purse. Near the front door."

I watch him walk back into the dark living room. Apologizing has always been a habit I couldn't break. I'm not sure why it pops out without a second thought; it just always has. Probably some pathetic tendency to want to make everyone around me comfortable.

"You mind if I get it out myself?" he asks, returning and holding my purse up in the air.

"Go ahead. Promise there's nothing exciting in there."

Chuckling, he opens the zipper and begins to walk towards me but trips on one of my boots in the middle of the floor and sends the bag into the air. "Fuck," he yells, catching his balance as the sound of all of my belongings scattering across the wood floor fills my room.

"You okay?"

"Shit, yeah," he says. "I'm sorry. Can you hand me my phone?"

"It's fine." I climb out of bed with both of our cell phones. "Here, let me help you."

Turning on the flashlights, we begin picking up the contents and place it all back in my bag. After a moment, he pauses. I flash the light in his direction to find his lips curved upward. "Are these... trading cards?" he asks, gesturing to the three cards strewn across the floor.

Oh, fuck.

"Yeah, but I was given them tonight at the game. I don't collect them or anything. I'm not a psycho."

He picks up all three from the ground, scanning them with the light coming from his phone. "I had no idea you were so obsessed with me." He grins and flashes them in my direction.

"Am not."

"Then why do you have three trading cards with my face on them?"

"Coincidence." I shrug.

"You can admit it."

"I'm not obsessed with you," I deadpan. "They were handing them out at the game. I obviously got you so many times because there aren't too many noteworthy Crowns players."

"Not true, but glad to know you think I'm *noteworthy*." He chuckles, and his shoulders move up and down, causing his laugh to turn to a wince.

"You okay?"

"I'll be fine," he says, returning them to my bag. We stand, and I hand him the small bottle of ibuprofen. Setting my purse on the nightstand, I climb back into bed. The lid of the plastic bottle scrapes as he opens it, and the rattling of the pills fills the silence. He dumps them into his hand and throws them into his mouth, swallowing them dry.

"You don't want some water?"

"Nah," he says, climbing back in to join me.

We both settle into the bed on our respective sides. Disappointment starts to creep in as his breathing becomes steady.

"Hey, Ev?" I whisper.

"Yeah?" His voice is a little groggy, and I find it endearing.

"Thanks for tonight."

The sound of him turning over causes me to turn as well.

"Are you thanking me for sex?" he asks, his eyes finding mine in the dimly lit space.

"No...I just meant...I don't know. Being with you really turned my night around and...I don't know..."

"You're welcome for the sex."

"Good night." I giggle, rolling back over.

"Night."

After a few minutes, his breathing begins to even again, and I watch the pink that's still swirling outside my window, reflecting on everything that happened today and still unsure what it all means.

Chapter 14: Morning

Everett

December Eighteenth

The morning sun streams through the window, casting a soft glow throughout Claire's room. She's still asleep, curled into the crook of my body. Her pillow is nowhere to be found, and instead, she's taken over one of mine. Inhaling deeply, the sweet scent of her hair fills my nostrils and makes all of my muscles relax.

It's a very foreign feeling, and I'm not sure what the protocol for this sort of thing should be. My past doesn't include many moments like this one.

There's a part of me that doesn't want to move. A part of me that enjoys holding her like this—like I've never held her before. The steadiness of her breathing and the warmth of her skin put me at ease.

Four and a half years ago, she and I would've never *cuddled* because I would've never considered spending the night, and she would've never allowed it. We would've fucked, and then I would've gathered my things and left. But, now it's morning, and I'm still here, unmoved, with the girl who, twenty-four hours ago, I never thought I'd see again, in my arms.

Do I attempt to get up without waking her and make her break-fast? Maybe leave to grab us both coffee and a bagel? Or do I hold her until she wakes up and savor the rare, quiet moment we're sharing?

There's no doubt in my mind that she's going to hate the realization that we slept like this last night, which makes the not moving option all the more tempting.

Still deep in her sleep, she subconsciously nestles tighter against me. Her mostly bare ass rubs against my dick and causes it to strain against the thin fabric of my boxer briefs.

Well, she's really gonna hate that.

Fighting the urge to pull her in closer, I roll to my back to put some space between us. Because as much as I would love to lay here holding her like this all morning, I don't know what she's thinking. She's fresh out of the thing with Raph, still hurting, and I have my own shit to deal with. My days in the league are numbered, and thanks to that reporter, rumors of my premature exit are rampant. Who wants a washed up hockey player? She didn't want me at my best; no way in hell she'll want me at my worst.

Carefully, I try to move my arm, but she starts to stir.

"Morning, Ev," she says, a sleepy chuckle escaping with her words. She rolls further away, freeing my left arm, and rubs her fingers over her eyes.

"Morning." Sitting up, I stretch my arms above my head, and to my surprise, my shoulder doesn't feel stiff. I roll it a few times, and I feel nothing. It feels better than it has in months. It feels normal.

That ibuprofen is really working overtime.

My eyes scan her room, and I take in my surroundings for the first time in the morning light.

"I didn't know you liked pink so much," I say, shifting to face her. She doesn't look at me though. No. Instead, I turn to find her staring at her hand. Specifically, the ring on her hand. Her left hand.

Blinking, I double-take. On her left ring finger sits a large diamond ring with a matching diamond band.

"You're married?" I hear myself question as I jump out of bed.

"No," she says. "You heard me break up with Raph last night."

"Right," I say, running my hands through my hair. "Sorry, I saw the rings and thought they were…" My voice trails off as I watch her scan her room. The look on her face shifts from confusion to horror. Her chest begins to lift with quick, panicked breaths. She nervously fidgets, gripping the fabric of the comforter tightly between her fingers.

"You okay?" I ask, unsure why her face has gone so pale.

"Where are we?" she asks, frantically.

"Your bedroom."

"No, this isn't my room." Her voice cracks as she speaks, her eyes scanning the space again.

"What are you talking about? You sure you're okay?"

"Everett, this isn't my place," she yells, her eyes falling back to the ring on her finger.

"Well, it's not my place," I argue. "And I'm pretty sure you unlocked the door with a key last night."

"This isn't funny," she says, her eyes beginning to well with tears.

"Shit, um, it's okay." Climbing back onto the bed, I reach out, trying to feel her forehead with the back of my head, but she swats me away.

"Don't touch me," she bites out, scrambling out of bed.

"Look, I'm not sure what's going on, but you're worrying me, so maybe we should get dressed and go see a doctor." I attempt to keep my voice calm and even.

"I don't need a doctor. I know we're not in my apartment. How do you not know that?"

"This is my first time here, and with the power out last night, and all of our, um, activities…" A smirk forms across my face. "I didn't really pay attention to your decor."

"Activities?" she scoffs. "God, you are just as insufferable as you used to be. You can say the word sex. We were both consenting adults."

I let out a chuckle, and she flips around and stomps toward the large window. Drawing the blinds, a gasp falls from her mouth as she reveals a snowy landscape and no city buildings. She's right. We aren't in New York.

My mouth falls open as I try to find the words, but instead, nothing comes out, and I move to join her. There's nothing but snow and trees.

What in the actual fuck is happening?

"I don't think we're in Kansas anymore, Toto."

She lets out a groan and turns to move past me, but I stay stuck in place, looking out at the winter wonderland.

"Um, Ev?" her voice shakes.

"Yeah," I say, turning to face her.

In her hand is a framed photo of the two of us. She's in a light pink, floor length gown, and I'm wearing a tuxedo. A large bouquet of flowers is in her hand. My eyes shift back and forth between the photo and the rings she's wearing. Slowly, I turn my gaze downward to my own hand, where a simple gold band wraps around my left ring finger.

When did we get fucking married?

ACT 2:
Sugarplum Park

Chapter 15: Are We Dead?

Grasping the edge of the sink, I stare into an ornate, rose gold-framed mirror, assessing every little thing about myself and looking for anything that might be different or any clue to what's going on.

My long black hair is still wavy from the curls I wore to the game last night. My lace bralette and thong are what I fell asleep wearing. The dainty silver chain and initial charm are still around my neck. Mascara is smudged under my eyes from where I didn't wash my makeup off before going to bed.

Everything's the same, except it's not.

I'm in a room I've never been in before, wearing a diamond on my left hand, and according to the photo on the bedside table, I'm Everett Nuttall's wife.

This is a dream. This has to be a dream.

Blowing out a frustrated breath, I try to calm my racing heart rate. There is no need to panic. I just need to wake up.

Turning on the faucet, I splash cold water on my face, but when I open my eyes, I'm still standing in the bathroom.

Pumping some facewash into my hand, I cover my face with the gentle suds. Splashing more cold water on my cheeks, I wash away the night before, fully expecting to open my eyes and be safely in my bed in New York, but nothing changes.

I'm still here—wherever here might be.

Grabbing for a towel, I wipe away the water and turn around, leaning against the counter top.

The date on my phone reads December eighteenth, which is correct because yesterday was December seventeenth. Swiping up, I tap on my sister's name. It goes straight to her voicemail. I try texting her, but it doesn't deliver. Trying my parents, my heart sinks when the same thing happens.

Pulling up the map on the phone, I attempt to find my location, but the map won't load.

Fuck...what is going on?

Flipping around, I stare at my reflection, slapping my cheeks until they both turn red. "Wake up! Wake up! Wake up!" I yell at myself, but it's no use.

No matter what I try, I'm still standing in this bathroom, half-naked, and Everett Nuttall—*my husband*—is on the other side of the door. Or at least I think he is. How long have I been in here? Twenty minutes? An hour? For all I know he's left me here to fend for myself alone.

A small knock startles me. "Claire, you okay in there?" Everett asks from outside the bathroom. Concern laces his voice.

Okay, so he's still here. That's good. I think.

Running my hands down my face, I try to collect myself. Don't panic. Worst case scenario, we're both dead and this is some sort of Hell. Best case, this is a dream and we'll wake up any minute and laugh about it.

Shit, are we dead? Is this some sort of pink Hell?

"Claire, um, maybe we should talk and try to figure this out."

I swing the door open and take in the man before me. He's leaning on the door frame. His dark hair is messy, like he's been running his hands through it more than a few times. He's wearing nothing but black boxer briefs that outline his cock. My eyes dip to his bulge and his leg tattoo, and I bite my lip.

"I'm up here." He chuckles, his lips tipping upward on one side.

Focus. Now is not the time. Where was I? Right. What's going on? Is this a dream or...

"Do you think we're dead?" I blurt out. My eyes finding his.

"I hope not," he says, shrugging.

A small smile ghosts my lips as I breathe out a laugh. Moving past him, I walk back into the bedroom and scan for any more clues, but it just looks like a regular bedroom.

A large king-size bed, with a snow-white velvet tufted head-board, sits in the middle of the room covered with plush white and pink bedding. It's framed by two large mirrored bedside tables. Each is adorned with a crystal lamp and a rose gold-framed photo of me and Everett—memories that don't exist because, despite the rings on our hands, we aren't really married. None of this is real. It can't be.

"We should get dressed," I say, turning to find him leaned up against the door frame, watching me. "It's freezing."

"Really? I was thinking we could just stay in our underwear all day and take advantage of being here alone. Think about it," he says, wiggling his eyebrows and pushing off the wall. "No one knows we're here, which means we don't have any responsibilities for the first time in a long time. We could repeat last night as many times as we wanted and never be interrupted." The side of his mouth tips into a sexy grin.

"How do you know no one knows we're here?"

"I can't get a hold of anyone back in New York, and according to my phone, my location can't be found. You?"

"Yeah, it goes straight to voicemail and none of the texts will deliver. My map won't even load."

"See, so we could just hold up in bed until everything goes back to normal."

Fucking men. I shake my head and pinch my brow together.

"No, we have to figure out what's going on. This isn't some vacation from our lives. We went to sleep in New York last night and woke up, *married,* in a place neither of us has ever seen before. We can't just pretend like nothing weird is happening."

"What if it was the sex. Maybe if we try doing it again, it'll transport us back to New York."

"Glad to see you are as unbearable as before," I deadpan.

Walking past him into the large closet off the bedroom, I'm met with women's clothes that aren't mine. Gosh, this version of me owns a lot of ballet pink. "I think this goes without saying, but I don't think it was the sex," I say, grabbing a chunky, knitted sweater from a shelf and pulling it over my head.

"You don't know that," he yells from somewhere else in the house.

"Yes, I do," I shout back.

Quickly locating a pair of jeans, I tug them on and then slide my feet into a pair of fleece-lined boots.

I walk out to find Everett also fully clothed.

"I don't know—we were always pretty magical together." His mouth curls into a one-sided grin.

This. This is why we didn't work before. How could I forget how incredibly cocky he was and apparently still is.

My eyes rake down his body, taking him in. He's wearing a taupe turtleneck sweater and black jeans. The sweater is practically painted on him, highlighting every cut line on his sculpted body, and if we weren't in the middle of a total crisis and he wasn't being one hundred kinds of annoying, I'd peel it off of him.

Forcibly closing my mouth, I do my best to divert my gaze away from him.

"You don't like my outfit?"

"No...um...no...it's," I stammer.

"Words, Sugar." He smirks.

"I just didn't peg you as a turtleneck guy, that's all." Blush creeps up my neck and covers my cheeks. I hate how attracted I am to him, but I also kind of love it.

"Sure." He chuckles. "It was either a turtleneck or a Christmas sweater. I thought this was the better option."

Given how it looks like it's painted on his perfect body, I'd say it was definitely the better option. No doubt about it.

Fuck, I need to focus.

I move towards where I left the wedding photo, running my hand over the fur throw draped over the edge of the bed.

"Everything feels so real, but I know we aren't married," I say, picking up the frame. The dress I'm wearing is stunning—*pink*, but stunning. The blush corset bodice fits me like a glove. Matching tulle straps are layered over it, creating a deep V. My champagne colored heels peek out from beneath the full skirt. Everett is in a classic black tuxedo. A bouquet of pink roses, anemones, and greenery hangs in my hand as he dips me into a kiss.

"I mean, look how in love we seem. How do you explain us being here and having no recollection of our marriage or our life together?" I turn to face him.

"I'm as lost as you are," he says. "Maybe if we think through the night, then we can get some answers. What do you remember?"

I attempt to replay my evening. I was at the hockey game with my sister. I broke things off with Raph, then ran into Everett at the bar. He asked me if I wanted to get out of there, and I did. We went back to my apartment in New York and hooked up. He stayed over because the power was out.

"The power went out. That's why you stayed over."

"Yeah. The snow and those northern lights were insane. So pink they didn't seem real."

Pink. Everything is fucking pink.

Oh.

My.

God.

"Stella!" The photo falls from my hands and onto the mattress in front of me.

"Who?"

"I knew there was something weird about her, and then I saw her at the arena," I explain, my words rushed, and I begin to pace around the room. "Well, not her, but a version of her. And then there was that woman in the bathroom. She had pink hair too, and now everything in this place is pink."

I pull at my sweater. "Pink."

I grab a pillow off the bed. "Pink"

I point to my wedding dress. "Pink"

I gesture to the rug on the floor. "Pink…it's all pink!"

"Slow down. I don't understand," he says, walking into my path. He firmly grabs both my arms, squeezing gently. The tension building between my shoulder blades eases, my pulse slows, and my breathing evens out.

Inhaling deeply, I try again.

"Stella is a witch—I think—and she's cursed us, and now we're stuck in some place that doesn't exist, married to each other."

"A witch?" One of his eyebrows lifts and his hands fall to his sides.

"Yes."

"Not possible." He shakes his head.

"Some might say waking up in a house that's not yours, married to a person you hooked up with the night before, is impossible, but here we fucking are, Everett." I gesture my arms out to the side. "Did you have any weird run-ins with any pink haired women last night?"

He studies me for a minute, sliding his hands into his pocket. I can see the wheels turning behind his eyes, and I do my best to think of any other explanation for our peculiar situation, but the only thing that makes sense—and I'm using the term *makes sense* very loosely here—is Stella.

"You know, now that you mention it, before the game started, I saw a woman with pink hair in the stands watching me. And then, when she and I made eye contact, the arena felt colder for a minute." He chuckles. "Theo thought I was nuts, but do you think that could've been her?"

My eyes narrow. "Yes, I think that's exactly who that was."

"And then after the game, one of the reporters had pink hair. Well, she was blonde, but she had pink strands in it." He rolls his shoulder, and his eyes seem to drift off somewhere behind me.

"Did she say anything weird?" I ask.

"Who?" His eyes focus back on me.

"The pink-haired reporter?"

"Oh. She seemed to know about my shoulder, but I doubt that was magic."

"Or it was," I argue, crossing my arms.

"Okay, let's assume that's what happened," he begins.

I nod.

"Why would this Stella woman curse us?"

"I don't know. Maybe she was bored."

"Bored?" His head tilts to the side, and another chuckle escapes past his lips.

"I don't know why witches do what they do." My arms fly into the air, and I shift my weight. "I'm not a witch. But I know that women with pink hair seemed to be common last night, and Stella had pink hair. I don't have any other leads."

"This is ridiculous. Witches aren't real." He throws his head back, running his hands up his face and through his hair.

"You don't know that."

"I think I do. But I'll keep playing along. So, what's your game plan?"

"What's *my* game plan?"

"Yes, how do you propose we find a witch?"

"I don't know. What's *your* game plan?"

He just stares at me, and I wish he would speak. I wish he would say something helpful, but he doesn't.

"Great, so neither of us has a plan."

As the reality of our situation begins to settle in, pressure builds behind my eyes. We don't have a plan. We may never get back to

New York. I might not get to dance on Christmas. I may never see my family again.

Tears break free and begin to run down my face. Wiping them away, I do my best to push the fear aside and formulate a coherent thought, but my mind is too muddled by my emotions, and all I can think about is how badly I wish I was home.

"I know this is strange, but we have to stay focused," he says. "Crying about it isn't going to get us home."

"Crying about it isn't going to get us home?" I scoff. "Forgive me for trying to process this incredibly insane situation we're in." I wipe my eyes with my fingers and turn to walk away.

"Wait, where are you going?" he asks, following me out of the bedroom and into the living room.

Unsurprisingly, everything is pink. A rose-colored couch covered in different pink-hued pillows is positioned across from a small brick fireplace that is painted white. Snow flocked Christmas garland decorated with pink and silver ornaments hangs on the wooden mantle. Two pink velvet stockings hang below. More faux memories of me with Everett are framed and sit on every flat surface.

If I didn't know better, I'd think this bitch was taunting me.

Tall windows give a picturesque view of the snowy backyard. Evergreen trees tower over a small clearing where a hot tub and small fire pit are set up. Lights are strung above it all.

Moving across the space, I walk into the kitchen and begin opening the white cabinets.

"What are you doing?" he asks.

"I need coffee and maybe something to eat. I think we need to process what all this actually means. Try to dig deep. Figure out why she may have put us here."

"Dig deep?"

"Yeah." Grabbing a canister of coffee, I flip around to face him. "Like maybe I'm here because I clearly cannot make good decisions when it comes to my love life, and she's trying to teach me a lesson."

"What does that mean?"

"Well, I don't think dating Raph and then jumping into bed with you literally while I ended things with him was the best decision I've ever made."

He rubs his hand on the back of his neck and shakes his head.

"Is there something going on with you that could've been the reason she sent you here with me?" I ask.

The hand that was still resting on his neck drops to his side, and he moves his right shoulder again. "No, I'm the happiest I've ever been," he says through a smile. "I woke up married to you."

This *fucking* man. I set the coffee container on the counter, sighing heavily. "Actually, I changed my mind. I think I'm gonna go try to find a coffee shop."

"Out there? You don't think we should get a plan together before we go gallivanting off into the snow?"

"No, I'm not thinking clearly, and coffee will help me do that. I just need to get out of here and clear my head."

"Well, then I'm coming with you."

"You really don't have to," I snap, marching towards a door that looks like it might be some sort of coat closet. Swinging it open, I'm relieved to find that I was correct. I scan the coats, trying to decide which one to wear, but everything is—you guessed it—pink.

Everett walks up behind me, and we both reach into the closet at the same time, grabbing for the only black coat. Our hands collide against the fabric, and he lets out a low chuckle.

"This one is mine," he says. "I think it'll be a little big on you."

"I know that," I say through a clenched jaw, moving to the blush coat next to it.

"Trying to hold my hand then, Wifey?"

"No. No. No. No. No. We aren't doing that." I pull the coat from the closet and begin putting it on. "We aren't really married. I'm reinstating the no nickname rule."

Straightening the jacket, I move my hair from under the collar. I need to clear my mind, and being around him isn't helping.

"But we were never good at following that one." He smirks.

"Why don't I run and find us a coffee, and you stay here and start working on your *game plan*," I suggest, throwing air quotes around the final two words.

"I'm not going to let you go out there by yourself," he says, batting his eyes at me. "What if this witch finds you and eats you?"

"We aren't Hansel and Gretel. She's not going to eat me."

His laughter gets louder, and with it, my blood pressure begins to rise.

"Oh sure, mock me. That's incredibly helpful. I'll be back soon."

"We will be back soon," he corrects. "What kind of husband would I be if I left you all alone to fend for yourself out there?"

Exhaling, I turn and reach for the crystal door knob of the front door.

"Like it or not, we're stuck together until we make it home," he says from behind me.

Spinning around to face him, I'm surprised to find him incredibly close. He takes a step towards me, crowding my space even more. I attempt to take a step away, but my back hits the door. His eyes find mine, and my breath hitches when I inhale his expensive cologne. Leaning forward on both of his arms, he cages me in, and my body betrays me like it always does when he's nearby.

"You said she's trying to teach us something…what if it's that we're meant to be together? We did wake up married after all."

"She's a witch, not a matchmaker. And if she is a matchmaker, it appears she's not a very good one."

Bringing his mouth to my ear, his warm breath tickles the exposed skin of my neck and causes goosebumps to erupt across my arms. Dropping his voice to a whisper, he says, "I'd have to disagree. I think we could be really good together."

"You do?" My voice shakes, and I swallow hard. My knees threaten to buckle underneath me as I try my best not to give away the effect he has on me, but it's no use.

A hum escapes from his lips. "We were pretty good together last night."

The door clicks open, and my eyes follow the sound to find that his hand is no longer on the frame, but on the door knob.

"After you, Wifey" he says, chuckling.

"Ugh, can you try not to be so annoying." Letting out a frustrated breath, I push him away from me. If I'm not already dead, then this man will surely be the death of me.

CHAPTER 16:
THE NUTTALLS

Claire pushes me backward, scrunching her nose and scowling, which I have to admit is pretty cute. Pulling one half of the French doors open, I watch as she walks through it.

The Victorian-style house is pale pink with white and teal trim. It looks like a gingerbread house or something out of a storybook. It doesn't look real. It's everything I hate about this time of year—over the top and cliché.

Lights are strung around the banisters and outline the roof. Evergreen wreaths with pink velvet ribbons adorn every window. A life-sized pastel nutcracker stands guard by the door.

The doormat catches my eye, and I chuckle as I read the words printed on it. Under a row of gingerbread houses are the words *The Nuttalls* in script.

Glancing down at the gold ring circling my finger, I spin it. I don't have any idea why we're here, but I can't shake the thought that maybe this Stella woman is trying to push us together and that maybe that's the key to getting home.

The pink-haired reporter was interested in my shoulder and when I planned on settling down. Could she have taken my abrupt exit from the media room as an invitation to meddle in my personal life? Is that what this is about? Or, maybe the feeling I have is just my deepest desires bubbling to the surface.

"Did you hear me?" she asks.

"Oh…um, no…sorry. I got distracted by the doormat." Her eyes find our name, and she lets out an annoyed breath.

"Does that mean my name is Claire Nuttall now?"

"What, you don't like the sound of that?"

She shakes her head in disbelief and buttons her coat to keep out the cold. "I was saying we should probably exchange phone numbers since you are so insistent on us sticking together."

"Okay, what's yours?" I pull out my cell phone and begin to type in her phone number as she says it out loud. Grinning, I turn the screen in her direction. "Looks like you're already in here, *Sugar*."

"How do I know that's me?" she questions, placing a hand on her hip. "For all I know, you call everyone that silly nickname."

I don't. She's the only woman I've ever called that nickname. Or any nickname for that matter.

Flipping the phone, I tap the contact that reads "Sugar" with my thumb, and her phone begins to ring.

"Who's calling you?" I smirk. She flips the phone in my direction, and another wedding photo flashes on her screen along with the name Ev. "Would you look at that? Looks like we do have each other's numbers."

Rolling her eyes, she ignores the call and moves past me down the small set of stairs. The large yard is covered in an untouched blanket of snow. We walk across it towards a sidewalk, leaving a trail of footprints behind us. The street is lined with houses similar to ours. Each one is a different color. The light posts are decorated for the upcoming holiday. From my vantage point, I can see that we're close to what appears to be some sort of town square.

"Want to walk?" I ask, nodding down the street.

"I don't see a car," she says. "So, I guess it's our only choice."

We move down the sidewalk, my steps falling into a steady rhythm with hers.

"I'm sorry," I begin at the same time she says the same thing.

She giggles nervously, and I shake my head. "I'm sorry this whole morning has really thrown me. It's not an excuse, but I shouldn't have ignored how you were feeling. If you want to cry, that's completely valid."

"And I'm sorry for trying to leave without you. You're right that we need to stick together."

"Your husband *was* kinda being a dick," I half-jest.

"He kinda was, wasn't he."

"I've never been good with feelings," I admit. "My parents were gone a lot growing up, and my sister and I were raised by nannies. Hockey became my life from the minute I learned to skate, and it's not necessarily a sport that promotes anything other than being tough."

She nods as we continue to walk.

"I expect that same toughness from my team, but I shouldn't expect it from you," I explain.

"It's okay to feel things," she says. "But, I shouldn't have taken it out on you. We aren't going to get home unless we work together."

"I think you're onto something with the 'Stella is trying to teach us a lesson' thing."

"What do you mean?"

"Well, if this Stella person is the one who put us here…" I pause and take a deep breath. "The reporter with pink hair really went in on me about my shoulder injury and my future. She asked if I had plans to retire and settle down, and the team's publicist kinda rushed me out before I could fully answer her."

"Why didn't you say that back at the house?"

"Because my shoulder injury and what it means for my career isn't really something I want to talk about."

"Okay…" She clenches her jaw. "But, what do questions and your future have to do with being here with me?"

"The settling down part. I mean, we woke up married. That's kind of as settled down as you can get."

"But why me?"

Because I've been pining over you for years. That doesn't make sense though. My closest friends don't even know that, so how could a total stranger. She wouldn't. She couldn't.

"I don't know. Do you remember anything she said or you said that was along the same lines?"

She plays with the chain of her necklace and then pauses suddenly, covering her mouth.

"What is it?"

"Oh…um…" Blush covers her face, and she turns away from me.

"Come on, the retirement discussion isn't something I want to think about either, but we gotta dig deep, right?"

"Okay, well…" she begins, flipping back around to face me and crossing her arms. Her eyes lock somewhere over my shoulder. "In the cab, she gave me this crystal, and it was super weird. I ended up spilling my guts to her, and then when I set it down, it was like I came to and realized everything I said," she rushes out.

"Which was what?"

"Huh?"

"What did you say to her?"

"It's a little blurry, but it had something to do with wondering what it would be like if you and I ever got a second chance."

My whole face breaks into a grin, and my stomach swoops.

"Is that so?"

"I was clearly under a spell or something, because the minute I put the stone down, I realized what I had said, so don't let it go to your head." Her eyes find mine. "Stop," she whines.

"Stop what?"

"That goofy ass grin and that twinkly thing you're doing with your eyes. It was the magic, not really how I was feeling."

My heart sinks, and I try to push the sting of her words away.

"Maybe, but unfortunately for you, I do think this means we're going to have to fall in love."

"Nice try." Laughing loudly, she starts walking again, leaving me to have to catch up with her.

"You know I'm right."

"I don't think you are."

"Then why make us married?"

"Everett, I…" she begins, rubbing her hand across her eyes. "You can't force love."

"Who said anything about forcing it?"

She laughs, and her head falls into her hands before finding my eyes.

"You did when you suggested we fall in love. Love is supposed to be spontaneous. It's supposed to knock you off your feet because you weren't expecting it. It's not supposed to be prescribed."

"And you don't think that's possible?"

"I think Christmas is in a week, and I need to be back in New York. Falling in love takes longer than that."

"Challenge accepted." I wink.

"You're useless. This isn't funny. I can't miss Christmas, and honestly, the sooner we can get back the better. I can't imagine any world where you and I fall in love in a year, let alone less than a week."

Damn. She really knows how to cut deep.

"Why Christmas? It's not that great of a holiday."

"You don't like Christmas?"

"Not really," I admit. "I'm usually pretty busy through the holidays, so I've never bothered to really get into all that."

"I thought the league didn't schedule games on Christmas?'

"They don't."

"Oh, so you're just a huge scrooge?"

"What do you mean?"

She shrugs. "You were always a little grumpy and grumbly, so it makes sense you would hate being jolly."

"I guess that means you like Christmas?"

"I love it, which is why your plan will never work, because whoever I fall in love with has to love it as much as I do."

I rub my hands down my face. "You do realize how insane that sounds, right?"

"I don't care. It's one of my favorite things, and I can't imagine marrying someone who thinks something I love is silly."

Nervously turning the gold band on my finger, I turn my gaze to Claire. I take a moment to admire how incredibly beautiful she is. Her dark hair flows down her back. Her blue eyes draw me in like they always do. She's stunning.

Mildly infuriating, but stunning.

"So, is that why you need to get back to New York? Because you want to celebrate Christmas in the city?"

"No."

"Okay…" I breathe out a long breath and try to calm myself. "Then why do we have to get back for Christmas?"

"The Sugar Plum Fairy in The City Ballet's Christmas production of *The Nutcracker* has been my dream since I was five and saw the ballet with my mom." She blinks back tears, and her nose makes a little sniffling sound. "Yesterday before the game, I was given the role after the dancer I was understudying hurt her ankle."

"Wow. That's incredible."

"It was. Until we ended up here." She throws her hands out and gestures around. "If we don't get back, then everything I've worked for will have been a waste, and my chance at any other lead role in the future will be ruined."

She blinks her eyes shut and takes a deep breath.

"I'm already missing rehearsals, at this rate I'll be lucky if he hasn't already given my part to another dancer."

Looking down at my watch, I say, "It's not even nine. I'm sure you haven't lost the part yet."

"Rehearsal starts at ten, so assuming we're in the same time zone as New York, which, who could know because this place doesn't show up on any map, I have one hour before I no-call no-show the biggest rehearsal of my entire dancing career."

"Then we'll get back," I promise.

"In an hour?"

"Well, maybe not an hour, but we'll get back in time for you to perform. I'm missing hockey too, so I get it, but it's going to work out. I promise."

She forces a smile and so do I. I'm not sure if I just lied to her or told her the truth, and that's a very humbling thought.

CHAPTER 17: CANDY-COLORED HELL
CLAIRE

I hope Everett is right, but if falling in love with one another is the answer, then I fear we are most certainly fucked.

Turning a curve in the sidewalk, we make it to the entrance of a small town square. The street sign reads Main Street, and a large mural painted on the exterior side of the first shop greets us. *Sugarplum Park: The Sweetest Town There Ever Was* is written in large, curly letters and is surrounded by pastel colored sweets. Different lightly-colored buildings line either side of the long street. Each store front is adorned with a large window, giving each passerby a glimpse of what's inside. Garland and wreaths decorate the lamp posts that are perfectly spaced down the cobblestone side-walk as far as the eye can see. It looks like we stepped into a holiday card. It's the quintessential Christmas town, and despite never being here before, there is something oddly familiar about it.

"Sugarplum Park?" Everett questions pointing at the wall. "I think you may be right. It's like we stepped into candy-colored Hell."

"More like Candyland," I say, gesturing towards a fudge shop called The Chocolate Bar, and then across the street to Gum Drop Sugar Shop. "Maybe she's trying to help you find your Christmas spirit."

"If that's the case, then this is a really dramatic way of doing that," he says.

"Morning, Everett. Hi, Claire," a tall stranger says as he walks by us. He's wearing a long, khaki trench coat, chocolate-colored pants, and an argyle scarf. A brown fedora sits on top of his dark hair. His umber skin is smooth, and round olive glasses rest on his nose, framing his dark brown eyes. A newspaper is tucked under his arm.

We both offer him a wave and watch as he crosses the street toward the candy shop.

"Should we follow him?" Everett asks.

"Why would we do that?"

"Because he seems to know who we are, and he's holding a paper that could give us more information about where we are."

"Okay, Sherlock. How do you suggest we ask him any of those things without sounding like we've gone insane?"

"I have a way with people."

"Something tells me your charm isn't going to get us out of this one."

"Look, I'm still working out the details on how to get us home, but no matter what, we have to try to trust one another. There is no getting home without each other."

Inhaling deeply, I then let out the breath slowly.

"You're right. We're in this together," I say through a forced smile.

"Good, now come on." Before I can react, he grabs my hand and starts pulling me across the street.

If I'm honest with myself, I like the feel of my hand in his, and despite my insistence on not falling in love with him, I could see that maybe it would be possible if our circumstances were different. If instead of waking up in Sugarplum Park, we had woken up in New York and shared a bagel.

He tugs me closer, so that we are walking side by side, and lets go of my hand. Folding my arms across my chest, we follow the man down the sidewalk, and I do my best to take note of the shops as we pass.

Gum Drop Sugar Shop is first. It's painted light purple, and a long awning in a similar shade covers both windows and the plum colored door. A display of pastel candy canes covered in faux snow is set up in both windows, and a closed sign hangs on the door.

The next shop is painted a light blue. The round wooden sign bolted above the door reads: The Music Box. It's also closed, and the blinds are pulled shut so that we can't see inside.

The man is a few yards ahead of us, and he doesn't seem to notice that we're following behind him.

"So, what's your plan?" I whisper, nudging Everett with my shoulder.

"I want to see where he's going."

"Brilliant."

"Do you have a better one?"

"No," I grumble.

"You're cute when you're frustrated." He smirks, causing me to grumble again. "See? So cute." He taps the tip of his finger against my nose, and I swat him away.

We pass by an orange storefront that belongs to The Book Rack. Next door is a green storefront that belongs to a quaint little flower shop called Dewdrops and Daisies. Vines crawl up the front of the store, and despite the frigid temperatures, the flower boxes are overflowing with different colored blooms. Both stores are closed.

Pausing in between them, I pull out my phone to check the time.

"Why'd you stop?" Everett asks, turning to see what I'm doing.

"It's just that it's after nine, and every shop is closed." I turn and look across the street. From my vantage point, I can make out the chocolate shop, a toy shop, a coffee and tea shop, and a ballet studio. Each storefront is painted a different pastel color, but all the lights are off. The doors I can see have closed signs hanging in the windows.

"Maybe things don't open until ten?" Everett shrugs.

"Not even the coffee shop?"

"Shit, we lost him," he says.

I look over to find that the tall man is gone, and Everett and I are all alone.

"Come on." He tugs on my hand again. Moving past the flower shop, we make it to the final building on this side of the street.

"Well, that was easier than I thought it would be," Everett says, looking up at the sign above the door that reads Stella's Diner.

"A bit too easy, don't you think?" I question, still turning over how quiet the street seems for a mid-morning weekday.

Both windows are painted with a Christmas mural and topped with snow flocked garland. A warm yellow glow spills through the blinds, and muffled conversation and music comes from the other side of the door.

"Shall we?" he asks.

"I don't know." My pulse begins to quicken, and my throat goes dry. "We have no idea what is on the other side of this door."

"Probably a diner that's owned by Stella." He nods up toward the sign.

"You don't know that for sure."

"Seems pretty clear that it is. You want to get home, right?"

"Yeah."

"And you think Stella is responsible for us being here?"

"Yeah."

"Then I think we need to try to talk to her—unless you've changed your mind about falling in love with me?"

I shake my head, and his chest moves as he laughs.

He grabs my hand again, but this time he doesn't let go. Lacing his fingers with mine, he squeezes it, reassuring me it's all going to be okay. "Plus, I'm sure there's coffee." He shrugs his shoulders and lifts one of his eyebrows. A nervous giggle bubbles out of me, and I nod.

"Together," he says.

"Together," I repeat, feigning confidence.

He swings the door open. The sound of a woman's voice drifts by us and then abruptly stops as we step inside to meet no less than fifty people staring back at us with wide eyes.

The walls are painted a soft pink. Large white and black tile covers the floor in a checkered pattern. A matching border of smaller tiles forms a chair rail around the entire restaurant.

It's completely decked out for the upcoming holiday. Garland and lights cover every inch of the ceiling. Ornaments in different sizes and shapes hang down, catching the light and refracting it in every direction. Pink Christmas trees are centered in front of both windows and decorated to match the rest of the space. Christmas music plays low over a speaker. It reminds me of one of those Christmas pop-up bars in the city.

Every chair and booth is full of people I've never seen before, except for the tall man we followed here. He removes his hat and tilts his head in our direction before placing it back on his head.

Two women I don't recognize offer me a wave and a big smile, and I return the gesture, confused as to why anyone here would act like they know me.

"The man and woman of the hour," a pink-haired woman at the front of the diner sing-songs. Her hair is cut into a short, choppy bob and curled. A black knotted headband sits on top of her head. She's wearing dark-wash bell-bottom jeans and a black top that shows a bit of the golden skin of her abdomen. A long, flowy, lightweight cardigan covered in silver stars grazes the floor when she moves. Chunky mixed metal jewelry hangs from her neck and wrists, clanging together as she gestures for us to walk forward. A star tattoo peeks out from under one of her sleeves. "Come in; come in. We just started talking about the Christmas Extravaganza."

Everett steps in front of me as if he's readying himself for some sort of attack, but despite how I felt before we walked in, I don't feel in danger. It feels like we're exactly where we're supposed to be.

He leads me, hesitantly, toward where she stands. And I suppress a laugh because it's clear this place is giving much more North Pole than Shutter Island vibes, so I seriously doubt anything bad is about to happen. But, nonetheless, him protecting me makes my heart skip a beat.

"Let's hear it for this year's king and queen of Sugarplum Park's Annual Christmas Extravaganza," the woman chimes.

The what?

Everyone stands and begins to clap and cheer. The two girls who waved at me are the loudest in the crowd.

Reaching forward, I grab ahold of Everett's bicep and squeeze gently, causing his gaze to shift to mine. I offer an encouraging smile, and the tension he's holding between his shoulder blades seems to dissipate a little.

"Okay, okay," she says, quieting the crowd. "You two can sit right here." She points to two empty high-back chairs situated to her left. In each chair sits a silk sash and a crown.

The applause fades, and I let go of Everett's hand to move the items so I can sit.

"Put on the sash and crowns," one of the women yells.

"Yeah, let's see them," the other calls.

Looking towards Everett, he shrugs.

"Let's see it, you two," the pink-haired woman says.

Pulling the sash over my head, my eyes scan the room once more.

What the hell did we walk into?

A hand brushes mine, causing me to jump. Looking downward, it's just Everett. I turn to face him as I fidget with my sash.

"You okay?" he mouths.

I nod, and he forces a smile.

"Can I help you with the crown?" he asks.

"Oh…yeah…sure."

He places it on my head, and then I help him to do the same.

"Wonderful!" She claps her hands together. "Okay, so where were we? Oh, yes. The rules."

She pauses for a split second, walking over and retrieving a clipboard and a pen from a different pink-haired woman.

"If I contacted you, then your business was selected to participate in the competition this year as one of our seven finalists. If you weren't contacted, there's always next year, and I encourage you to try again." She pauses, fanning out her long cardigan as if it was the train of a dress. "Whatever you choose to enter must be presented to the town today and cannot be changed. Our king and queen will be judging your creations on appearance, taste, and overall Christmas cheer on Christmas Eve, so choose wisely."

Everett glances towards me and swallows hard, and I wish being here came with some sort of ability to communicate telepathically with him, but alas, it doesn't, and I have no idea what he's thinking.

He shifts uncomfortably in his chair, and his crown begins to slide off the top of his head.

"Oh, shit," he says, a little too loud, earning a chuckle from a few townspeople as he attempts to catch it. He succeeds in stopping it from falling, but it's no longer centered atop his head.

"You good?" I whisper, reaching up to help him straighten it.

"Yeah."

"Aren't you two just the most precious couple," the pink-haired woman trills. "Aren't they precious?"

More applause comes from the crowd, and she looks over at us with a proud smile. Her purple eyes find mine, creasing at the corners, and my pulse begins to quicken as I realize who she is. With absolutely no doubt in my mind, I smile back.

"Thank you, Stella. You're too kind."

Chapter 18: The Christmas Cup

Everett

When I opened the door of the diner, the last thing I expected was to step inside a place that looks like some type of Christmas bomb exploded or to be catapulted into the middle of the town's annual Christmas competition. Over-the-top doesn't even begin to describe what I'm looking at or what I'm hearing.

My stomach sinks when Claire calls the woman running the meeting Stella. She seems a bit too happy we're here, and with every curve of her lips, uneasiness settles over me.

I have a bad feeling getting back to New York isn't going to happen today—or any day soon for that matter—but I'm doing my best to take note of everything she says in case there's a clue on how to get us home.

"Anyway," Stella continues, turning to face the crowd, "this is all in good fun and a friendly competition. On the day of the Christmas Extravaganza, our king and queen will judge each of the entries and name the winner of The Christmas Cup. Are there any questions?"

She pauses for half a second.

"No? Good. If your business is participating in this year's festivities, please stand when I call your name and tell us what you plan on entering."

Her finger runs down the paper pinned to the clipboard and then she surveys the audience. Extending her arm, she points to the only familiar face in the crowd. "Chip, let's start with you."

He stands, removing his hat. "Thanks, Stella." Despite the way he's dressed, I'm surprised to find he doesn't appear to be much older than me.

"The Chocolate Bar's entry will be my famous peppermint bark," he continues. Gasps circulate through the crowd, and I glance over at Claire who just shrugs her shoulders.

"You can't enter your peppermint bark," a woman around his age scoffs, standing and causing everyone to look in her direction. She's one of the two who waved when we entered. She has dark brown skin, and her black hair is down, twisted into small braids. A tiny silver hoop is pierced through her septum, and she's wearing a bright orange sweater that contrasts against all of the pastel colors around us.

"I'm entering mine," she says. "But you already know that."

A loud laugh rolls out of Chip, and everyone's head swivels toward him like a group of cartoon characters watching a debate, and I begin to question my sanity. It's absurd to be fighting over something as trivial as peppermint bark, but then again, who I am to judge them. Maybe that's the worst thing that can happen here, and something about that is reassuring.

"There are no rules against two businesses having the same entry," he argues. "I've entered my peppermint bark every year for the last ten years, and I intend to do the same this year."

Every head swivels back toward the woman, but this time it's Stella who interjects.

"Now, now. Lolly, he's right. So, there is no need for any arguing, only festive cheer." She taps her pen against the clipboard on the last two words. "You can both enter your peppermint bark, and Claire and Everett will be happy to judge it fairly."

"Well then, I look forward to beating you in the name of festive cheer," Lolly says, taking her seat as Chip does the same with a bit of a huff. Stella writes something on the paper and then scans the page again. Looking up, she narrows her eyes.

"Okay, Joe and Cami. Do I have this right? Citrine Brews will have a coffee and a tea entry this year?"

A man with graying hair stands. He's wearing a brown apron over a flannel shirt. His smile takes up his whole face, exposing the wrinkles around his eyes and the dimples in both of his warm ivory cheeks.

"That's right. We thought a little competition could spice up the marriage." He chuckles and nudges the woman sitting next to him, drawing a few laughs from the crowd. She has a mix of blonde and gray chin-length hair and is wearing a matching brown apron over a loose cream colored sweater. She stands to join him.

"I'll be making an eggnog latte," he says.

"And I'll be beating all of you with my Christmas chai latte," Cami quips.

"Fabulous," Stella says, scribbling across the paper. "Okay, well Lolly, we already know what The Gum Drop Sugar Shop will be making. So that brings us to Reid from The Music Box." She surveys the crowd. "Reid, are you here?"

A man stands, clearing his throat.

He's young, around our age. He can't be taller than six feet, maybe a few inches shorter. He's got light skin, dark hair, beady eyes, a long nose, and a clean shaven face.

"I'm here," he falters. "I'll be making marzipan fruits."

"Sounds delicious," Stella beams, writing again. "Wow, you two are really going to have a tough competition." She glances over her shoulder.

"Alright, next up is Ginger."

A woman with red curls and fair skin stands. She is around five feet and her full figure is covered by a bulky coat. She is sharing a booth with six kids, all of whom have matching curls, and a man who I presume is her husband. "Sugar—" she begins while trying to hold two of her boys apart. "Boys, please," she orders and the boys freeze, straightening up in the booth. The older one sticks his tongue out at the other, and Ginger snaps her fingers in their direction. "Sorry about that. I'll be making sugar cookies."

Gasps and whispers circulate around the restaurant.

"None of your famous gingerbread cookies this year?" Stella asks, stunned.

"I wanted to switch it up," the woman explains. "Plus, I thought it would be fun for the kids to help."

"If you insist, but they'll be missed." Her finger trails down the piece of paper. "And that brings us to Aster," Stella says.

The other woman who waved stands. She's a few years younger and at least half a foot shorter than Claire. Her black hair is wavy and cut to frame her round face. Deep purple highlights shine through, and a dimple appears on the right side of her face when she smiles. Her plum puffer jacket hits just above her ankles, and a chunky hand-knitted sage scarf covered with flowers hangs around her neck.

"I'm gonna make a mistletoe kiss cocktail with some of the rosemary from my garden."

"Delightful," Stella beams, jotting something down on the paper. "So, I guess that brings us to the last thing on the agenda. Lolly and Chip have graciously volunteered to co-chair the decoration committee."

There is a groan from somewhere in the crowd, and someone else snorts. Lolly's arms are folded across her chest, and her lips are pursed. Chip mimics her body language and is shaking his head.

"I'm sure they'll need help the day of the Extravaganza, so please see either of them to volunteer. Let's not forget the Sugarplum Park way. We help one another, we're there for one another, and above all else, we love one another."

Her face brightens as she looks over the crowd.

"As you all know, this festival is an important part of our town's history and has been for over a hundred years, so I truly appreciate all of your enthusiasm when it comes to making it the best year yet. Merry Christmas!"

Everyone stands and begins layering on coats, hats, and scarfs. Stella turns to us and unclips the piece of paper from the clipboard she's been holding.

"Here's the judging schedule for Christmas Eve," she explains, handing it to Claire. "And all of the entries."

"Actually, we were wondering if you had a minute to chat," I ask, removing my crown.

"I don't. I have somewhere I need to be."

"But it'll only take a moment," Claire tries.

"Bye now," Stella says, waving toward a group of people passing by us. "I know you two must be feeling nervous about the judging, but I find the key to it all is just to really lean into the spirit of the town and give into the magic."

"Is that how we get—"

"Stella!" Another pink-haired woman interrupts Claire, calling out from the kitchen.

"Be there in a minute." Stella lifts her arm to acknowledge the other woman. "Alright, you two, I'm so looking forward to the Extravaganza," she says, beginning to walk away. "Be there at one o'clock sharp. I expect you to be in your crowns and sashes since an SDN photographer will be present."

Claire nods, and a knot forms in my stomach.

"Oh, and please for the love of Christmas, do not be late. The whole event revolves around the competition, and we can't have it delayed," she sings, looking over her shoulder. Without another word, she disappears into the kitchen, and my gaze shifts to Claire.

"Did she say SDN?" I whisper.

"I think so. Why, have you heard of that before?"

"The reporter with the pink hair said that was who she was with."

"Okay…" she says, blinking and looking around the restaurant. The wheels behind her eyes turn as she tries to process everything. Placing my hand on her lower back, I move us toward the door, not sure what our next move should be, but determined to figure it out.

CHAPTER 19: WHEN IN ROME
CLAIRE

My brain feels like it's in overdrive. Stella just disappeared before we could get any real information from her, leaving us with nothing but a piece of paper and more cryptic messages. I'm also in desperate need of coffee and, at this point, probably some food.

Exhaling, I fold the schedule and slip it into my coat pocket and remove the crown from my head.

"You want to go check out the coffee shop?" I ask, looking over at Everett as we move toward the front of the diner. His brow is knitted together and his hair falls messily across the top of this forehead.

"We can. What do you think the reporter being with SDN means?"

"I don't know."

"Do you think I'm right about falling in love?"

"I don't know," I repeat. "That was…"

"A lot?"

"Yeah."

"Okay, let's get some coffee and then we can try to make sense of everything."

"Table for two?" a woman standing behind us asks as Everett reaches for the door of the diner. She can't be over five feet tall, and her curvy frame is accentuated by the striped apron resembling a candy cane tied around her waist. Blonde hair highlighted pink hits right below her chin and brings out the rosiness of her cheeks.

"Oh…um…we were just heading out," I say.

"Nonsense," she says. "I heard you say you were grabbing coffee, and we have plenty. Plus we have food too, and I know Everett can always eat."

He shrugs. "I am a little hungry."

"Okay," I agree, my eyes landing on the waitress's name tag. "Thank you, Ruth."

"Wonderful," she sing-songs, grabbing two menus and then leading us to a booth where we slide in across from one another. "Two cups of coffee?"

"Please," I say, perusing the menu. "Actually, I think I'll try a gingerbread latte. That sounds good."

"I'll take one of those too."

My eyes find Everett's and narrow.

"Great, I'll be right back." She smiles at us both before heading toward the kitchen.

"A gingerbread latte?" I ask.

"When in Rome, right?"

"That's rich coming from Scrooge."

"Hey, just because I don't love Christmas doesn't mean I don't like the drinks associated with it. I don't know if you heard, but I was crowned the king of the Sugarplum Park Christmas Extravaganza a few moments ago, so I have to play the part, right?"

I roll my eyes and then drop them back to my menu. "I guess so."

Ruth returns and sets the two drinks on the table. They're both topped with a heaping serving of whipped cream, shaved nutmeg, and a tiny gingerbread cookie. His mug is shaped like some type of Christmas soldier, and mine is pink with the words *Son Of A Nutcracker* printed across the front in different shades of green. "Do you know what you want to eat, or do you need another minute?" she asks.

"Another minute, please," I say.

Ruth nods and walks away.

Picking up the mugs, we both take a sip of our drinks. Ginger and molasses swirl across my tongue. It tastes like it was made by one of Santa's elves, and honestly, the way our time here is going, I wouldn't be surprised if we found out it had been.

Glancing up at Everett, I giggle at the white cream now covering his mustache.

"What?"

"You have a little whipped cream..." Standing slightly, I lean over the table and wipe my thumb across his lips, making him freeze under my touch.

"Sorry, I shouldn't have done that," I stammer, sitting down and wiping my fingers clean with a paper napkin. "You're perfectly capable of wiping your own face."

"It's okay." He chuckles. "I liked it."

There's a beat of silence, and my eyes land back on my menu.

"Okay, you two," Ruth chimes, walking back up to the table. "What can we get you?"

"I'll have the eggnog French toast with a side of bacon."

Ruth jots down my order and then looks at Everett.

"Two eggs over easy, bacon, and French toast."

"Eggnog or plain?" Ruth asks.

"Surprise me." He wiggles his eyebrows, laying on the charm.

She giggles, her cheeks turning a deep shade of pink. "Anything else?"

"Nope," I say. "That's all for now."

She grabs our menus and walks away from our table. Crossing my arms, my gaze lands back on Everett.

"Copying my order is an improvement from the last time we ate together."

"What are you talking about?" He shifts in his seat.

"You don't remember stealing my food on our one and only date?"

"No, I don't remember being a thief."

"Oh, come on. You really don't remember telling the waiter you didn't want dessert and then proceeding to eat half of my crème brûlée."

"Oh, you mean eating the dessert you ordered for us to share after I was a gentleman and let you order for the table?"

"What?" I gasp. "It wasn't to share."

"I'm a little offended," he jests. "You've seriously thought for four and half years that I stole your dessert that night."

"You did steal it."

"The waiter brought two spoons."

"No, he didn't."

"Then where did the spoon come from?" He chuckles and lifts his brow.

"I can't believe we're arguing about this." I run my hands through my hair. "We have such bigger problems."

"You can admit I'm right." He smirks.

"I think I'll pass."

"Suit yourself, but I think you're going to start to realize I'm right about a lot of things. Like how I think you need to fall—"

"Don't." I hold up a finger. "That's not how we're going to get home."

His face falls slightly before he sips his latte and clears his throat. Playing with the handle of my coffee mug, I contemplate our morning. The house. The wedding rings on my finger. The meeting. His insistence on us falling in love.

"Any ideas on how we get out of here then?" he asks.

A long sigh falls past my lips, and my head hits the back of the bench seat. "No, I was hoping Stella would be more helpful than she was."

"Maybe I am right." Everett huffs out a laugh as he looks down into his mug.

"Nice try, but if that was the case, I think love would've been mentioned."

"It was mentioned. Remember?"

"No."

"She said it's the Sugarplum Park way to love one another."

"I don't think that's what she meant." I bite my lip. "What did she say after the meeting? Something about the key to it all being something."

"Oh, when she was talking about judging the competition on Christmas Eve? I think something to the effect of giving into the magic and leaning into the spirit of the town."

"Any idea what 'spirit of the town' means?" I ask, moving my head from side to side.

My phone chimes, and I look down to see a text.

The Naughty List

ASTER:

I'm still laughing about Chip's reaction to Lolly's
entry.

Aster? The flower shop owner.

LOLLY:

I know. He's insane. He was holding the article
spotlighting my peppermint bark. He knew, but he
just wanted to cause a scene. I swear he lives for
trying to infuriate me.

Lolly? The candy store owner.
The women that waved.
Are they…*my friends*?

ASTER:

So insane! Claire, it looks like you and your hubby
have your work cut out for you.

LOLLY:

For real! We looked for you outside Stella's after the
meeting, but you'd both disappeared. How are you
feeling about having to judge this year?

Muting the text thread, I don't respond. I can barely find people
who want to be my friend in New York. The last thing I'm going to
do is make friends with fictional people.

Nope. Not happening.

CHAPTER 20: TOUCHÉ
EVERETT

Stella's vague statements might as well be riddles with no answer because I have no idea what they mean or how to solve them so we can go back to New York. I'm not used to not having the answer. As captain, I lead my team, but I feel like I'm completely floundering when it comes to leading us home. The last thing I want is to disappoint her.

Her mouth falls open as she stares at something on her phone.

"Whatcha looking at?" I ask as she sets her phone on the table, screen side down.

"A couple of the girls from the meeting are texting me." She massages her temples and physically shakes off whatever thought is in her head.

"Did you respond?"

"No, I don't even know who they are."

I shrug. "Doesn't mean you have to ignore them."

"If strangers were texting you, would you respond?" Her gaze flicks upward as she takes a deep breath, reaching for her mug.

"To them we aren't strangers," I whisper. "Maybe they have information that could help us."

"This is all too much," she says, sliding her phone off the table and putting it into her coat pocket.

"I know it's a lot, but we got—"

"Here we go," Ruth says, approaching our table with our plates. She sets them down and then hands me a syrup container from an unused table behind her.

I cover my toast with the sticky substance and then pass it to Claire.

"Can I get you anything else?" Ruth asks.

A way home.

"No, I think that's it," Claire says, looking down at her food.

"All good here," I say. "The plain French toast is perfect. Good choice." I throw her a wink, and she blushes. Giggling like a school girl, she leaves and walks over to another table.

Leaning forward with my fork, I steal a piece of the bread off Claire's plate.

"Food stealer," she quips, slapping at my wrist as a laugh bubbles out of her.

These are the moments I wish I could hold onto. I like making her laugh, and every time her face falls, I desperately want to make the negative feelings go away—want to see her smile.

"I knew it," she accuses.

A wide grin paints my face, and she rolls her eyes.

"What? She gave me plain. I wanted to try the eggnog."

"Then you should've ordered it."

"Where's the fun in that?"

"Nothing is fun about this situation."

"I'm having fun." I chuckle, running the piece of toast through the syrup before putting it in my mouth.

Her eyes flick upward, and she shakes her head.

"Where were we before I got those texts?" she asks, picking at some of the whipped cream on the edge of the plate. "Oh! Spirit of the town and whatever the hell it means."

"Well, what do we know about the town?"

"Stella put us here. It looks like a Christmas card. We're married." She spins the rings on her fingers and I watch, mesmerized by the movements of her delicate hands. "People seem to know us. There's a town square with…" She counts the shops we saw earlier on her fingers. "Nine shops."

"Maybe we have to get to know the people here?" I shrug. "Like those girls texting you, maybe we befriend them."

"No, that doesn't make sense." She runs her hands through her hair, and once again I'm hypnotized by her movements. Pulling out the schedule Stella gave us from her pocket, she studies it.

"You think it's the competition?"

"Maybe," she says, biting her lip. "But why?"

"Could she have brought us here because they needed people to judge it."

Seems like a whole lot of trouble, but Stella doesn't seem like the type of person to do things simply.

Her eyes scan the paper, and I sip my latte, swallowing down the sweet liquid.

"Ha!" I laugh. "Could you imagine if she brought us all the way here just because no one else wanted to be the judges. Talk about going through a lot of trouble just to pick a winner."

"Yeah, I don't think that's it."

I reach for the schedule. "Can I see that?"

She nods, handing it to me. I do my best to make sense of what I'm reading, but the answer to getting us home doesn't seem to be on this piece of paper.

"This sucks. I wish I could call my sister," she says, picking at her toast.

"Is that who you tried to call this morning?" I ask.

She nods and looks back down at her food. "Well, her and my parents. You?"

"I tried the team doctor and then my coach."

"That's it?" Her sapphire eyes find mine.

"Yeah. I was supposed to go in today to have my shoulder assessed before practice. Figured I needed to let someone know I wouldn't be there."

"You didn't call any family or friends?"

I shake my head.

"Did you not try to call your ballet people?"

"No, I stopped when the calls wouldn't go through to my family." She goes back to eating, or rather just moving the food around her plate. Her gaze clouds, and her fingers toy with the silver chain around her neck.

"I'm not super close with my parents," I admit, my face falling.

"Oh? We don't have to talk about it if you don't want to."

"It's fine. I can see that look in your eye like you want to know." I lean back in the booth, my shoulders slumping a little.

"There's no look. I don't care," she feigns, her eyes finding mine.

"Yes, you do, but there's no story to tell. We just aren't super close. I see them a couple of times a year, and I try to talk to them monthly."

"That's it?" The hand that was still fiddling with her necklace falls to her lap.

"They don't live in New York, and they travel a lot for work. If I'm honest, I don't even remember where they are right now. Australia, I think…or maybe it's Austria."

I think back to the last time we spoke. Goodness, it had to be over a month ago.

"You have siblings though, right? You didn't want to call them?"

I nod. "A sister."

"What's her name?"

"Maren. We used to be a lot closer, but she lives in Wales with her husband and two girls now. We do our best to call, but you know how life goes. You make a plan, and then the next thing you know, two weeks have gone by and you still haven't talked."

"I'm sorry." Her blue eyes find mine again, and my heart skips below my ribs.

"Why?"

"I don't know. It sounds lonely. My little sister, Andi, is my best friend. We've never gone a day without talking."

I do my best to force a smile. "She and I are both busy, so it's okay. I get a lot of snail mail from her girls, but sometimes making time to talk or visit is hard."

"Like letters?"

"Yeah, her oldest, Elsie, is six and is learning to write, so I've been getting more hand written letters lately. They're a little hard to decode, but I do my best." I chuckle, and a smile spreads across my face. This time it isn't forced. Elsie and Iris have always had that effect on me. "In the last one, she was asking if I'd buy her a pomeranian because Maren told her no."

"And her little sister?"

"Iris is four, so she mostly sends me drawings and doodles."

My mind wanders to the art that covers my locker, and I wonder if I'll ever see them again.

"Is she who drew the picture in your wallet?"

"That one's actually from when Elsie was younger, but I keep it with me everywhere I go."

Setting her fork down on the table, she picks up her drink.

"Do you ever write them back?"

"Of course I do. Writing them back is the bare minimum."

She hums. "What about friends? You didn't want to try calling them?"

"They all went out last night after the game." I take a bite of my eggs. "No way they would've answered."

Her face falls, and her head tilts to the side.

"I'm not some lonely loser," I continue. "I have my team and my friends. My parents and sister are good people; they just stay busy, and that's okay because I'm busy too."

"That's not what I was thinking," she says, sitting up a little straighter and sipping her latte.

"Then stop looking at me like I am. I'm good with it. I've never known any different, so it's cool. And honestly, after all these years of the media's attention, it's nice to be alone sometimes."

She presses her lips together and studies me.

"Will you tell me more about your nieces?"

I smile, and my body relaxes. "Elsie wants to play hockey like me, and Iris loves everything that sparkles."

"That's sweet. Have they ever done ballet?"

"I don't think so. Elsie definitely wouldn't go for it." I chuckle.

"Why not?"

"She's a real tough cookie."

"And you don't think dancers can be tough?" She blinks, cocking her head.

FUCK!

Talk about inserting my foot into my mouth. Why the fuck did I say that?

"No, that's not what I meant," I try, shaking my head and running a hand through my hair.

"It's fine. I know the tutus and glitter don't really give off a tough vibe, but I think you'd be surprised how tough we are. How much we put our bodies through to do what we love, all while not wearing helmets and pads." She smirks.

"Touché," I say. "I promise I wasn't shitting on what you do. I think what you do is incredible. I'm sorry. I shouldn't have said that."

She moves her toast around, but doesn't look up at me. "How about the younger one? Is she tough enough to be a ballerina?"

"Oh, definitely."

"Well then, I think she and I would get along splendidly." Her eyes find mine, and a soft smile breaks across her lips.

"I think you would too."

My heart expands at the thought of Claire meeting the two little girls who mean so much to me, but I shake the thought as quick as it comes. She was clear that falling in love with me isn't a possibility, and I shouldn't get ahead of myself.

"Are you finished?" Ruth asks, returning to clear off the table.

"I am," Claire says, pushing her breakfast away.

"Oh, dear. You barely touched your food. Was everything okay?"

"Oh, it was delicious. I'm just full."

Ruth nods and sets the bill on the table then clears both of our plates.

Pulling out my wallet and flipping it open, I freeze for a moment. My thumb brushes over my niece's drawing, and then I chuckle as I spot a pink debit card and pull it out. The surface of the card shimmers in the light as I turn it toward Claire. In the top right corner, Sugarplum Park Bank is stamped into the glitter, and along the bottom is my name.

"You think that will work?" she asks.

"Only one way to find out." I place it on the small tray with the bill, and Ruth returns to grab it. Silence falls between us as we wait for her to return.

"So glad you two stayed to eat," she says, setting the card and receipt on the table. "I'll see you around."

I sign, and then we both make our way out of the restaurant.

CHAPTER 21:
ABSOLUTELY NO
SAFETY AWARENESS
CLAIRE

Everett holds the door of Stella's, and I walk past him out onto the snow covered sidewalk, zipping my jacket.

"I really feel bad," he says, meeting me outside. His head turns down and his shoulders slouch. "I'm sorry again."

"For what?"

"For insinuating ballet wasn't a tough sport."

"You aren't the first person to think that," I say. "It's really okay."

"But that's the thing—it's not okay. I see how tough you are and can only imagine how hard you train back in New York. I don't ever want to make you feel like I don't see you. I never want to diminish anything you do."

I stare at him a little stunned. I was honestly just giving him a hard time and joking around, but his sincerity has me feeling a way I've never felt around him before.

"I believe you," I say as we begin to cross the street. "But thank you for saying all of that."

"I mean it." Our eyes connect, and without a doubt I know he does.

I offer him a reassuring nod and a small smile. "So, you want to head back to the house? Maybe see if we can find any clues there?"

"That sounds good."

We turn to head toward the house when shouting coming from the three young boys who were wrestling in the booth causes us to freeze.

"Coach! Coach!" one of the boys yells as they all sprint toward us from the outdoor ice rink that's situated at the top of the street in front of a town hall. Red curls bounce as they run through the snow.

"Coach, look at my new hockey stick," one who is a little taller with similar red, curly hair shouts.

"I got a new one, too, but I hit Maple with it this morning, so Dad said I can't have it back until tomorrow," the youngest of the three whines, not taking a full breath until the last word falls from his mouth.

"Hi?" I say, looking from the three children back to Everett. It's clear these boys know us, or they think they do.

"Are your parents around?" I ask.

"They're over there," the boy holding the stick says, pointing to where a small group of adults is huddled together, laughing. "What do you think, Coach?" He shows off the new piece of equipment proudly, pretending to shoot a puck across the street.

"Claire! Everett!" Their mother, Ginger, waves. "Hold on. I'll be right there. Boys, give them some space." She's holding a baby on her hip, and two little girls follow after her like miniature shadows.

My attention turns back to the boys. All three of them are talking so fast that I can't catch more than every third word. Everett nods along as they talk like he understands what they're saying.

Their mother makes it to us and immediately wraps me in a one-sided hug.

"Hi, Mrs. Claire," both of the little girls sing-song from behind her.

"Oh, hi," I stammer, doing my best to return Ginger's gesture, but I'm certain I've already made it awkward.

"Don't you look pretty," she says, stepping back and smoothing her coat. "Pink really suits you."

"Thank you." I fidget with the chain of my necklace.

"Cori, Dill, Fen! Stop talking so fast and let them be. You will have all of Coach Everett's attention Monday at practice. Now run along." She waves them off.

Coach Everett?

Why does the idea of him coaching little kids make my heart beat a little quicker? Fuck, I bet that's cute. My eyes flit over to

Everett standing and listening intently as Ginger speaks. Both of his hands are casually in his pockets, and he nods and smiles like this is some normal conversation between old friends.

The three boys run back toward the rink, yelling, "Bye, Coach" in unison, and Everett lifts his hand.

"The girls are so looking forward to dance classes starting back up after Christmas," Ginger continues.

"Oh! They dance?" I ask, eyeing both girls, who are peeking out from behind each of their mother's legs.

"What are you talking about, hun?" She cocks her head to the side.

I frantically search the street for any clue that could help me sound less crazy. My eyes dart down to the two little girls.

Mrs. Claire.

They called me Mrs. Claire.

Looking up, my eyes land on the ballet studio situated across the street from Stella's Diner.

I teach dance.

Blush creeps up my face. "Oh…um…I just…I just meant…" I force a laugh, trying to cover my mistake, but I can't think of anything to say that would make sense. Ginger's brow knits together. "Are you okay, sweetheart?" she asks.

"We didn't get a lot of sleep last night," Everett cuts in. "Isn't that right, babe?" He nudges me with his elbow gently.

"That's right." I nod and force a smile.

"Oh, I remember what the first year of marriage was like. So young and so in love." She laughs. "How do you think Rusty and I got all these kids? I think I came home from our honeymoon pregnant with…well, you get it." She laughs again and moves the baby to the other hip.

"Oh, no that's not what he meant. We're just both in desperate need of some more coffee. Right, *babe*," I say, gritting my teeth.

"Ginger, have you seen Cori's gloves?" a man, who I assume is Rusty, yells from where the three boys are now rolling around in the snow.

"One second," Ginger yells back. "Well, I'll let you two get going. You'd think I'm the only one in this family who knows where anything is. We'll see you two later."

The four of them make their way back to the rest of their family, leaving me alone with Everett.

"Okay, so that was…"

"Informative," Everett finishes for me.

"Yeah." The street is full of people coming and going from each shop. My eyes settle on the dance studio. I wonder if this version of me is happy teaching dance. If she ever knew what it was like to dance on the stage at Lincoln Center. "I can't believe it's mine."

Everett turns to see where I'm looking. "No? Have you ever considered owning your own place before?"

"Not really."

"Should we go check it out?"

"Really?"

"Yeah, I mean what else are we going to do?" He shrugs.

We finish crossing the street and arrive at the door of Pirouettes and Plies. The exterior is painted a light pink, and the trim is a shade slightly brighter. Above each window is a small white and pink striped awning.

"We don't have a key," I say, laughing and moving up to one of the windows. Placing my hands above my eyes to block the sunlight, I peer into the dark studio.

"I'm sure there's a spare somewhere around here," Everett says, digging in one of the small potted Christmas trees that frames the door.

"And if there isn't?" I ask, turning to look at him.

"Then I'll break a window," he deadpans.

"Right. Because breaking and entering will surely help us here."

Shaking my head, I try to channel where this version of myself would've put an extra key, but I'm not sure. I know nothing about the me who lives here other than she is married to Everett and owns a dance studio. Neither of which I ever saw myself doing.

"Is it under the doormat?" he asks.

"Do you really think I would leave the key where anyone could find it? The New Yorker in me knows better than to put it there."

He glances around the street. "I mean, I can't imagine this town is full of hard criminals."

"We still don't know that."

He chortles.

Poking and prodding around, we try to find a trick rock or lock box or literally any place a key might be, but there's nothing.

"What are you two up to?" a voice says from our right. Whipping our heads in the direction of the sound, we find Cami standing with a foldable chalk board outside the doors of Citrine Brews.

"Claire wanted to dance today," Everett explains, gesturing in my direction. "But would you believe that she can't find her key anywhere?"

Cami giggles as she begins to set up the sign she's holding. "Is the spare you keep under the doormat not there?"

A snort erupts from Everett, and I cut my eyes in his direction. "Yeah, babe. Did you check under the mat?" he asks, trying to hold back more laughter.

"How could I forget," I grit out through a forced smile. Swallowing my pride, I bend down and lift the doormat, revealing a small silver key.

Dammit. Apparently this version of me has absolutely no safety awareness.

"You two have a good day," she calls, disappearing back into the shop.

"The New Yorker in me would never leave the key under the mat," Everett mocks as I unlock the door.

"Stop it," I warn, spinning around to face him with my hands on my hips.

"Say it with me," he quips. "Everett. Was. Right."

"You're ridiculous."

"Hey, I told you I'm right about a lot of things." He steps toward me. My breath hitches as he bends down and his lips tickle the side of my neck. "You starting to come around to my idea yet, Sugar?"

Breathing in deep, I push him away. "The only thing you were right about was suggesting we check out the dance studio."

My stomach dips as his mouth breaks into a grin, and I turn around, pushing the feeling away.

Opening the door, we walk into the small studio. Flipping the switch, the chandeliers across the ceiling illuminate and reflect off the mirrors casting sparkles of light all around. The light wood floors stretch across the entire room. Framed photos of different aged children hang on the wall. Each age level is wearing a different costume from what appears to be a spring recital. I'm in each photo, posed and smiling. Dozens of different colored tutus hang from a clothing rack along the back wall.

"This is a cool place," he says, looking around.

"Yeah, it is." My fingers trail across the glass of one of the photos, and I take it all in. The tension between my shoulder blades begins to loosen, and my head feels a little clearer. For the first time since I woke up this morning, I feel at home. Like everything might actually be okay.

"Alright, well I'm gonna go explore, and I'll meet you back here in a little while?" he says, still standing near the door.

"Explore?"

"Yeah. You're welcome to come with me. I just thought you might want to dance or something. I know skating always seems to calm me down when I'm stressed."

"Really? You don't mind?"

He shakes his head. "No way. I'll go walk around and see if I can find anything worth our time, and then I'll swing by and we can walk back to the house together."

"Yeah…okay…thank you."

"I'll be back soon," he says. The corner of his mouth tips up, and then he turns, disappearing out of the studio and leaving me alone.

I lock the door behind him and begin to shed my jacket and then my bulky sweater. My bralette covers just as much as a bathing suit, and I want to be able to move freely. The jeans aren't ideal, but I've danced in them before. Kicking off my chunky boots, I walk over to the large stereo sitting on the ground in front of one of the windows. I connect my phone to the aux cord and scroll until I find Tchaikovsky's "Dance of the Sugar Plum Fairy" and click play.

If I'm forced to be stuck here, then I can use my time to prepare for the show, or at least do what I can without my dance partner. The music begins, and I start to train the part I know so well.

Over and over, I run through the dance, and with every move-ment I feel a little more settled and my mind feels a little more clear.

CHAPTER 22: GIVE INTO THE MAGIC

EVERETT

DECEMBER NINETEENTH

My eyes flicker open as the sun pours into our bedroom. Stretching, I turn to find Claire asleep on the other side of the bed. Her pillow is pushed up above her head, and she's laying on her stomach with her head directly on the mattress. Her hair is sprawled wildly around her.

She looks beautiful.

Her body begins to stir, but I can't look away.

"Are you watching me sleep?" she asks, peeking through her silky strands.

"Caught me," I admit, my lips curling into a soft smile.

"Freak." She laughs. Her gaze moves around the room, and her face falls when she realizes where we still are. "Part of me was really hoping yesterday was a dream."

"I know."

Breathing in deep, her eyes flutter closed. I shift my body, so that I'm now just a couple inches away from where she is.

"What are you doing?" she asks, her eyes popping open.

"Well, I was going to try to comfort you, but if you'd rather me not, I can give you a minute."

"Comfort me?" Her voice wobbles slightly, and a few rogue tears run down her cheeks.

"I don't have any ulterior motives, just thought you could use a hug." I reach out and trail my fingers down her arm.

"I could."

"Then come here," I say, pulling her into me. She melts into my embrace, and I inhale her sweet scent. Her body shakes as she begins to cry, and I hold her tighter.

"It's okay," I assure her, rubbing my hands up and down her back. "We'll figure it out today."

Rolling back, her eyes find mine, and I bring the pad of my thumb to her cheek, wiping away the tears.

"You think so?" she sniffles.

"Yes, and I was thinking. Maybe we go explore the town together today and see if Stella will talk to us. I came up empty handed yesterday, so I think the key to this is us doing it together."

She moves away from me and inhales deeply, looking up at the ceiling, and my heart sinks.

"I'm not suggesting the love thing again, but I do think we're better together than apart," I explain.

"I agree." She turns her head. "And for the record, I'm not opposed to your idea. I just don't think it's the solution that's going to get us home before Christmas."

Holy fucking shit. She's not *opposed* to falling in love with me.

"Don't look at me like that," she says, covering her face with her hands and shaking her head.

"Like what?"

"Like I just told you I love you."

"Didn't you?" I smirk.

"No…" She huffs a breath and sits up. "I said that I'm open to the idea of you and me in the future. I just don't think it's going to happen before Christmas."

"I'm hearing I have a chance."

She rolls out of bed, laughing. "You truly can be so incredibly—"

"Amazing?"

My chest expands as a smile brightens her face.

"Not the word I was going to use," she quips.

"No? You're not crying anymore," I boast, climbing out of bed and turning to face her.

"No, I guess I'm not."

"See? Seems like someone pretty amazing made you feel

better." I can't help the arrogant curve of my lips. She may not want to admit the effect I have on her, but I can see it. Like maybe she's realizing I could be more than the cock that makes her feel good.

"Let's get dressed," she says, walking toward her closet. Her hands flex by her sides as she moves, but she doesn't look at me.

I turn to walk to mine holding on tight to the thought that if I keep showing her the man I really am, she and I might actually have a chance this time.

The weather is a little warmer than it was yesterday but still too cool to melt the snow. Nervous energy pulses through my veins like electricity through a wire as we approach the doors of Citrine Brews. We have to figure this out today, and I don't know what we're going to do if we don't.

I look over toward Claire, hoping to calm some of my nerves, and I find her staring back at me holding in a laugh.

"What?" I question.

"Your sweater," she says. "It's just funny that that's what you picked to wear."

The sweater I'm wearing peeks out from beneath my open coat. It's dark green, and on the front, red lettering says that I'm *On The Naughty List*. A Santa hat tops the "O," and some type of tinsel is sewn into the fabric, making it incredibly itchy.

"It was this or a light-up sweater with a large reindeer head on the front, so I went with what I thought was the less obnoxious option."

"Oh man!" She giggles. "I wish you had worn the other one."

"Laugh all you want, but we're supposed to be giving into the spirit of the town, and I felt like this did the trick."

"Okay," she says, putting her hands up. "It *is* actually kind of cute on you." She smirks, shifting her eyes to mine.

"Oh yeah? You think I'm cute." I stand up a little taller and puff out my chest.

"You know I do. Just don't let it go to your head."

"Oh, it's definitely going to my head." Glancing down at my dick, I wiggle my eyebrows.

"How do you do that?" she asks.

"Do what?"

"Make me want you even when I should want nothing to do with you?"

"You want me?"

She sucks in a sharp breath. "Stop," she scolds, blush covering her cheeks.

"That's not a word I've heard you say before." The corner of my mouth tips upward.

"Don't flirt with me when we're supposed to be focusing on getting back to New York. We have so much to figure out."

"But the flirting is fun."

"The flirting isn't going to get us anywhere but back in bed, and the only place we need to be going is back to New York."

"It's that hard to resist me?" I nudge her as we continue to walk.

"Um…"

"You can admit it."

She shakes her head. "Yes. Okay. It's hard to resist you, and while we're both used to distracting one another from a bad day, this is different. We need to try to focus, and you flirting is making that really hard."

My eyes find hers, and I lift an eyebrow.

"We'll figure it out," I assure her. "Plus, if we took a detour to the bed on the way back to New York, would that be the worst thing in the world?"

"Everett," she warns.

"Okay. Okay. I'll stop." I put my hands up and shake my head.

For now.

I can't help myself when I'm around her, and as much as she wants to pretend like she doesn't like our little back and forths, I know she does.

"Shall we go figure it out?" I ask, pulling the doors of Citrine Brews open. Following her inside, we're met with immediate warmth and calm.

The lighting is dim, and exposed brick surrounds the space on three sides. Worn wood floors are covered by mismatched vintage rugs. Along one of the walls is a large bar. The veining of the wood and raw edges add to the woodsy charm of the shop. Behind the bar is a cluttered counter covered with espresso machines, pour-over coffee makers, canisters filled with ingredients, syrups, mugs, and more. Hanging plants, novelty signs, and Christmas trinkets haphazardly decorate the shelves above it. Two large chalk boards list the seasonal menu, and twinkling lights are strung across the ceiling. A small glass case to the right of the register is full of seasonal pastries.

An array of leather and jewel-toned furniture is mixed with a few tables, laid out so that people can gather with one another. The shop is busy with people, and the instrumental Christmas music can barely be heard over their conversations and occasional laughter.

"Well if it isn't two of my favorite people," a man who I recognize as Joe says, chuckling from behind the counter. "Can I get you both your usual?"

Usual? We have usuals here?

"Sure," I say, looking over at Claire and lifting an eyebrow. "Thank you."

We explore the store while we wait.

Along the wall opposite the bar, minerals are displayed on glass shelves with small descriptions of the glittering rocks. To the right is a display case full of stacked baskets filled with smaller stones of varying shapes. Each one is smooth and easily held in your hand. On top of the case is handmade jewelry.

"Claire! Everett!" a woman says as she walks toward us.

Shit, what is her name? Carrie? Kim?

"Hi, Cami," Claire says as the stranger wraps her in a warm hug, and she awkwardly returns it.

"Don't tell me you two are finally interested in my crystals."

"Oh, we were just waiting on our drinks," I explain.

She hums to herself but doesn't walk away.

Perusing the smaller crystals, Claire picks up an ocean-colored stone.

"Actually, what's this one called?" she asks, smoothing her thumb over the surface.

"That one is a blue apatite crystal."

"It's pretty. What does it do?"

"Oh, apatite is a powerful stone. It can help you communicate truths, and some believe it can even help you manifest your deepest desires."

Claire abruptly throws the stone back into the basket she pulled it from and then glances over at me.

"Is that so?" she asks.

Cami hums again. "You should get one. Apatite is a good choice, but if I were you, citrine might be better suited for you two." She plucks a reddish-orange stone from one of the baskets.

"What does it do?" I ask.

"It helps with sorting through complex problems and with making decisions."

Like figuring out how to get home?

"And why would we need help with that?" Claire asks, no doubt having the same thought I'm having.

Does she know we aren't from here? Ginger didn't seem to, and neither did the girls texting Claire, but maybe…

"The Christmas Extravaganza competition of course." A wide smile breaks across her face. "It's a tough competition and a long day. I saw the look on your face when Stella announced you two as the king and queen. It seemed like you two could use all the help you can get." She puts out her arm, handing Claire the small stone. "You should take one home on me. Think of it as a good luck charm."

"Oh, we couldn't," she says, not taking the stone.

"Why not?"

Claire hesitates, peering over to me.

"Uh, Stella asked us not to accept gifts," I interject. "Something about bribing the judges."

Claire offers me a thankful smile and then plays with the silver chain around her neck. "Yeah, she's being really strict."

"Well you know what Stella doesn't know won't hurt her, but I understand." She places the stone back where she retrieved it. "They'll be here if you change your mind. You'd be surprised what can happen when you give into the magic."

Give into the magic. Isn't that what Stella said?

I open my mouth to question her, but she's already walking away.

"Everett. Claire. I've got those drinks," Joe calls from behind the counter, holding up two paper cups and then setting them down for us.

"How much do I owe you?" I ask, walking over.

"Ten," he says, tapping on the cash register.

Reaching into my coat pocket, I pull out my leather wallet and freeze when I see my niece's drawing. If I could ever use the luck this little flower could bring, it's now.

"You good?" he asks.

"Oh, yeah," I say, handing him the debit card.

"I swear Cami is going to get you to buy into her crystals one of these days." He chuckles, swiping the little pink card and handing it back.

"I don't know about that."

"My wife can be very persuasive. Receipt?"

"No, we're good. Thanks, man."

I grab the drinks and turn to find Claire already waiting for me by the door.

CHAPTER 23:
OH...NO...POISON
CLAIRE

"How much money do you think is in that account at the Sugarplum Park Bank?" I ask as Everett holds the door open and we walk back outside.

He shrugs. "Hopefully enough to get us through our time here," he says, chuckling. "Did you hear Cami say '*Give into the magic*'?"

"I did."

"Stella said the same thing."

"I know…I just have no idea what it means."

"Me either." He looks around the street at each of the stores. "Where do you want to start?"

"I don't think it matters," I say, looking around. "Maybe the bookstore?"

"Okay," he agrees.

We begin to cross the street toward The Book Rack.

"You know? I don't have any idea what drinks he gave me," he says.

"Me either. You think we should be afraid or excited?" I giggle as we walk.

"I'm not sure. If we were still in New York, what would be in your cup?"

"I'm a sucker for whatever seasonal drink is on the menu, but my usual is a brown sugar latte with oatmilk."

"Why? Are you lactose intolerant?" he asks.

"No, I just like the way oatmilk tastes. What's your go-to drink?"

"What do you think it is?"

"A cappuccino," I guess.

"Try again."

"Ummm…I don't know. A latte?"

"I bet you'll never guess it." His lips curl into a smirk.

"Then why are you making me play this silly game?" I huff.

"Oh, come on." His body bumps into mine as we move. "I'll give you a hint. It's a lot like me."

I tap my chin pretending to think.

"Oh, I know! You like it black, just like your heart?"

"Hilarious," he deadpans. "No. It's a large whole milk latte, with three pumps of caramel, two pumps of vanilla, no whip, light foam, and caramel drizzle."

"You're joking."

"Dead serious."

"In what world would I be able to guess that drink?"

"I gave you a hint."

"A bad one. How is that drink anything like you?"

"Because I'm really sweet."

"Ha!" I roll my eyes and run my free hand through my hair. "A vanilla latte is sweet. Whatever you just listed only proves that you're an incredibly high maintenance man."

"Maybe. Or I just know what I want." His eyes trail down my body, and he raises his eyebrows. Heat crawls up my neck and covers my face under his stare. I physically attempt to shake the effect he has on me away, but it doesn't work.

"I thought you said you'd stop flirting with me."

"Oh you meant forever?"

I clench my jaw, not sure what to say to him because honestly… I like the flirting. I like it more than I should, but I know we need to stay focused or we'll never get home.

"Should we try our mystery drinks?" he asks.

"Sure." I study my cup feeling grateful for the shift in our conversation. "You go first."

"Ha! You would ask me to go first."

"Who's gonna get us back if I die," I tease. "The best idea you've come up with is falling in love. We need me to live."

He cuts his eyes at me, shaking his head and trying not to laugh.

Hesitantly, he takes a sip from the cup and immediately grabs his throat.

"Uh…no…poison…ugh…" He sputters dramatically, falling to his knees in the snow and catching the attention of a few strangers walking by.

"Hilarious," I deadpan, holding back a laugh. "You're not funny."

"Keep telling yourself that," he says, standing and knocking the snow from his knees. "I think he switched them. This one is definitely yours. It's gross."

"Is not." I giggle as we trade cups, each then taking a sip of the drink that should've been ours to begin with. "So, if you like sweets so much, which Christmas Extravaganza item do you think you'd like the most?"

"I think Chip's peppermint bark."

"Not Lolly's?" I laugh.

"I don't know. I get a good vibe from him. I think I'll probably like his better."

"You get a vibe from him? You don't even know him."

"No, but it's his aura. He's like a cool, young grandpa."

"And that means he makes good peppermint bark?"

"I think so. What about you?"

"The eggnog latte." I sip my drink, and swallow hard.

"Why?

"My dad makes eggnog French toast every year for Christmas dinner, and it's one of my favorite things."

"Breakfast for dinner?"

"It's tradition."

"Sounds like a good one."

"The best." My voice drifts off, my heart aching for my family. I'd give anything to see them again. To hear about my dad's latest prank. To be able to hug my mom and sister. But I can't even call them.

"Maybe I'll get to try it sometime," he says.

"You know you have to be a fan of Christmas to try it," I tease. "It's a prerequisite for getting invited."

"Dang." He chuckles."Any non-holiday traditions I could try?"

"No, I'm from a family that's obsessed with every holiday there ever was. I'm talking matching Halloween costumes, those turkey-shaped hats, and Christmas sweaters that make the one you're wearing look like child's play."

"Ugh, sounds like I'd hate it."

"I don't know—you keep surprising me. Maybe you'd be surprised to find that you actually love it."

"Maybe."

Silence falls between us as our laughter fades, and I try to organize my thoughts as we make it to the door of the book shop.

Everett pulls the door open. Placing his hand on the small of my back, he leads me inside the well-lit space.

To the right, and taking up half the store, is a section for adults full of various genres of books— the largest appearing to be romance. On the back wall to the left are shelves covered in puzzles and games. A square wooden table is situated in front with pieces scattered across the top. In the front left is a children's section. The shelves are lined with books and small stuffed animals of all kinds. Homemade paper garland and stars hang from the ceiling.

"Welcome," Ginger says, greeting us. She's dressed in a blue sweater decorated with a family of friendly looking snowmen on the front. On her head sits a headband that resembles colorful Christmas lights. It flashes on and off.

"Hi," I say.

"Can I help you find something?" she asks.

"We're not sure," Everett says. "Thought we'd just look around—"

"Oh my! Would you look at that?" Ginger says, pointing out the window to the sidewalk outside her shop.

Chip and Lolly are stopped. Her hands are on her hips and his are crossed over his chest. She looks like she may be yelling, but it's hard to tell because we can't hear them.

"Don't you think they would make the cutest couple?" Ginger asks.

"Huh?" Everett questions.

"Lolly and Chip," she clarifies, tipping her chin in the direction of them. "Did she not tell you what happened?"

We both shake our heads.

"Well, according to Ruth, Chip asked Lolly out when she first moved here. She turned him down and then opened that cute little candy shop, and now they pretend like they hate each other, but I know better. I think they secretly like one another and are just playing hard to get."

"Maybe," I say.

"Sometimes people just need to take the time to talk to each other to realize they have more in common than they assume." She looks back and forth between me and Everett.

"I couldn't agree more," he says, locking his stare on me. I swallow hard and my stomach swoops.

Ginger begins to laugh. "They're going to have to spend lots of time together thanks to Stella!"

"What do you mean?" I ask.

"The decoration committee, of course."

"Didn't they volunteer to do that?"

"Oh, goodness no. They were voluntold and weren't very happy about it, but they'll just have to work through it." She smiles and her eyes gleam. "Anywho, let me know if you need help finding something."

We both nod and then walk toward the section of the store with books we hope might have clues for us to get home.

"Seems like people with pink hair *do* like to play matchmaker," Everett whispers.

I shake my head and roll my eyes.

"You're so much better than me with all of these strangers. It's taking all of my energy to smile and pretend like I know them. How do you do it?"

"I don't know. I've had a lot of practice from being in the spotlight the way I've been, but that doesn't mean it's not weighing on me too. You found me in a pinball bar, trying to escape my inevitable retirement, remember?"

I offer him a half-smile.

"Where do you think we should start?" he asks, running his fingers along the spines of some of the books.

"I don't know. I just keep thinking about what Stella said, so maybe books on magic or books about the town."

"Good idea," he says, beginning to peruse the shelves. We maze up and down each aisle looking for anything remotely resembling a book on Sugarplum Park or magic, but there's nothing.

"Do you like to read?" he asks, bending down to search a lower shelf.

"I do, but I don't have a lot of time for it with dance."

"I get that. Hockey doesn't leave a lot of extra time for hobbies either."

He stands, and we continue down the aisle, turning the corner to the next one.

"I have so many books in my apartment, but I think the last time I sat down and enjoyed one must have been at least a year ago."

"So, why buy books if you don't read them?"

"Well, I plan on reading them one day," I explain. "I'm also just a sucker for a pretty cover or special edition, so I own a lot of duplicates of my favorites. Do you read?"

"Not really."

"Do you have any hobbies?"

"I travel a little during the off season, but when I'm home I don't do much. Most nights it's either Fritz's or a puzzle at home."

"A puzzle?"

He winces.

"Yeah, I find them relaxing."

"Wait." I stop walking and turn to face him. "You. Everett Nuttall. Professional hockey player. Do puzzles in your spare time?"

"Yeah."

"Huh." I start moving again, leaving him by a section of cookbooks.

"Are you judging my hobby?" he asks, catching up to me in one long stride.

"No, not at all. I'm just surprised that's what you like to do."

He shrugs. "I'm gone a lot, so I buy the ones with thousands of pieces and work on it when I can. If I'm on the road for a while, it's easy to pick back up once I'm home."

"I guess I could see how that's appealing."

He stops again. His hands dip into his pockets as he leans back on his heels and looks up toward the ceiling. "Did I just ruin all of my sex appeal by admitting that?"

"No," I say, my mouth tipping up. "I don't think anything could do that."

He steps toward me, enclosing us amongst the shelves, and I look over my shoulder. We're completely hidden, and I swallow hard, inhaling his warm cologne.

"Is that so?" he asks, leaning forward, caging me against the shelf behind me.

I nod my head slowly. "I think it actually sounds kinda hot."

His mouth breaks into a grin.

"Tell me more."

"You, sitting at a table, thinking hard about which piece goes where." I reach up and run my hands over his chest. "Add some slutty little glasses and one of those turtlenecks you wore yesterday, and oh, my godddd." Dropping both of my arms, I fan myself with one hand and roll my eyes into the back of my head.

His mouth finds mine in a chaste kiss, and my eyes shoot open just as he's backing away.

"Sorry," he says. "I shouldn't have…"

Swallowing hard, my fingers brush against my tingling lips.

"No, it's okay."

He begins to move away from me down the aisle. Need pulses through me, and I wonder if maybe I was wrong to tell him we needed to stop the flirting and skip the sex until we get back. Maybe that's exactly what I need.

I try to shake the thought and focus as we turn the next corner.

"Oh, you've got to be kidding me," I mutter as the rows of sex and intimacy books come into view.

"What—" Everett begins, looking over his shoulder.

"You two good over here?" Ginger asks, popping up out of seemingly thin air and causing me to jump.

"Oh, shit! You scared me."

"I'm sorry. Just wondering if you two needed help finding anything."

Everett's eyes shift to me, and he chuckles.

"We're looking for a book on…um…magic," I explain.

Ginger starts to giggle. "My, my you two." She begins to walk down the aisle and bends down to a lower shelf. "This one always seemed to make things a little more magical for Rusty and me," she says, blush painting her cheeks. She stands and hands me a book titled *How To Have Mind Blowing Sex And Keep Having It.*

"No," I blurt out, not taking the book and waving my hands. "I didn't mean that. I meant actual magic. Sorry."

She giggles again. "My mistake. You two probably don't need any help in this department." She begins to bend down to put it back on the shelf when Everett stops her.

"Actually, I think we might get that one too." He wiggles his eyebrows in my direction.

"No, we won't."

"Couldn't hurt," he quips.

"No!" I say a little too loudly. My face heats, and I cut my eyes in his direction. Given the goofy grin plastered across his face, it's clear he thinks he's hilarious. "We don't need it, but thank you," I assure her a little more calmly.

"Okay," she muses, shrugging. "If you're sure. It is a good one though."

She replaces it on the shelf and then stands, cocking her head to the side in thought. "Let's see. Magic? Magic. Magic. Magic. I know we have a book on magic tricks over in the kids section, but I'm guessing that's not what you're looking for?"

"No," Everett says.

"Hmmm," she hums to herself and begins to walk to the back of the store. "Follow me."

"Should we get a puzzle then?" he asks as we follow her.

"Why?" I question.

"So we can live out your fantasy," he explains. "I think I saw a second turtleneck in my closet, and I'm sure I could find some glasses if you're into that."

"You're insufferable sometimes. You know that?"

"Maybe, but I know it turns you on," he whispers.

"Does not."

It does.

"Then why do you have that look in your eye?"

My mouth falls open, and a chuckle rumbles his chest.

"Here we are," Ginger chimes as we approach a small shelf full of discounted books, stuffed pumpkins with faces, and craft kits. "This is what's left over from Halloween. There might be something on here." She scans the spines.

"Tarot cards, crystals," she mumbles to herself. "Oh what about this? *Magic 101 for the Modern Witch?*"

Everett and I glance at each other. "Sure, that sounds interesting," he says.

Ginger giggles again, pulling it from the shelf and handing it to him. "Why are you two suddenly interested in magic?"

"Claire's looking into becoming a part-time Etsy witch to help pay the bills," Everett says, throwing his thumb in my direction.

Ginger shakes her head, and I roll my eyes. "You sound like you've been spending too much time with Cami," she says. "Anything else I can help you find?"

"Any books on the town's history?" I ask.

She begins walking, and we follow her again. "Let's see," she says as we arrive at a small section. "This one." She pulls out *A Brief History of Sugarplum Park* by Stella Crumb and hands it to me.

"Or, if you want something more thorough, I have this one." She hands Everett a thick book titled *Sugarplum Park: A Complete History* by Stella Crumb.

She pulls a third book from the shelf, and my heart aches when I see that it's *The Nutcracker*. "I swear," she complains. "People will just put books anywhere they want. I spend half my day putting things back where they go." She exhales a short breath. "You two ready to check out?"

"This should do it," Everett says. "Unless Claire wants to get a puzzle."

"No, I'm good. Maybe next time."

We follow her back up to the front of the store with all three books in hand, and I send a silent prayer to whoever will listen that the answer to getting us home is within them.

CHAPTER 24: HI
CLAIRE

Climbing the stairs to the house, exhaustion covers my every move. "I was not expecting today to be so tiring," I say, following Everett into the house. "I feel like I'm peopled out, and we didn't even make it to Lolly, Aster, or Reid's shops.

"I can't believe Stella is conveniently out of town."

"Oh, I know."

"Sorry it was more dead ends," he says.

"We don't know that. We still have to look through the books we bought, so maybe something will be in there."

I remove my coat, hang it in the closet, and then kick off my shoes by the door. Moving across the living room, I collapse onto my stomach on the couch.

"I'm tired, but it wasn't all that bad," he says. "I had fun getting to hang out with you today."

Sitting up, I watch as he takes off the Christmas sweater and throws it over the chair, revealing his abs. My eyes rake over him. "Do you always undress the minute you get home?"

"If you had been in that torture device all day, you'd be half-naked right now too."

He scratches his fingertips over his bare skin, and his biceps flex as he moves.

"So, should we look through the books now? Or do you want to wait?" he asks.

"Honestly, the idea of reading and talking sounds miserable." My eyes find his bare abs again, following the line of dark hair that disappears below his waistline. "Any ideas of activities that don't require talking?"

I shouldn't want him right now, but I do. I've been the one drawing the line in the sand, but suddenly everything I've said is flying out the window. Maybe it's because he's standing a few feet from me, shirtless. Maybe it was the kiss in the bookstore that's been fucking with me all day. Or, maybe it's because part of me is desperate for some normalcy after a very abnormal couple of days. But whatever the reason, my pulse is beating a little faster, and my skin feels a little a warmer, and between my legs feels a little wetter.

He shakes his head. "You want to jump in the shower with me?"

"Shower sex?" I blurt, my mouth tipping into a grin. Flutters begin somewhere low in my belly.

"No. Just a shower." He shakes his head.

"Oh." My cheeks heat. Definitely miscalculated that. Fuck. "Yeah, if you want a shower, that's fine. I'll take one after you."

"That's not what I asked," he says, walking towards the bedroom and pausing right outside the door. "I asked if you wanted to take a shower *with me*."

"But you said—"

"I know what I said. You look tired, and I know you're stressed. I thought it might be nice to jump in the shower and let me take care of you in a different way." His mouth forms a sexy grin, and my body heats again.

"A different way?"

He nods.

"Just you and me. No talking. Let me help you relax."

"Okay, yeah."

"Good." He turns, disappearing into the bedroom. Standing, I hear the shower turn on, and I try not to overthink why he doesn't want to have sex with me.

Pushing away the negative thoughts, I walk the rest of the way to find that his pants and boxer briefs have already been left on the bathroom floor.

"You ready?" he asks, causing me to look up to where he stands in all of his naked glory.

And every bit of him truly is glorious.

Maybe this was a bad idea.

Need gathers in my core, and I breathe in deep, reminding myself he said this wasn't going to lead to sex.

Letting my gaze wash over him again, the metal in the tip of his cock catches the light, and I wonder how hard it would it be to convince him to give in?

"I'm up here." He chuckles.

"Sorry...I..."

"Got distracted?"

Blush paints my cheeks. "Yeah."

I slowly strip my clothes off under his stare and then walk across the tile floor joining him outside the shower.

"Hi," he says, reaching up and tucking a strand of my hair behind my ear.

"Hi."

He opens the door and grabs my hand, helping me step inside. The warm water cascades over me, easing the tension in my shoulders and neck. Everett follows after me, moving in close behind.

"Can I touch you?" he asks.

I nod, and his hands find my shoulders. I let out a low moan as his hands trail down my upper arms and then back up, grazing my skin softly. Goosebumps erupt across my body, and he laughs to himself as he begins rubbing the tight muscles across the top of my back.

"That feels good."

"Good." He continues to massage me, and I let my eyes close. I knew he knew how to use his hands, but I didn't know he knew how to use them like this. His touch is tender and full of care. My stomach flutters. Another moan escapes, and I allow my mind to quiet. Moving down my back, he then runs his hands just above my ass and relieves the stress I'm holding there too.

"Is that okay?" he asks.

"Mmhmm," I hum.

He pauses, and my eyes open.

"Why did you stop?"

"Hold on. I'm just getting some soap." He chuckles as he pumps some body wash into his hand. "May I?"

I nod again, and he rubs the soap between his palms. The sugar cookie scent fills the steamy shower, and he begins to work my body under his touch. His hands are gentle yet firm, and my body continues to melt as he lathers every inch of my upper half, except for my breasts.

Kneeling behind me, his hands find my leg. He moves from my

ankle to my upper thigh, stopping just short of touching me where I wish he would. This whole massage is starting to feel like a tease, and with every touch, my desire for him builds.

I let out a disappointed moan as he moves to my other leg, repeating the same motion.

"You can touch me," I say.

"I am touching you," he says, pumping some shampoo into his hand.

"You know that's not what I meant."

"I know, but this isn't about that," he explains. "Trust me, I've been dreaming about fucking you again since we finished the other night. It's why I kissed you today, but right now I want to help you relax. This is about you."

Butterflies swoop low in my belly with his words.

"I didn't know you could be this sweet," I jest.

"There's a lot you don't know about me, Sugar," he says, his hands finding my scalp, and he begins to massage the shampoo into my hair. The feeling is euphoric, and my head lolls back as he continues to knead his fingers through my wet locks. Carefully, he rinses out the shampoo and then adds conditioner. He repeats the same steps, then washes the soap away when he's finished.

His strong hands move back to my arms, and he gently runs his fingers up and down, softly tickling my skin. My hands find his, and I pull his arms around me, leaning back into his firm body. There is something comforting about being wrapped up in his arms. It feels safe and reassuring. It gives me hope that if we stick to the plan, together we'll make it home.

We stay like that for a few long moments, letting the water fall over our embrace, and he takes me by surprise when he kisses the side of my head tenderly.

"You feeling a little better?" he asks.

"I think so. Thank you. I wasn't…um…anyway, that was really nice."

"I'm glad you liked it," he says. "Anytime you need me to help you relax, you just say the word, and I'll be your man."

I'll be your man.

Pulling away, I open the door and climb out of the shower.

"I'll be out in a minute," he says as I grab for a towel and wrap it around me.

Nodding, I leave him to finish.

I didn't know shower massages were a thing, but I could definitely get used to them happening more often—especially if Everett was the one giving them. Something about the tenderness he showed warmed me in a way I wasn't expecting. He was so careful not to make it sexual, but it felt more intimate than anything he and I have ever done before, and that's left me confused.

Doubt starts to creep in that maybe I should have returned the favor. Or maybe all of that was a lead up to shower sex, and I just awkwardly fucked up his plan by getting out and walking away.

Shit.

Turning, I begin to head back into the bathroom as he shuts off the water and steps out.

"Forget something?" he asks, grabbing a towel and running it over his dark hair. Water rolls down his tan skin and beads in his chest hair.

"No. I'm sorry. I should've offered to give you a massage or—"

"Don't apologize," he says, drying off his body. "That shower was to help you feel good and to get me clean. I'd never expect anything from you."

"You sure?"

"I'm positive." He wraps the towel around his waist and walks over to where I'm standing. Grabbing me by the arms with both of his hands, he looks me in the eye. "I promise."

"But your shoulder. I'm sure you could have used a massage too. I feel bad."

He chuckles. Letting me go, he rolls his arm up and over his head in a circular motion. "Honestly, it's weird. It hasn't bothered me since we got here."

"Really?"

"Yeah, I don't know. I'm trying to not think about what it means too much. Let's get dressed and see what we can find in those books?"

"Sure."

We both move out of the bathroom to get ready, and I can't help but wonder why he didn't mention the shoulder thing before now. Yesterday and today were a little nuts, so maybe it just didn't come up, but then again, I feel like it should have. Shaking the thought, I walk into my closet and begin to get dressed. We need to buckle down and see if any of these books unlock the secret way back home.

Chapter 25: Magic 101

That shower was torture. The minute she walked out of the bathroom, I slammed the water to freezing to take care of the raging hard-on I had. I don't know what I was thinking when I offered to touch her naked body like that. It took all of my restraint not to take it further, but I know she has to start seeing me as more. For me to have a real chance with her, I have to show her the man I really am.

Walking back out into the living room, I find Claire sitting on the couch with her knees tucked underneath her. Her gaze quickly shifts to me and then diverts to somewhere else in the room.

"You good?"

Sitting up slightly, she runs her hands down her face. "I think we need to talk and put some guidelines in place," she says.

"What do you mean?"

"Well, the town thinks we're married, and that shower was confu—that shower was interesting. And I'll be honest, I don't really know how to act around you here. On the one hand, I like flirting with you and kissing you and touching you, but then on the other, I know we need to focus on getting home. I don't know what we're doing."

Her brow knits together as she talks, and I smile at how cute she is when she's a little flustered.

"If we were in New York, what would you want to do?"

"That's not a fair question because this isn't New York and we're both wearing rings on our left hands."

I stare at her, contemplating what I want to say. If she's saying she thinks we should give us a real chance, then I'm in. Sign me up. But, if she's setting me up to tell me she thinks we can't have more moments like we just did, I don't want any part of that plan at all.

"Four years ago, what happened after I walked away?" I ask, sitting next to her.

"What does that have to do with anything?" Her head tilts to the side, and a memory seems to play behind her eyes.

"I think it has everything to do with what you're asking me."

"I don't know. I focused on dance and my family."

"You know that's not what I meant."

"What are you talking about?"

"Fine, I'll go first. I considered turning around and asking you out on a real date, but I knew that's not what you wanted, and I was leaving, so I didn't. I've regretted that decision every day since."

"Oh." Her mouth falls open. "Why?"

"Because nothing has ever been like it was when we were together."

"We hated each other back then," she argues.

I shake my head and chuckle. "No, you hated me. I...well...I definitely didn't hate you."

Her mouth parts, and her eyes get a little glossy.

"I didn't hate you," she says quietly. "You were, and some might argue still are, mildly infuriating and way too cocky for your own good, but I didn't hate you back then."

She hesitates for a second, and my heart expands behind my ribcage.

"So, what happened after I walked away?" I push.

She shakes her head.

"Claire, you can tell me. I can handle it."

"I cried," she admits, her eyes finding mine.

"You cried?"

"Yes, I closed the door behind you, and then I cried for the rest of the night while I ate a pint of mint chocolate chip ice cream and watched *10 Things I Hate About You*."

"Why?"

She leans against the back of the couch. "I don't know...because at some point it started feeling like more than hook-ups, and I was sad you were leaving."

"I'm sorry I left."

"It was a long time ago." Her mouth twists and her shoulders rise slightly.

"Why didn't you tell me?"

She shakes her head. "I don't know. I was too proud. Too focused on dance, and you were moving to Texas. Plus, I was under the impression you were only interested in being fuck buddies. It seemed like a surefire way to be disappointed, and I didn't think my heart could take it. I already had to say goodbye."

I press my lips together, trying to hide the smile that's threatening to break free.

"If I had known, I would—"

"You would've what? No. You were traded halfway across the country. It wasn't like you could've just stayed. You know as much as I do that long distance wouldn't have worked, and I was never going to give up living in New York, and you were never going to give up your hockey career to stay there."

"No, I guess not."

"Plus, I vividly remember telling you to call if you were ever back in the city, and you didn't."

I wince at her words, guilt climbing up my throat and catching my breath.

"I almost did, but when I found you on social media, you looked really happy, and I don't know. I figured you'd met someone new, and because of what we used to be, I was scared I'd be rejected too."

"You? Scared?"

"I don't know. I told you I struggle with expressing my emotions."

"Hmm," she hums. "So, what does all this mean? I know we've kind of been playing along with this whole marriage thing, but—"

"I don't think we have to think too hard about it. The kiss earlier felt right, so I did it. The shower felt right, so I offered. If something feels forced, we don't have to do it."

"But do we need rules or something? Parameters?"

I chuckle.

"Nah, rules didn't really work before. I think we just *give into the magic* and see what happens."

She bursts out laughing, covering her mouth with her hands.

Moving closer to her, I pull her into me, hugging her tight. Her body seems to relax a bit in my embrace, and I kiss the top of her head. "You ready to look through these books?"

"Yeah, let's do it." She pulls back, and I stand, walking across the living room to where the brown paperback sits.

Picking it up, I walk it back over to the coffee table.

"Do you want some wine?" she asks, standing. "I think this might be easier if I had some."

"That sounds good." She disappears into the kitchen, and I pull out *Magic 101 For The Modern Witch.*

"What are we looking for?" I call, skimming the table of contents.

"I don't know. Anything that looks familiar."

Claire walks out with two glasses and hands one to me. Joining me on the couch, she picks up one of the history books and starts flipping through the pages. We sit in silence for a few moments, sipping our wine and reading.

"Looks like Sugarplum Park has quite the history in mining rare gems." She flips the book toward me, showing me a chapter titled "The Great Gemstone Rush."

"Didn't you say Stella handed you a crystal in the cab?" I ask, and she turns it back around and continues to read.

"Yeah, Cami said it was called apatite. It's the blue stone I was looking at this morning. Why?"

"Crystals and gems are the same thing, right?"

"Maybe."

Turning the pages, I stop at the section on crystals and begin to read.

"This says apatite can help people manifest things and reveal truths," I say, looking up at Claire.

"Mmhmm," she says, not looking up from her book. "Did you not hear Cami say that earlier?"

The wheels begin to spin in my head, and she slowly looks up at me as she sips from her glass. "You said you told Stella you wondered what it would be like to get a second chance with me while holding it."

"Did I?" Her eyes shift back down to her book. I can't believe I hadn't put it together before.

"So, that would mean…the crystal made you tell the truth, and by saying all that, you manifested being here married to me."

"Maybe."

"No, not maybe. That's definitely what happened." A wide grin erupts across my face.

"Stop looking at me like that." She shakes her head. "I knew it. I knew I'd never hear the end of it if you put that together."

She sips her wine, and my heart blooms in my chest.

"What does that being the truth have to do with getting us home?"

"Because I think the crystals are the answer."

"What?"

"Think about it. Stella gave you a crystal that brought us here. When I told Ginger you wanted to be an Etsy witch…" She lets out a little snort, causing me to chuckle too. "Stop, I think I'm onto something."

"Sorry, go ahead."

"Ginger said it sounded like you had been hanging around Cami too much. Cami sells crystals, and the coffee shop is named *Citrine Brews*. Isn't that one of the crystals she tried to sell us?"

"Oh, my god." Claire squeals, grabbing my arm. "And she and Stella said the same thing about *giving into the magic.*"

"Right." I nod. My eyes find her hand, and she pulls it away. "Stella also said to give into the spirit of the town, and if its history is rooted in mining gemstones, then maybe…"

"Holy shit, you're right."

"This says that they all have different purposes, so what if there's one that could get us home?"

"Okay, but which one?"

"I'm not sure."

Claire sets the books she's holding down and moves closer to me, so she can read what I'm reading.

"Maybe it's the apatite crystal," I suggest.

"That doesn't make sense though. I have one of those in my purse. If it would send us home, wouldn't we already be back?"

"Not necessarily. You stopped telling Stella the truth when you put it down, right?"

She nods.

"So maybe we have to hold it and tell it what we want. Manifest getting back to New York, if you will."

She blinks at me.

"Like a wish?"

"It seems like it's worth a shot. Doesn't it?"

She jumps off the couch and moves into the bedroom.

We finally have a lead. My pulse begins to climb as I wait for her return, and I take a few large sips of my wine. If she has this crystal, we could be home by morning. This whole thing could be over, and instead of focusing on getting home, we could focus on one another.

She walks back into the living room with her face turned downward and her shoulders slouched.

"What's wrong?"

"It's not here," she says, lifting the bag she's holding.

"No?"

She digs in her purse. "I dropped my purse at the arena before the game. Maybe it fell out there?" She sits back on the couch and picks up her wine, taking a long sip. "Fuck, another dead end."

"I don't think so."

"No?" Her eyes find mine. "If I don't have the crystal, then I don't think it's how we got here."

"I disagree." I scoot a little closer to her and set my glass down. "What if your admission about being madly in love with me while you were in the cab—"

"That's *not* what I said in the cab."

"That was the gist."

She laughs. "Do you have a point?"

"What if you holding it in the cab is what started all of this, and now we just need to find another one to end it?"

She rubs the side of her hand across her forehead. "I think it could be worth a try."

"Me too. Tomorrow we'll go to Citrine Brews and buy a crystal."

"Yeah, okay." She nods, tears welling in her eyes. "That sounds good."

"Why are you crying?"

"It just feels like we might actually have a chance of getting back for the first time since we got here."

Taking her wine, I set it down and pull her into me.

Fuck, I really hope I'm right.

Chapter 26: That's Comforting. I Guess?

Claire

December Twentieth

"Slow down," Everett says, the two of us hurrying down the sidewalk toward the coffee and tea shop.

"Sorry, I'm just eager to get the crystal and get home," I say. "I barely slept last night because the anticipation was killing me."

"I get it," he assures me. "We're going to get it, and then we're going to go home."

I stop moving a few feet from the door, then spin around to face him.

"What if it doesn't work?"

"It'll work."

"But if it doesn't?"

"Then we'll figure out another way to get back." He pulls me into him. "Breathe, Sugar. It's going to be okay."

"You promise."

"I promise" I peer up at him, and his soft eyes assure me that he's right. "Besides, what's the worst thing that could happen if it didn't work?"

I take a step back.

"Let's see. We could lose the careers we love, never see our families again, and be forced to live out our remaining days here until we both die."

He snorts. "That was very specific, but that's not going to happen."

"You don't really know that."

Reaching out, he places both hands on my shoulders, easing the tension there. "Take a deep breath and think positive. We're almost there. It's going to be fine. And if we do get stuck here, then at least we're together."

That's comforting. *I guess?*

I inhale deeply, then exhale a long breath as he smoothes his hands down my arms.

"Come on," he says.

We begin moving again, and he grabs for my hand, squeezing it gently before letting go.

Pulling the door of Citrine Brews open, we're greeted with rich notes of coffee and the sounds of an espresso grinder drowning out the music coming through the speakers.

"Morning," Joe calls from behind the bar. "Want an early taste of my eggnog latte?"

"Careful, dear," Cami warns, walking over to greet us. "Stella has ears everywhere. Can't have her thinking you're trying to cheat."

"We're just here for our usuals," Everett says. "She's right. It's important to Stella that the competition stays fair, and although it sounds tempting, we're gonna have to wait until it's time to judge it."

"You got it," Joe says as he begins to work behind the counter. "I know you can't discuss anything. I think Stella knew what she was doing when she made you two the judges."

"What do you mean?" I ask.

"You both mean a lot to everyone here," he explains. "And I know out of everybody, you two will judge it the most fairly."

"Thank you," I say as blush crawls up my neck and my stomach turns with uneasiness. Everyone seems to know us so well, and I hate that we don't know them at all. I feel guilty, which is silly because these relationships don't really exist. These people aren't really real, and after tonight, we'll never see them again.

Pulling out my phone, I run my thumb over the little red thirty that tops my messaging app, signaling a heap of text messages from The Naughty List group chat I've ignored.

"I'm looking forward to helping you with practice on Monday,"

Joe says to Everett as he pours espresso into a cup. "I'll head over once I'm done here. It starts at four?"

"Uh…yeah…that sounds right," Everett says, glancing at me and widening his eyes.

"The Polar Bears are looking really good this year," he says. "You coaching them has made all the difference. You're a natural."

"Thanks, man."

"You know jade is believed to bring good luck," Cami says, walking over. A small green stone is in her hand. "Could help the team bring home the championship this year."

Everett chuckles. "Funny that you mention that. Claire was reconsidering those crystals of yours. Right, babe?"

"That's right."

Cami's whole face lights up.

"Ginger said you two were snooping around for magic books yesterday. Honey, if you had questions, you just had to ask."

"I knew Cami would convince you two one of these days," Joe chuckles, continuing to work.

"Come, come. Which ones were you considering getting?"

Walking over with her, I peruse her collection again. The apatite immediately catches my eye, but I want to be sure it's the right one. Maybe there's another that could work with it to ensure we get home.

"These pink ones are pretty," I say, pointing at a basket full of long, cylindrical pink gems. "What do they do?"

"Oh, rose quartz." She hums, glancing toward her husband. "They're the heart stone."

"Heart stone?"

She walks over to where I stand, picking one of them up.

"They help you attract love." She turns the stone in her hand and lowers her voice. "How do you think I got Joe to fall in love with me?" She giggles.

"Hmm."

"Doesn't seem like you need any help in that department," she says, her voice still hushed.

"No?"

"Baby girl, I've never seen a man look at a woman the way your husband looks at you." She offers me a soft smile and hands the stone to me. "You two are incredibly lucky to have found one another."

I peer over my shoulder to where Everett stands. He sure likes to talk about falling in love with me, but I know neither of us are there.

"Do they work together?" I ask, placing the pink crystal back into the basket.

"What do you mean?"

"Can you pair two of them together to make their effects stronger?"

"Some of them. Which one were you considering getting?"

"The apatite crystal."

"Hmmm," she hums. "What are you looking for a pairing to do?"

"Just make the effects stronger."

Her eyes squint. "Okay, well then…um…clear quartz can amplify its energy, so, in a way, that would make it stronger."

"That sounds good," I say, my eyes shifting back to Everett. "I'll take one of each and maybe the jade too. We could all use a little good luck."

She giggles. "I'm just thrilled you're interested in them. Any other questions?"

"What's the best time to try them out?" I ask.

"The moon is believed to charge them, so I often like to hold them at night and meditate then. Apatite works well under your pillow."

"At night?" My heart sinks, and I roll my neck. We're going to have to wait until tonight.

Fuck.

"That's what I would suggest. What is it that you're trying—"

"Did you find what you needed?" Everett asks, interrupting her question. "Drinks are ready, so I was going to pay."

I nod. "Yep." Cami helps us back to the register with the three stones.

Taking my paper cup, my free hand taps against my thigh as I watch Cami package each stone carefully and Everett pays for everything.

"Thank you," I say as she hands me the bag.

"Of course. We'll see you two soon," Joe says.

Everett leads me from their shop and out the door.

"To the house?" he asks as the door closes behind us.

"She said we shouldn't use them until tonight."

"Tonight?"

"Yeah, something about putting the apatite under our pillow."

"Okay." He sips from his cup. "That's okay."

"I was just hoping we could be done already."

"That makes sense though. We woke up here, so I'm sure we have to wake up in New York too."

Sipping my drink, the brown sugar and oatmilk swirl across my tongue, putting me a little more at ease. "Since we have the day, would it be silly if I went and danced for a little while?"

"Not at all. I might actually go skate for a bit if you're going to do that."

I drum my fingers on the side of my cup. Just one more day. I can do this one more day.

"Why don't we walk back to the house and get changed."

I nod, and we begin to walk back down the street in silence.

"What if we made tonight a little special?" he asks after a few moments.

"What do you mean?"

"We can both do what we need to do to clear our minds, and then I can come meet you in a little while. Maybe we can grab some dinner at Stella's tonight before we head back?"

"Ugh," I groan. "Maybe we can do take out instead? I don't know if I'll have the energy for Ruth."

"Sounds like a date."

There's an awkward pause, and then he reaches out and grabs my hand. He doesn't let go, and I find myself not wanting him to. I'm finding his touch seems to ground me in a way nothing else does.

Chapter 27: Floating

When I arrive at the dance studio, the vision of Claire dancing around the well-lit space stops me in my tracks. Beautiful isn't a good enough word to describe her. She's in light-pink tights. A matching leotard fits her snuggly, and a sheer skirt flairs around her hips. The ribbons of her pointe shoes wrap around her ankles and draw me in. Her movements are effortless.

She looks happy. She looks at peace.

Every spin and leap make it clear that she's a talented dancer, and I wonder why it's taken me this long to really watch her dance. Four years ago, the thought never crossed my mind, but then again, neither of us was really interested in what the other was doing. She's completely enchanting, and at this moment I want nothing more than those crystals to work, so she can continue to live out this dream.

She stops dancing and turns to walk toward a bulky stereo situated near the window. Our eyes lock, causing her to freeze on the other side of the glass. Lifting her hand, she offers me a small wave, and I lift a paper bag full of to-go containers.

She glides toward the door and swings it open.

"You out here in the cold watching me?"

"Hard to take my eyes off of you when you look like that," I tease.

"Come on," she says, gesturing for me to come in. "If you stand out there much longer, our food will be cold."

"You ready to head out?" I ask.

"Let me just grab my coat and boots," she says, moving out of the way and letting me pass. She crosses the floor. Undoing the ribbons of her shoes, she removes them, pausing to massage the arches of her feet. She stands, sliding her feet into her fur lined boots, and then pulls on her coat.

"What time is it?"

"Almost seven. The food took longer than I expected."

"Goodness, I was here all day. Thanks for letting me dance," she says, meeting me near the door. "Helped keep me sane."

She turns off the lights and closes the door behind us. Locking it, she drops the key into her coat pocket.

"How do you do that?" I ask.

"Do what?"

"Move like you were. I knew you were flexible…" I smirk. "But you're incredible. It looked like you were floating."

"Floating?"

I nod. "I don't know, I've just never seen anyone look so beautiful as they move. I was trying to think of a word to describe it, and I guess my vocabulary isn't big enough because nothing seemed adequate. You're stunning, Sugar."

Her eyes find me, and they sparkle in the moon light and she lets out a nervous giggle.

"What?"

"Sometimes I feel like I know you, and then you go and say things like that and you take me completely by surprise."

"I'm just stating the truth."

"What did you do today while I was at the studio?"

"Not much. I went for a run and then headed to the rink for a bit. Explored the town a little and ended up running into Chip. He's actually a really cool guy."

"What did you two talk about?"

"He vented a lot about Lolly and her shop and having to co-chair the decoration committee with her."

"Oh yeah? You think Ginger was right and they're going to fall for Stella's scheme."

"Ha! Actually, maybe. He really was trying to act like he didn't like her, but I think she might be on to something. I could see it happening."

"Really?"

I nod. "Have you texted those girls back?"

"No. Why?"

"I don't know." I shrug. "I'd be interested to know what Lolly thinks about him. I'm a little invested now."

"No you're not."

"I am," I jest. "They remind me a little of us, and I'm dying to know if that's going to work out too."

"You're ridiculous."

Silence falls between us for the next ten yards or so.

"Have you thought about this hockey practice you're supposed to coach on Monday?" she asks as we walk off the main street to our small neighborhood.

"Not really. We shouldn't be here for it, right?"

"Yeah, no. You're right." She looks over at me, pressing her lips together.

"Were you thinking about teaching dance?"

"Yeah, while I was at the studio, I was imagining what it might be like. There are all these pictures on the wall with me and kids. I look really happy in them. I never considered teaching dance, but I don't know…something about being there the other day and today has me wondering what it would be like."

"For what it's worth, I'd think you'd make a great dance teacher."

"You don't have to be this nice to me," she muses.

"It's true."

"Do you ever think about what you'll do when hockey is over?"

I shake my head. "I don't know. It's weird. When I was in New York, I was doing everything in my power to avoid any talks about the future, but since we've been here, it's all I can think about."

"What do you mean?"

"What life might be like once I retire."

"Is that going to happen? You said your shoulder is feeling better, and you just got back to the Crowns. You really think you'd hang up your skates?"

"I don't know. I think I'm realizing that there are things that could fulfill my life other than hockey."

"Like what?"

You.

"Building a life with someone."

"That does sound nice doesn't it?" Her eyes find mine, and for a split second, it seems like she knows what I'm insinuating. "Do you think you'd try to coach or commentate or something like that? I can't imagine you leaving hockey entirely."

"Maybe. So, do you think you would teach dance once you're done?"

"I have a lot more goals that I'd like to reach before that day comes, and it would be a huge learning curve. I haven't taught dance since I was in high school, but I think it could be really fulfilling to help kids reach their dreams. I mean, I've wanted to dance as the Sugar Plum Fairy since I was five…"

Her voice trails off, and she looks down at her feet.

"You're going to get to do that," I assure her, squeezing her hand. "All we have to do is make the rocks do their magic, and we'll wake up back in New York tomorrow."

"I hope you're right."

We climb the stairs of the house, and I unlock the front door. Pushing it open, she walks inside. Setting the food down, we both remove our winter layers.

"What do you think about turning on the fireplace and us eating in the living room?"

"I like that idea," she replies, a smile lighting her face.

She grabs the bag of food, and I work to start a fire. When I'm done, I turn to find her setting up the to-go containers on the coffee table.

"Want some wine?"

"Yes, please."

I walk into the kitchen, grab a bottle of pinot noir from above the fridge, and open it.

"Heavy pour or light pour?" I call.

"Always a heavy pour," she calls back.

I fill the glasses, then walk back to join her.

"Did you notice we don't have a Christmas tree?" she asks as I sit down next to her and hand her wine.

"No." I chuckle. "It does seem weird that Stella left out that little detail."

"Very," she muses, taking a sip. "My Christmas tree has been up since November first."

"Of course it has," I say over my glass.

"Don't tell me," she says. "You don't have one."

"I don't."

She rolls her eyes dramatically. "That's insane."

"I told you I'm rarely home this time of year, and when I am, I'm usually resting and trying to recuperate before my next game."

"Excuses, excuses" she tsks. "Goodness, do I need to come over to your apartment when we get back to New York and help you set one up?"

"You can come over to my apartment whenever you want. You don't need an excuse."

"That's not what I meant."

"No?" I tease. "Sounded like you were trying to come up with a reason to spend time with me."

"Can I confess something?" she asks, giggling.

"Please," I say, a little too eager.

"Contrary to popular belief, I do like spending time with you," she whispers.

"You do?"

I try to mask my excitement, but it's no use. I like the sound of what she just said too much.

"I know. I was surprised to figure it out too."

Scooting closer to her, my eyes find hers, and my hand connects with the soft skin of her cheek.

"I like spending time with you too, Sugar. I like it a lot."

A soft smile breaks across her face, and she leans forward, closing the gap between us. Her mouth parts slightly, and her tongue wets her lips. The energy around us shifts, and my heart rate beats wildly behind my ribs, anticipating my next move.

Our lips connect, and I push my hand through her hair, gripping the back of her head and pulling her into me. She tastes like the wine we've been drinking. The sweetest sound escapes from her throat as our tongues tangle and a wave of warmth covers my body.

Happiness overwhelms me, and I feel like I'm floating. For the first time since we've been here, I let myself believe there's a chance she's starting to fall for me too.

CHAPTER 28: WE AREN'T WITCHES

CLAIRE

Everett walks into the bedroom holding the brown bag from Citrine Brews. He climbs onto the mattress next to me, and I watch as he slowly unpacks it, unwrapping each crystal as he sets them on top of the comforter.

"Alright, so what do each of these do again?"

"The blue one is the apatite crystal. The clear one is quartz and is supposed to make the other crystals work better. And the green one is jade. Figured we could use a little good luck."

"Right. So how do we do this?"

I shift in the bed, crossing my legs and sitting across from him. He mirrors my position, and I study each of the crystals.

"I held the apatite in the cab and then said what I wanted. So, maybe we hold it together and say we want to go home."

He smirks.

"What?"

"Just remembering you said you wanted me."

I exhale. "Of all the times I need you to focus, it's right now."

"You're right." He picks up the blue stone and then sets it down. "What?"

"Should we light a candle or put on some music? I don't know, the vibe seems off. Doesn't feel magical enough."

"What are you talking about?"

"Well in the movies, the witches are usually sitting in the dark by candle light and music plays in the background while they say their spells."

"We aren't witches."

"Hold on."

He jumps out of bed and jogs out of the room. The sound of cabinets and drawers opening and closing drifts through the house, and then a few moments later he returns holding two candles and a lighter.

"What are those?"

"All I could find was a Christmas tree scented candle and a cookie scented one, but I think it'll work."

He walks around the room setting one candle on each bedside table and lighting it. Then, he flips off the light and joins me back in bed.

"Okay, where were we?"

"We were going to hold the stone and say what we wanted."

"And then what do we do?"

I think back to my conversation with Cami at the coffee shop. "Cami said we needed to put the apatite under our pillow, and then I guess we go to bed and wake up back in New York."

He picks up the stone and holds it out towards me. Reaching out, I grab it, and he wraps his hands around mine, causing electricity to pulse through my body. My pulse quickens, and I attempt to control my breathing and stay calm.

"On three?" I ask.

He nods, beginning the count. "One."

"Two," I say.

"Three," we say together. He nods, encouraging me.

"We want to go home," we say in unison, both freezing and looking around the space, but nothing has changed.

This is just the first step. We still have to sleep.

"Maybe we say it a couple of more times to be sure," he suggests.

I nod again, inhaling deeply. The mix of pine and sugar cookies fills my nostrils.

"We want to go home," we repeat two more times.

Pulling away, I turn and place the little blue stone under the pillows at the top of the bed and then the other two stones on the nightstand.

We both move to blow out the candles then nestle under the covers. He reaches out, pulling me into him.

"Night," I say.

"Good night," he says, kissing the side of my head. "I'll see you in New York, Sugar."

I exhale, melting further into his embrace. Our breathing begins to even out, and I close my eyes, hoping that we're right.

CHAPTER 29: STELLA!

"Everett!" Claire's panicked voice jerks me awake.

"What? What is it? Did it work?" I say, blinking my eyes open and trying to orient myself to what's going on.

"We're still here." Her voice falters, and I turn to see her sitting up in bed with tears streaming down her face.

"It's okay," I say, sitting up and taking in all the pink that still surrounds us.

Fuck. It didn't work.

"You don't know that," she says, collapsing against my chest. Her whole body shakes as she cries, and I soothe my hand over her spine, trying to calm her.

"Maybe we missed something," I suggest. "We can figure it out."

She pulls away from me, and I rub the pads of my thumbs across her cheeks, wiping away her tears.

"But we were so sure. Everything pointed to the crystals. Why would they have worked to bring us here but not bring us back?" Her voice is rushed, and she doesn't seem to come up for air until the last word.

"I don't know, but maybe there is more to it or maybe…" I try to come up with a reason as to why we woke up in Sugarplum Park this morning and not New York, but I honestly have no idea.

"It just doesn't make sense," she says, wiping her nose with the back of her hand.

"Then I think we need to get some answers."

"Stella?"

"Stella." I nod. "Come on, let's get dressed, and then we'll head into town."

Rolling out of bed, she grabs all of the stones and throws them back into the paper bag, setting it by the trash.

"What a waste of time," she says.

"I'm gonna get you home. Don't worry." Leaning forward, I brush my lips across her forehead. "All hope isn't lost."

We both walk to get dressed. The idea that maybe we are just meant to stay here creeps in, but I push it away. It doesn't matter that being here with her makes me happy. It doesn't matter that my shoulder is healthy. She wants to get back, and that's what we have to do.

I pull on jeans and a light blue sweater, then walk out to the bedroom to wait on Claire. She emerges a few moments later wearing a white sweater, cranberry-colored trousers, and boots.

We walk to town in silence, hand-in-hand. My blood pressure rises the closer we get to Stella's. She better be there, and she better talk to us.

The diner comes into view a few yards away, and we both watch as the woman herself walks out the front door. She's wearing a black long-sleeved, flowy maxi dress. The front is cut into a deep V, and around her neck sits a star-shaped crystal. She pulls on a long black coat and hat, then turns to walk away from the main square of town.

"Come on," I say, pulling Claire. We both break out into a jog.

"Stella!" I yell, but she ignores me.

We round the building and see her walking ahead.

"Stella!" Claire calls, this time catching her attention. She flips around, a wide grin spreading across her face.

"If it isn't my king and queen," she says, walking back toward us. "Can I help you two with something?"

Looking around, I check for other people and am relieved to find that the three of us are alone. "You could start by telling us how to get back home," I challenge.

Stella starts to laugh. "Are you feeling alright, Everett?" She blinks back and forth between Claire and me. "You know where your house is."

"Look, it's just us three," I say, my body heating. Claire tugs at my hand and peers up at me. Taking a deep breath, I attempt to calm the rage bubbling inside me. She's really not going to stand here and gaslight us into thinking we're the crazy ones. "Let's cut the bullshit. We all know what's going on, so it would be really great if you could stop avoiding the conversation and tell us how to get home."

"Whatever are you talking about?" she asks.

"Stella," Claire tries. "We just want to know what to do."

"I already told you what to do," she says. "Remember? When it comes to the competition you just have to lean into—"

"The spirit of the town and give into the magic," I finish. "We're not talking about your competition. We're talking about our lives. We tried playing your game, but we're still here."

"Where else would you be?" She shrugs, offering us an unnerving smile. "Claire, I'm shocked that you of all people haven't figured it out."

"What...what does that mean?" Claire stammers. "Are you saying you did put us here, and I should know the way to get us home."

"You're already home." Stella looks from me to Claire. "When I look at you, I see two people who have everything they've ever wanted and all the answers to all of their questions. I'm really not sure why you're both so upset."

Holy shit, this woman is maddening.

"I'm sorry," Claire begins. "I'm confused. Are you agreeing with us that you put us here?"

Stella's whole upper body moves as she laughs. "Where else would you want to be on this beautiful day?" She looks up at the clear sky.

"Home." I snap. "We would like to go home."

"That's understandable. I know that as the king and queen of the Christmas Extravaganza, there is a lot of unwanted attention on you two. It makes perfect sense that you'd want to hide away in your house together until the day of, but I really think the best way to do it is to lean into the town spirit." She claps her hands together on the final two words.

Claire's gaze finds mine, and I massage my temples.

"Alright," she says. "It's a busy day, so I'm going to let you two get going. I'll see you at the Extravaganza. It should be a really good time."

She turns on her heels and moves away from Claire and me without another word. We watch in silence until she disappears around the back of the building.

"Well that wasn't helpful," I say, turning to find Claire. Her eyes are glossy with tears. She turns and starts moving back toward the street, pulling her coat around her tightly.

Fuck.

"Claire?" I yell as I gain on her.

"Please, I just need some time to process everything," she calls back.

"Stop moving!" I shout.

"Everett, please just give me a second!"

Catching up to her, my hand connects with her wrist. "Please stop and talk to me," I say, spinning her toward me. Her face is red and puffy. She sniffles, and her eyes find mine.

"I just need a minute," she snaps.

"No."

"No?" she questions, becoming more frustrated with me.

"No. We need to figure this out together, and I know that was frustrating and not helpful, but running away from me isn't helping anything either."

"And I just need a minute to gather my thoughts," she says, spinning and walking away from me again.

"Claire," I huff out, but she ignores me and keeps walking.

I follow her into town, restraining myself from trying to stop her again. The town is busy with people going about their day. Each person pauses as we walk by, watching and taking note of our body language and the fight I guess we're having.

Making it to the ice rink, she sits down on one of the benches and folds her arms across her chest. I take a seat on the other side, and the cold air burns my lungs as I inhale and exhale slowly.

"Can you please tell me what's going through that head of yours?"

"You heard her. She said I should be able to figure it out, and then she kept saying the word home, like we're never leaving. This isn't home."

"Claire, she essentially talked in circles. Nothing she said made any sense."

"But if she's right…what if I'm the one who has to get us home, and I don't know how. Or what if there is no getting us home and this is it. We're just stuck here."

Her face falls into her hands, and she shakes her head.

"I was so sure we were right about the crystals, and we weren't, so what now?" she asks.

I move closer to where she sits. "I don't have an answer, but I think if we just take a minute, take some deep breaths, we can figure this out."

Her hands run through her hair, and she looks around the town.

"Why don't you go dance for a little while, and I'll go talk to Cami. See if we did something wrong with the crystals. I'll get us some coffee, and then we can go back to the house and see if we missed something in one of those books."

"I can come with you."

"I know that, but I think you need to take a break. Clear your head. Forget all that nonsense that she just spewed. We're going to figure this out, and we're going to do it together. It's not going to fall all on you, and we definitely aren't staying here."

"I'm sorry," she says, her body crumbling against me. "I'm so sorry."

"Shhh." My hands rub up and down her spine. "It's okay. Waking up here this morning was a lot, and you freaked out. She was no help. It's okay."

"I'm sorry," she says, sitting up. The cold wind wraps around us, causing her to shiver, and she wipes her face with the back of her hand.

"You don't have to keep apologizing," I say.

"Yes, I do. I just acted like a complete lunatic." She shakes her head. "How are you being so understanding?"

"Because I can tell you're scared and overwhelmed."

She swallows hard.

"Plus, I like when you're a little crazy." I smirk, then start to chuckle, causing her to laugh too.

Leaning down, my hand finds the side of her face, and I kiss her. Her lips part, and she lets me in as another breeze blows by us, sending a shiver through us both.

"Come on," I say, pulling back. "Let's get you inside to warm up."

Standing, I reach out and take her hand. We begin our walk

toward her dance studio. We pass by a small group of people who stop talking the second we're in ear shot.

"I think we put on quite the show for everyone," she whispers. Her cheeks turning a bright pink. "I feel like they're all staring and talking about us."

I chuckle. "Just ignore them. They have no idea what they heard." I squeeze her hand and lean down, placing a kiss on top of her head. The word *home* swims around my brain, and I attempt to shake the thought that we might actually be stuck here, and although I'm beginning to think I'd be happy living out my days here with her, I know she wouldn't feel the same.

CHAPTER 30: THE NUTCRACKER

CLAIRE

A knock on the glass door startles me, and I whip around to find Everett waving and pointing at the lock on the door. Snow is coming down all around him. His face is a little red from the cold, and two paper cups are in his hands

I click the lock and let him in.

"Sorry," I say. "It's freezing out there. Hopefully that was the first time you knocked?"

"It was," he assures me, making his way inside the studio and dusting off some of the snow from his jacket. "How are you feeling?"

"Better." My eyes find the clock. "Shit, has it really been an hour?"

"Yeah."

"Did Cami have any insight into the crystals?"

"No," he says, handing me one of the cups. "I don't know. The way she talked about them kind of made me think they're bullshit."

I snort. "I think we're supposed to be believing in the magic, not questioning it."

He shrugs. "I guess it made me realize that we better come up with a different solution."

Sitting, I begin to unlace my shoes, and he sits next to me.

"Did dancing help you feel better?" he asks.

"It did. Thank you for knowing it's what I needed," I say,

focusing on the knot of one of the ribbons. "So, if it's not the crystals, what do you think it is?"

He shakes his head. "Other than you and me falling—"

I let out a chuckle. "Everett!"

"Hey, it's the best lead we have."

"So we're back at square one?"

"I'm sorry."

"It's not your fault." I exhale. The music fades and the next song begins to play.

"This is interesting music," he says. "What is it?"

"*The Nutcracker.*"

"Hmmm. Is this the song you dance to?"

"No," I laugh. "This is Mother Ginger and her polichinelles. Have you never seen the ballet?"

"Polichinelles?"

"Like clowns, but sometimes they're called gingerbread children."

He shakes his head and chuckles. "Did you say Mother Ginger?"

"Mmhmm. Why?" I remove both shoes and set them to the side. Picking up my latte, I take a sip.

"Nothing. It's just funny that Ginger is named Ginger and has a bunch of kids, so I guess it's like she's the town's very own Mother Ginger."

"Oh my god!" I shriek.

"What?"

"What if that's it?" I pop up and move across the floor to my coat, digging out the schedule for the competition that's still there. My pulse quickens as the pieces start to click together.

"What if what's it?" Everett asks.

Unfolding the paper, I scan the words. I can't believe I didn't see this before. It was literally right in front of me the whole fucking time.

"Can you please tell me what's going on?" he asks.

"Sorry, but I think I figured it out."

"Figured what out?" His eyes crease and he tips his head as I walk back to join him.

"We're in *The Nutcracker*," I marvel, sitting back down next to him.

Laughter shakes his whole chest.

"I'm sorry?"

"Specifically act two," I clarify.

"What?"

"We. Are. In. Act. Two. Of. *The. Nutcracker.*"

He sits up a little straighter and rubs his hands over his face and down his beard.

"Claire, that's impossible."

"Says the man who woke up here a few days ago married to me in a place that doesn't exist on any map anywhere."

"First, Stella was a witch who trapped us here with crystal magic and now we're in the—"

"I think we were wrong about that. I think she's the Sugar Plum Fairy," I say. "That's why the crystals didn't work."

"And who does that make me then? The Nutcracker?" he asks, sipping his latte.

"Yes."

Liquid sprays from his mouth. "You can't be serious."

"I am. And I think that would make me Clara."

"Forgive me because I'm not too familiar with the ballet, but I don't remember The Nutcracker and Clara fucking in it."

Massaging my temples, I breathe in deep and clench my jaw.

"You haven't fucked me since we've been here."

"No, but we did the night before we got here."

"Well, technically she does fall asleep with it and the rest is the same."

"How?"

"For starters, we went to sleep and we woke up in Sugarplum Park, and in the ballet, Clara falls asleep and then they go to the Kingdom of Sweets," I explain.

Standing up, I move to the stereo and unplug my phone. I begin to tap on the screen and join him back on the floor.

"The shops on Main Street coordinate with the dances in act two, and so does the schedule. See."

I scoot closer to him, pointing to each dance on my phone screen as I list them. "Chocolate, Coffee, Tea, Candy Canes, Marzipan, Gingerbread, Flowers."

"I don't know. It seems a little..." He hesitates. "Far-fetched. Don't you think?"

"No. I think it's the only thing that makes sense. What else could 'spirit of the town' mean? The town is called Sugarplum Park, and all the stores on Main Street coordinate with the ballet. You said yourself that there is literally a mother named Ginger who lives here."

"Maybe."

For fuck's sake, how is he not getting this?

"Look, I know this ballet really well, and Stella said we needed to lean into the spirit of the town and that she was surprised I hadn't figured it out. Of the two of us, I'm the only one who could put this together because you've never seen the ballet."

His hazel eyes blink at me, and his mouth parts slightly.

"If it's *The Nutcracker*, which I'm pretty certain it is, then we have to finish it to get back to New York."

"What does that mean?"

"Stella said that we would be judging the competition on Christmas Eve, so I think each time we judge one of the entries we complete a dance."

"So what? We just start by eating Chip's peppermint bark and then tick off each dance until we're done."

Finally.

"Exactly."

"Okay, but that would mean we wouldn't get back until Christmas."

"I know," I say, sipping my drink.

"And you're okay with that?"

"At this point, I just want to get home, so if that means you and I have to spend a little extra time together here, then I think there are worse things."

"Are you saying you like spending time with me here?" His eyebrow raises.

"Maybe a little." I hold my hand up, pinching my fingers together.

Sliding toward me, he takes my coffee and puts it to the side with his. He pulls me in between his legs and wraps one of his arms around my back. The other grips the side of my head, helping his lips find mine. Our tongues swirl together, and my whole body ignites.

Pulling back, his hazel eyes bore into me, and I try to catch my breath under his touch.

"You ready to head back to the house?" he asks.

"Yeah, any ideas of what we can do?"

His whole face lights up. "I have a couple," he says. "Come on."

We throw our cups away, lock up the studio, and he grabs my hand. Neither of us says anything, and I find myself liking these quiet moments. The ones where he's touching me tenderly. There's no pressure to say anything or act a certain way. No insane schedule occupying all of our time. We can just be—*us.* And *us* is starting to sound really nice.

A little over half-way to the house, Everett lets go of my hand, stops, and crouches down to look at something in the snow.

"What is it?" I ask.

"I'm not sure," he says, rounding his body over and blocking my view.

"Everett, if it's a snake—"

"It's twenty something degrees out here." The air in front of his mouth freezes into a white puff of smoke as he laughs. "Snakes hate the cold. Relax."

"Then what are you doing? If it's an animal or a bug or something, I think it's best to leave it alone."

I move to try to see what it is, but he stands. In his hand is a perfectly round snowball, and a wicked grin spreads across his face.

"Don't you dare," I say, giggling and backing away from him.

He lets out a low chuckle, tossing the snowball into his other hand. "Come on, Sugar, have a little fun with me."

"Everett *I don't know your middle name* Nuttall, do not start a snowball fight with me because you will surely lose."

"Is that so?" He brings up his arm, releasing the snowball, and says, "I like my chances." The cold icy sphere hits me smack in the upper arm, crumbling on my coat.

Grumbling, I bend down to prepare for my counter attack. Carefully, I form a ball, but when I look up to find my target, he's disappeared, leaving behind a trail of footprints.

"Where did you go?" I call, surveying the snowy landscape. "This isn't funny. Where are you?" He peeks out from behind a tall spruce tree and attempts to throw another one in my direction but misses completely.

"Ha!" I yell out, running in his direction. He moves away from me, and I throw my snowball, hitting him in the back. "Got you!"

My eyes go wide as he turns around, and I realize he already has three more prepped. I duck behind a tree just as one comes spiraling for me and explodes against the trunk. Working quickly, I build a little arsenal and ready myself to get him back.

He might be a big, strong hockey player, but he underestimated how competitive I can be.

Picking two up, I peek out to see if I spot him. He's standing out in the open with a smirk painting his face. I attempt to throw one of my snowballs and miss.

Dammit.

He sends both of the ones he's holding my way, and I duck behind the tree again. The crunch of his boots grows louder as he moves toward me, and my pulse quickens as I anticipate his next move.

Spinning around, I turn to face him with two balls in my hands. "Fuck!" I scream as I run into his toned chest and drop both of my snowballs. "How the hell did you sneak up on me that quick?" I laugh, peering up at him. "You scared the shit out of me."

Without warning, his hand comes up and he crushes a snowball on top of my head. "I think I win," he says, chuckling. The icy flakes send a shiver down my spine as they freeze my scalp.

"You're so dead," I warn.

"Not if you can't catch me." In the blink of an eye, he takes off through the snow and jogs back toward the house.

Sprinting, I chase him, gaining on him quicker than I thought I would. At the same moment I catch up to him in the front yard, he turns. Our bodies collide once more, and we fall into the snow together. My lungs burn from the cold air as I try to catch my breath, but I'm laughing too hard and so is he.

Rolling to face him, his warm eyes find mine, and electricity pulses between us. The snow sticks to his hair and coat, and I run my hand through his brown locks, knocking some of it away.

"Aldrin," he says, returning the gesture and tucking a fallen strand behind my ear.

"Huh?"

"My middle name is Aldrin. What's yours?"

"Elise."

"That's pretty," he says, rolling closer to me so that our bodies are snug up against each other. I'm completely lost under his touch. His hand caresses the side of my face, and the other wraps around my back.

"Claire Elise Nuttall, I'm going to kiss you now," he whispers, causing me to smile.

"Everett Aldrin Nuttall, I was really hoping you would."

His mouth takes mine in a heated kiss, warming me down to the tips of my toes.

Need builds in my core, overtaking me. I moan into him and roll my body up on top of his. Straddling my legs across his hips, I grind downward. His hands rake through my hair and then move down my back, finding my ass and squeezing it firmly.

"Fuck, I missed this," he says against me.

I moan as he rotates his hips upward, creating the perfect friction between us.

"Me too," I pant, before our mouths connect again.

The world around us melts away, and I completely forget where we are. It doesn't matter—all that matters is that I like the way his hands feel on my body and how his mouth feels on mine.

CHAPTER 31: TWO TRUTHS AND A LIE

EVERETT

Kissing Claire takes me by surprise every time it happens. Even here in the snow, our tongues tangling and our hands exploring each other's bodies, we should be freezing, but I feel completely content and warm with her on top of me. She brightens everything she touches and sets my body on fire. I'm quickly learning just how incredible she is—a fact I already knew but love rediscovering.

She's sexy as hell when she gives me shit. Stunning when the sun hits her hair just right and makes it almost sparkle. Her smile and laughter are addictive, and I shouldn't be falling this hard, this quickly, but I like who I am when I'm with her here.

At this point, I feel like I've been edging myself. Her soft skin in the shower the other day, the innocent kisses and touches, her sapphire eyes that draw me in, her smart mouth, this kiss. Fuck, this kiss is everything.

I'm wound so tight that I don't think I'm going to be able to restrain myself much longer, but I'm trying my best to show her who I am without sex being involved.

Sitting up, she begins to laugh as she looks down at me. A shiver runs up her spine. Her cheeks and the tip of her nose are pink from the cold, blush covers her neck, and her lips are swollen from the kisses we just shared. "We're soaked," she says, brushing some of the snow from my hair.

"I always did have that effect on you," I tease.

"I meant from the snow." She playfully swats at my chest. "I'm also freezing, so can we maybe continue this inside where it's warm?" Her teeth begin to chatter, and she pulls her jacket a little tighter across her chest.

"I have a better idea."

"Oh yeah?"

"Care to take a dip in the hot tub?"

Her eyes glimmer with desire, and she stands. Reaching her arm out, she helps me up off the ground, and we both dust the wet, half-melted snow from our clothes.

Without any warning, I playfully throw her over my shoulder and take off toward the backyard.

She lets out a loud laugh and another shriek as I almost trip over a dip in the ground. And just like I do every time I'm with her here, I feel free.

The cool air stings my cheeks and cuts right through my clothes as I run. By the time we make it to the tub, we're both shivering, and I send a silent plea to Stella that the hot tub is ready to go. Lifting the lid, I'm relieved to find that it is.

The steam rolls off the top of the water, and Claire and I quickly undress down to our underwear. Her soft blue lace bralette and thong bring out her eyes, and I watch, mesmerized as she climbs into the hot water.

"You coming in, Ev?" she goads, smirking.

The contrast between the cold outside and the temperature of the water makes my skin break into goosebumps as I climb in to join her.

"It's so cold out," she says, a shiver running through her as I settle across from her on a bench seat.

"It's freezing, but this feels good."

"So good," she says, tying her hair into a high bun. She sinks under the water so that her shoulders disappear below the hot surface. "You want to come over here so we can finish what we started?" she flirts.

She has no idea how badly I want her, but I remind myself that this is about more than just some fleeting moment together. I need to convince her we could be forever.

"I thought maybe we could play a game?"

"A game?"

"Yeah, maybe get to know each other a little better."

"I was hoping we would be doing something else," she says.

My cock throbs, and her words threaten to put an end to me right here. Her foot reaches out, making contact with my leg, and I swallow hard, doing my best not to give in.

"I know, but this could be fun too."

I can't believe what I'm saying.

"Okay…uh…what did you have in mind?"

"Two truths and a lie?"

"Fine," she agrees.

My mind shuffles through all the possible things I could tell her. The thoughts are mostly surface level things, but I know I need to dig deeper. I need to risk showing her who I really am because love isn't surface level. It's deep and messy, and that's what I want with her.

"You want to go first?" I ask.

"Okay," she grumbles and thinks for a moment. "Let's see, when I was nine, I fell out of a tree and had to get stitches on my elbow. My favorite flower is an—"

"Anemone," I finish for her.

Her mouth parts. "How do you know that?"

"I remember a lot about you."

"That's not how you play the game. You're supposed to wait until I've listed all three things."

I chuckle. "The stitches story is true too."

"You haven't even heard my third thing."

"I don't have too. You still have a scar from it on your right arm."

She sits up out of the water, and her fingers find the small white scar above her elbow. "How…"

"I told you I remember everything about you."

Smiling, she gently traces the scar.

"Come on, tell me something about you no one knows. I want to get to know you, not the person you show everyone else. None of that surface level shit."

She bites her lip and looks away from me in deep thought.

"Okay," she says, after a moment. "Um…despite getting my dream role, I'm embarrassed that I had to understudy for a girl three years younger than me to get it."

"And the second thing?" I encourage her to continue.

"Let's see. My best friends are my sister and my parents because I've never felt like I fit in, no matter how hard I've tried."

My heart breaks that she's been carrying this around. That, despite her fun and bubbly personality, she's been hiding so many feelings of low self-esteem and doubt.

"And the third thing?"

"I hate that you are the person that I got stuck here with."

"The third one is the lie."

"How did you know?"

"Because I see the way you look at me. The way you're sitting over there desperate for me to pull you into my lap and kiss you again. I'd say you're very happy we're here together." A smirk breaks across my face.

"Ha! Cocky son of a bitch."

"Am I wrong?"

"No," she admits. "Do you think I'm pathetic after hearing my truths?" Her smile seems to disappear as she talks.

"Never. You have nothing to be embarrassed about."

She hums.

"Want to talk about it?"

She hesitates for a moment, finding my eyes.

"We don't have to—" I begin.

"No, it's okay. We can. I'm not very young by ballet standards, and I should've achieved roles like this a while ago, but I didn't. I was promoted to principal dancer later than the other girls I started with, and since then, it has just felt like an uphill battle trying to prove myself. Not only to Dimitri, our creative director, but to the other dancers."

I nod, encouraging her to continue.

"I see the looks on their faces, hear the whispers when they think I'm not listening. Everyone in the company has their friend groups. I feel like I'm not good enough to be included with the other dancers my age, and I feel too old to be hanging out with the ones who started after me."

"Principal dancer is a big deal though, right? Who cares when you achieved it? I think it's incredible that you're doing what you always wanted."

She shrugs. "You're right. I guess I should be grateful. Not everyone gets to where I am."

"That's not what I meant. Both things can be true. You can be proud of what you've accomplished and still wish for more. And for what it's worth, if people can't see how incredible you are, then that's their loss, not yours."

"Yeah, I guess so."

"What ever happened to that girl you were living with? What was her name? Scarlett?"

"Charlotte?"

"Yeah. Wasn't she a dancer too?"

"She was, but she moved out about a year after you left and stopped talking to me. I don't know. It was weird, and it bothered me for a long time, but you can only reach out so many times before you start to feel pathetic, so I stopped."

My heart breaks at the thought that anyone wouldn't want her in their life.

"The girls here seem to want to be your friend. You should text them back?"

She shakes her head. "They aren't real people. I'm just trying to keep my head down. Focus on getting home."

"Maybe," I agree. "But Stella did say we needed to give in to the spirit of the town. Maybe she wasn't just talking about *The Nutcracker*, but also the relationships with the people here."

"It's possible, I guess." She shrugs. "Alright, it's your turn, and don't you dare give me anything other than the deep shit." She lowers her voice pretending to be me and throws in some air quotes for effect.

"Ha! Is that your impression of me?"

"I think it was pretty good. Now stop deflecting. I told you my deepest, darkest secrets; now tell me yours."

"I'm afraid my shoulder injury will be the end of my hockey career, and with it, I'll also lose the relationships that mean the most to me. It doesn't bother me that my sister moved halfway across the world with her family, and I never get to see them."

My eyes find hers, and I hesitate before telling her my second truth.

"Okay, and the third thing?" she asks.

I'm falling in love with you, and I'm terrified you'll never feel the same.

"Earth to Everett." She moves her arm up and down. "You okay?"

"Oh, yeah. Let's see...I'm starting to see the appeal of Christmas."

She smiles brightly. "Okay, the third one is definitely a lie."

I shake my head.

She gasps. "Okay, so then the second one that's about your sister. That's the lie."

I nod.

"I imagine you feel a lot like I feel right now being so far away from your family. I'm so sorry that you feel like that all the time."

"It's okay. I know it's just not all on her. But, maybe if my hockey career is really over, then I'll get to see her more often." I try to laugh despite myself, but it's no use. There is nothing funny about potentially having to retire. It feels too heavy. Too big to handle.

"Who are you afraid you're going to lose without hockey? I mean, the league loves you. I'm sure if you aren't playing, they would snatch you up in a second to do something else."

"Maybe. Hockey is like my family. My whole existence is out on the ice. It's my entire world, and from a young age, I've allowed it to define a lot of my self-worth. I met my best friends through hockey, but sometimes the relationships feel really transactional. Like I'm only good for them as long as I can play and help my team win."

She shakes her head.

"I don't think that's true. There's no hockey here, and there's no one else I'd want to be doing this with. You make me feel safe and calm. You make me laugh." She pauses. "And for what it's worth, you're really hot." Her lips tip into a sexy grin.

"You think I'm hot?"

"I think you're so much more than that sport you play."

She has no idea how badly I needed to hear that.

"Come here?" I say, not able to wait any longer. I need to touch her. I need to hold her, and right now, she feels too far away.

She nods, pushing through the water. Her lace bra clings to her breasts and taut nipples. Straddling my lap, she says, "You're a good man, Everett Nuttall. A really good man."

She runs her hands through my hair and cups my face. Her lips find mine, and I open, letting her in. My arms wrap around her back, pulling her into me.

I lose myself in her kiss, and hope expands in my chest, that maybe, just maybe, even if she doesn't want to admit it, she's starting to fall for me too.

CHAPTER 32: FLOWERS
CLAIRE

DECEMBER TWENTY-SECOND

"Morning," Everett says as I nestle back into him.

"Morning."

His strong arms wrap around me, pulling me in tight as he nuzzles against my neck, causing goosebumps to erupt down my arms and legs. My mostly bare ass moves against his length, and lust gathers low in my core. The memory of us making out in the hot tub yesterday assaults me. The way he gripped my body with his hands, the way his mouth owned mine, and the feel of his cock grinding up into me. I wanted him then and there, but that's where it stopped.

"What do you want to do today?" he asks.

"Anything you want," I reply, a little breathless.

"Good. I have an idea" he says. His lips find the side of my head, and he rolls away, jumping out of bed.

"Wait, where are you going?" I ask, sitting up.

"I'm gonna jump in the shower since you took one last night. Want to get ready and then we can head into town?"

"Head into town?"

That's not what I wanted to do.

"Yeah." He walks away, disappearing into the bathroom, and I fall back into the bed feeling incredibly sexually frustrated and a little crazy that I might be reading all the signals I thought he was sending me wrong.

The shower turns on, and I roll from the bed to get dressed.

It doesn't take me long, and when I finish, the shower is still running. Maybe I should go join him, but then again, he didn't invite me, so I probably shouldn't.

Grabbing my phone, I shuffle into the living room and sit on the couch. Opening the text thread I've been ignoring for days, my fingers hover above the screen as I consider whether or not I should respond.

Deciding it's better not to muddle things this late in the game, I close out of it and put the phone on the coffee table.

"Oh, good, you're ready," Everett says, walking out of the bedroom.

Looking over to where he stands, my mouth falls open. The towel is hung low on his hips. Black ink is visible on the lower half of his leg. Small droplets of water bead in his chest hair, and he casually runs his hand through his damp locks, like the movement alone couldn't risk getting me pregnant.

Needless to say, I need his dick and I need it soon or I might combust.

"Hey, did you hear me?" he asks.

"No, sorry. I got distracted."

He chuckles.

"I was wondering what you thought about going skating with me?" he asks.

"Skating?"

"Yeah, I have that hockey practice later today, but I've been wanting to take you since we got here. We have nothing to do, so I thought it might be fun. Do you know how to skate?"

"I'm from New York and my favorite holiday is Christmas; of course I know how to ice skate. My dad used to take Andi and me to Rockefeller Center every year."

"Another tradition?"

I nod, my eyes raking down his body again as he walks further into the living room. "Could you get dressed? Seeing you in just a towel is really, really..."

"Claire?"

"Distracting. It's distracting."

"Is that so?" He smirks.

"Yes."

"Why?"

"Please, you know why. Look at you."

He glances down at his body and then back to me.

"Look at me? Look at you."

"What are you doing?" I huff out.

"I was trying to flirt with you. Is it not working?"

Standing from the couch, I massage my temples. "That's the problem. It's working too well," I groan. "I mean, fuck! Do you all of a sudden not want to have sex with me or something?"

"What are you talking about?"

I begin to pace in front of the couch, and my hands fly out in every direction as I speak.

"I mean yesterday, I was sure the snow would lead somewhere, and then we got in the hot tub, and don't get me wrong, I like making out as much as anyone, but we just kinda ended it there. And then I thought maybe when we went to bed, but no, it didn't happen then either."

Meeting me, he grabs both of my hands and causes me to still.

"Are you done?"

"No, I'm not done. I haven't even talked about the shower we took the other day. Or all of those kisses that made me feel like I was on fire. It's infuriating having to be around you when you look like that and not getting to do what I want to do. I just don't understand what's changed. The sex part is what we were always good at, and the not having it is driving me crazy."

"Are you done now?"

"I think so. Yes. That's all I had to say."

Stepping closer to me, he lifts his hand and runs it over the side of my neck and then through my hair. Gripping the back of my head tenderly, he says, "Do you really think I don't want to have sex with you?"

"Well…it's just…I…"

He bends forward, kissing my pulse point softly. Goosebumps erupt across my body, and my eyes flutter closed.

"Sugar, all I can think about…" he whispers before placing a kiss on my eyelid.

"Is getting you naked…"

He kisses my other eyelid, and I let out a moan.

"And worshipping every inch of this perfect body."

His mouth finds mine in a chaste kiss.

"Then why haven't you?" I ask, breathless.

"Because I want this to be more than we used to be." His lips graze my jawline and move back down my neck. Lifting his head, his hazel eyes find mine.

My breath hitches with his words, and our lips connect. Slightly tugging on my hair, he tilts my head back, and I open, letting his tongue into my mouth.

Need floods my system. One of my hands finds the back of his head, playing with the hair on the nape of his neck, and the other digs into the firm muscles of his back.

All the tension of the past couple days completely snaps, and the kiss turns filthier with every stroke of his tongue. I'll be damned if this doesn't lead to more. I need him. Fuck, I want him so badly it's starting to hurt.

Pulling back, I find the brown and green swirls of his eyes. Without looking away, I drop to my knees before him.

"Claire," he warns, swallowing hard.

"Shhhh," I say. "You keep taking care of me, and now I want to take care of you."

When I tug on the towel around his waist, it falls to the floor, and his cock comes into view. The stud on the tip teases me, and I bite my lower lip as I take in the sight before me.

"Is it okay if I touch you?"

"You better," he grits out.

Running my hands over his hips, I explore his body under his gaze, noting the details of his tattoo like I've never done before.

A lion's head is in the center of his thigh with a mix of flowers and greenery inked around it. I take note of each type of flower there—foxgloves, daisies, tulips, and...

I blink, not sure I'm seeing the fourth flower that's hidden among them correctly.

"It's an anemone," he says, as I peer up at him.

"Why?"

"I think you know why."

My hands trace the petals, and I lean forward, pressing a kiss to the center of the flower. I don't give myself time to try to figure out the meaning behind my favorite flower being tattooed on his body. We can unpack that later. Right now, his hard cock is already glistening with pre-cum just from me being on my knees, and I want to make him feel good.

He shudders above me as I lay kisses along his thighs, inching closer to his shaft. Looking up at him, I circle my tongue around the head, playing with each of the little metal balls of his piercing before taking him into my mouth.

"Fuck," he says on a moan as my tongue glides down this shaft.

One of my hands finds the back of his leg and the other finds the base of his cock, working him in perfect unison with my mouth. Watching him react above me is enough to do me in. I like having control over him like this, like being able to make his knees buckle as I swirl my tongue around the tip of his length.

His hips thrust forward, pushing him deeper into the back of my throat and causing me to gag a little, but I don't stop. I like this too much to care.

I like the way he tastes. The way he feels.

"God, you look so fucking hot on your knees like this for me," he praises.

Hollowing out my cheeks, I suck hard and his legs buckle again.

"Careful," he warns. "I'm not going to last…"

I cup his balls, massaging gently.

His head falls back, and a guttural groan escapes as his words stop mid sentence. Removing my mouth from his shaft, I continue to stroke him in my hand.

"What were you saying?" I croon.

"I was…uh…" He swallows hard, his eyes falling closed. "Sugar, you keep touching me like that, and I'm not going to last very long."

"No? What if I touch you like this?"

Grinning, my head dips forward and I run my tongue over this piercing.

"Claire," he warns, his eyes opening again.

"Or like this?" I ask, glancing upward.

Opening my mouth, I wrap my lips around his length, and a growl leaves him. His hands knot into my hair, holding me steady. Over and over, my hand and mouth work in perfect unison, bringing him closer to the edge.

Peering up at him, his eyes find mine as he watches me work.

"So pretty when you're desperate to taste my cum. Is that what you want?"

Pumping his cock in and out of my mouth, I moan around him.

"Do you want me to coat the back of your pretty throat?"

I hum against him, nodding my head, taking him deeper. Saltiness moves across my tongue as his cock begins to leak, and tears stream from my eyes as I continue to work him, giving him everything I've got.

"Fuck...fuck..." he pants as his legs tremble. His hand tightens in my hair, and I can tell he's almost there. Need coils in my own core as I become more desperate to taste him. His hips thrust forward at a punishing pace as he chases his climax and fucks my mouth.

Letting out a loud groan, he finds his release, and I drink down every drop he gives me, wanting more because holy shit I like having his cock in my mouth and his hand knotted in my hair.

I pull back only when I'm sure he's completely come down from the high, and he helps me to stand. His mouth crashes against mine in a charged kiss. Wrapping his arms around me, he picks me up so that my legs circle his bare waist. He moves us toward the bedroom, and I grind against him, aching for my own orgasm. When he makes it to the bed, he throws me on top of it and grabs the leggings I'm wearing, yanking them off of my body in one swift motion.

Standing back, his lustful gaze works over me and takes me in. My fingers find my center, and I begin to play with my clit just the way I like it.

"That's it," he says. "Show me what you like. Show me what you do to yourself when no one else is around."

I move a finger inside of me and gasp at the feeling. Adding a second, I moan again. His eyes darken as he watches me pleasure myself.

"Who do you think about when you play with your pretty cunt?"

"You," I breathe out. "I've always thought about you."

"Fuck, you're perfect," he says, kneeling in front of me. Removing my hand, he sucks my fingers into his mouth, swirling his tongue around them. They make a popping sound as he removes them, and my pussy flutters with anticipation.

"Fuck, can I taste you?" he asks.

"You better," I quip.

He pulls my hips forward, and I let out a moan at the roughness of his touch.

"You like it when I'm a little rough with you, don't you?"

"Yes," I agree, panting.

His firm hands trail up my legs, and he moves both of them over his shoulders.

"Please," I beg. "Fuck, I can't wait any longer."

And I can't. I need his mouth on my clit like I need oxygen, and if it doesn't happen soon I might just perish.

His lips press soft kisses up the smooth skin of my upper thighs, and the rough hair of his beard tickles me in the most delicious way.

I'm not going to last long either. I'm about to come completely undone from just the anticipation of his mouth.

Flattening his tongue, he licks up my center in one long, languid stroke.

"Ahhhhhh," I moan, as he sucks my sensitive bud into his mouth, gently nipping it with his teeth. There is nothing gentle about how this man devours pussy. It's rough and feral and...

"Oh...fuck...fuck..." I gasp as the tip of his tongue circles my clit slowly. One of my hands finds his hair, and the other grips the soft sheets on the bed.

His fingers find my entrance, and he pushes two in, causing me to gasp at the sudden full feeling. His mouth and hand work in perfect tandem, causing my back to arch and my hips to thrust forward.

Over and over he pumps into me, torturing me with the perfect licks and flicks of his tongue. Pressure builds at the base of my spine.

"That's it," he says, pulling back slightly but not slowing his hand. His fingers curl against my most sensitive spot, and my whole body jolts. "Soak me."

His mouth returns to my clit, and with one stroke of his tongue, my eyes roll back, and I fall. My legs shudder around him, squeezing together, as he takes me through the waves of my release. And then when I've completely come down from it, he moves up to the bed to join me.

Our mouths tangle in another heady kiss. His tongue moves over mine, and I moan into him as I taste myself. Pulling back, a wide grin breaks across his face as we both attempt to catch our breath, and I'm certain he's just ruined me forever.

It may have only been a few days since we hooked up in New York, but I know I can never go that long without us touching like that again.

I move so that my body lazily drapes over the top of his. My hand draws circles up and down his thick bicep, and our breaths, still slowing, begin to sync into perfect rhythm with each other.

"How long have you had an anemone tattooed on your leg?" I ask.

"I started working on the sleeve during my first off-season in Texas."

"Hmmm," I hum, thinking back to the elaborate ink that I studied earlier.

"What do the other flowers mean?"

"Well, the foxgloves are for Iris because she loves fairies. The daisies are my sister's favorite, and the tulips are for Elsie."

"And the anemone?"

"It's for you."

"But why?"

"Because I missed you. Because I thought about you every damn day I was in Texas."

My hand stills.

"But you never called."

"I should've."

"What would've happened if I hadn't walked into that bar though? If Stella hadn't intervened and pushed us together here? You would've just…what? Married some other woman one day with my favorite flower tattooed on your leg?"

"I thought you hated me back then, remember," he explains. "There were rules. No nicknames. No strings. No sleepovers. The last night I was in town, you told me you wouldn't miss me. I think your exact words were that you'd miss only my dick. It's not like you were blowing up my phone either. We both had our careers. You said that yourself the other day."

"So why get the tattoo?"

"Because you meant a lot to me, Claire. Because no matter what, you will always be someone I want to remember. Because even if I never saw you again, it wouldn't change how I felt about you. Fuck, how I *feel* about you."

"And how do you feel about me?"

He closes his eyes and inhales deeply.

"Everett, how do you feel about me?" I repeat.

"I'm falling in love with you."

"You're falling in love with me?" I sit up, my mouth parting slightly.

"Yes," he says, sitting up to meet me and taking my hands in his. "I know that's a lot, but you're right, I should've told you how I was feeling all those years ago. I should've told you yesterday when we were playing that silly game. I've been letting my insecurities get in the way of me being honest with you. So, forgive me for the blunt delivery, but I don't want to keep it to myself anymore. I want you to know how I feel."

"Everett...I..." My eyes shift down to his tattoo, and my fingers trace the black center of the anemone.

"You don't have to say anything back. I just need you to know that I am falling for you," he says softly.

"Falling for me," I breathe out as my eyes lock on his.

"Yes."

I reach forward, cupping his face, and kiss him tenderly. Pulling away, I open my mouth to say something, *anything,* but he speaks first.

"Let's get ready and head to town," he says, his face falling.

"Everett...I..."

Guilt overwhelms me. I should say something. I should tell him I'm starting to fall for him too, but like a coward, I don't.

"It's really okay." He shakes his head and moves from the bed.

As I move through the motions of getting dressed, I silently reprimand myself for not having the courage to say what I should have, but the fear that this still isn't real, and he doesn't actually mean what he said, consumes me.

CHAPTER 33: WE CAN'T LOSE

EVERETT

Since this morning, today has felt like it's running away from me. I have no idea where the time has gone, and I can't shake the feeling that I fucked up when I told Claire how I was feeling.

When we got to town, we were stopped no less than half a dozen times by people wanting to catch up and see how we were doing. We opted to have brunch at Stella's, but it was very crowded and the service was extremely slow, probably because Ruth couldn't help but gossip with us and everyone else about some big development with Chip and Lolly and what that could mean for their blossoming romance. After we left the diner, we were stopped some more and cornered by Rusty, Ginger's husband, who was asking for advice on how to help the boys train for hockey.

Claire mostly just smiled and nodded along with everyone, but other than some small talk here and there, she's been quiet since we left the house. I wish she would talk to me, let me inside her head, but I also don't want to prod too hard and risk pushing her away.

I realize admitting that I'm falling in love with her after a few short days probably sounded crazy, but the opportunity to tell her how I was feeling presented itself, and I couldn't imagine saying anything else, even if she doesn't feel the same way about me.

Looking down at my watch, I exhale. Today was supposed to go so differently. It's after three, and all I've managed to do is scare her away from me.

Walking together toward the rink, we find a nearby bench, and I lace up my skates. Glancing over at Claire, I find she's staring off into space, still wearing her boots.

"Need help with your skates?" I offer.

"Sure," she says, moving the pair of ice skates we found at the house into my reach, but continuing to look off into the distance. Kneeling before her, I carefully remove her boot and hold the skate steady as she pushes her foot inside. I take my time lacing them, then move to the other, completing the same steps.

I help her stand, and we step on to the slick surface together. Her legs wobble a little, and she lets out a nervous giggle as I grab both of her hands.

"Are you sure you're okay?" I ask. "You've been nearly silent all day. If I fucked up this morning, I'm sorry."

"You're sorry?" she questions, finding my eyes. "I'm sorry. I wasn't expecting you to say all of that back at the house, and I let my fears kind of take over, and then we came to town, and this is the first time all day that I've felt like we're alone."

"What fears?"

"If I'm honest, I feel myself beginning to fall for you too…"

My heart leaps in my chest. Damn, that feels good to hear.

"But…"

Fuck, of course there's a but.

"Um," she continues. "I keep finding myself wondering if the events here are actually real. Like what if you think you're falling in love with me, but it's because you're under some sort of spell. What if this is all just a dream, and tomorrow we wake up with no memory of this place?"

"Then I hope I never wake up, Sugar."

"You don't mean that," she says.

"In some ways I do. I don't want to live in a world where I can't remember our time here, but I will, if it means getting you back for Christmas, so you can live out your dreams." Pulling her into me, I wrap my arms around her, holding her close to my chest.

"That's why I didn't hold back what I was feeling," I explain. "There's a part of me that wakes up each morning expecting to be back in New York too. I want to make the most of the time we have together without all the noise that comes with being home, even if it's just for a few days."

"You're right," she says.

Pulling back, my lips turn upward. "I always am."

She swats at my chest, and my shoulders shake.

"Don't ruin this moment," she deadpans.

Bending down, I take her chin between my thumb and finger, lifting it slightly. Our lips connect in a kiss that says everything words can't.

"Come on," I say, grabbing her hand. "Skate with me."

We begin to move around the small rink, gliding together on top of the ice. It feels good to be out here, with her and in no pain.

She breaks away from me, moving ahead. Her movements are effortless, and she looks happy out on the ice with me. It's easy to imagine the two of us skating at Rockefeller Center every year.

She stops and turns to face me. Our eyes lock, causing her mouth to curve into a grin. Snow begins to fall around us. Putting her hands out to the side, she looks up to the sky and starts to laugh.

I skate quickly across to meet her. Snatching her up, I spin her around, settling her in front of me with her back against the boards. My hands weave into her hair, and I kiss her deeply.

"Sometimes this feels a little too perfect," she says, catching some snow on her glove.

"Or maybe it's just because you're realizing you and I are actually perfect for each other."

"You have no idea how badly I wish those cheesy lines of yours didn't have an effect on me," she says, pulling away and rolling her eyes.

"Just give in," I tease. Her mouth tips up, and her eyes gleam with mischief. "What's that look?"

"Want to play me in a little one-on-one ice hockey game?" she asks.

"That depends," I jest. "What does the winner get?"

Cocking her head to the side, she thinks for a minute.

"I'm not sure. What do you think?"

"How about if I win, I get to take you on a date tomorrow, and if you win, I have to plan a date for you tomorrow?"

"That's the same thing."

"Then it sounds like we can't lose." I flash her a goofy smile.

"You could just ask me on a date," she says.

"I could, but I like my chances better this way."

I skate over to where my hockey equipment sits, grabbing a puck and two sticks. "Okay, first one to get a goal wins," I say, tossing her one of the sticks.

"Okay," she says, putting the stick to the ice. She moves back and forth playfully, pretending like she knows what she's doing, but it's clear she doesn't.

"Have you ever played hockey before?"

"No," she says. "But, it doesn't look that hard."

Shaking my head, I move behind her. I wrap my arms around her and breathe in her sweet perfume. My lips find her neck in a tender kiss.

"I thought we were going to play a game."

"Sorry, I can't help myself," I murmur against her neck, making her body shudder. She tilts her head further to the side, exposing more of her soft skin, and I lay a few more up kisses up the column of her throat and towards her ear.

"Stop," she says, a little breathless.

"Why?"

"Because we're in public."

I place another kiss right below her ear.

"Come on, teach me how to hold the stick. You can kiss me wherever you want later."

"Wherever I want?"

She nods her head and shifts her hips back against me, causing me to groan and her to let out a giggle.

"This is torture," I say.

"Come on. Don't be dramatic. Teach me."

Exhaling, I straighten up behind her. "Grip the stick like you're going to shoot it."

"Which stick?" She grinds her hips backwards again.

A snort escapes, and I shake my head. "Yours."

She puts her hands haphazardly on the top of the shaft and looks over her shoulder. "Like this?"

"No." I chuckle. "Which hand feels more comfortable on top?"

"My right."

"Okay, so place it here, forming a V with the spot between your thumb and your finger." I point to the top of the shaft.

She moves her hand, following my directions. "Like this?"

"Perfect. Now, I like to grip it firmly, but not too tight."

"You like the grip firm, but not too tight," she purrs. "I'll keep that in mind."

My cock twitches at her words, and I try to will it away, but it's no use. She knows what she's doing, and I like it too much.

"Okay and what do I do with the other hand?" she asks.

"Place it underneath, and leave your grip loose until you're ready to shoot. Does that make sense?"

"I think so," she says, adjusting her hands slightly.

Releasing her, I turn, grabbing a puck and tossing it in front of her stick. "Okay, so I want you to try to shoot the puck toward that goal."

"Shoot the puck," she repeats. "Sounds easy enough."

She rears back, dropping her head. Her eyes land on the puck, but then she swings and misses, throwing her off her balance.

"Woah, woah," I say, moving back behind her, catching her waist. "Grip it the way I showed you, and then when you pull back, keep your head up and your eyes on your target."

"Can you show me?"

"Sure."

I cover her hands with mine and help guide the stick back and then forward. The blade makes contact with the puck, and it flies across the ice and into the nearby goal.

"I did it," she bursts.

"Good, now you think you can do that while moving?"

"I can try."

We both skate over to the middle of the rink and line up facing one another. I throw the puck into the air, and she immediately begins to fight me for possession when it lands in front of us. To my surprise, she wins out and moves past me toward her goal before I can react. Spinning around to follow her, I watch as she shoots and sends the puck into the back of the net like a goddamn pro.

What the hell was that?

Turning around, a proud, wide smile breaks across her face, and a laugh bursts out of her. "You can close your mouth," she teases.

"How did you do that?"

"I told you. It's not *that* hard."

"You played me."

"Like a fiddle," she jests. "I can't believe you thought I didn't know how to handle a stick. I feel like earlier in the living room, I clearly proved that I do."

A loud chuckle erupts, shaking my chest. Skating at her with my full force, she shrieks. I wrap my arms around her, and a melodic laugh escapes her as I spin her around and tickle her sides.

"Hey, you two," Joe says, skating toward us.

"Is it that time already?" I ask, setting her down carefully.

"Almost. Claire, I didn't know you knew how to play," he says.

"Barely." She laughs. "My dad is a big fan and taught me and my sister how to play when we were little. It's been a long time, and I'm a little rusty."

"Well, you sure gave Everett a run for his money."

"Hiya, Claire." Cami waves from off the side of the rink. "You ready for some wine?"

"Wine?" She glances over to me.

"Go," I encourage her. "We can walk back to the house together when I'm done?"

"I'd like that," she says.

"Good." Leaning in, I place a kiss on her forehead and then take her stick. I watch as she skates to meet Cami, relieved that today seemed to turn around and still drunk off the fact that she's falling for me too.

CHAPTER 34: WINE NIGHT

CLAIRE

The look on Everett's face when he figured out I know a thing or two about playing hockey was priceless. This playful side of him is making me fall harder by the minute. The way he challenges me stirs something deep in my soul, and I really hope when all of this is over, these feelings don't disappear with this town. I think that might completely break me if they did.

"Hey, stranger!" Aster yells, crossing the street with her arm linked through Lolly's. Both women are holding a bottle of wine. "We were wondering if you'd show up."

"I didn't realize I was imposing on your get together," I whisper to Cami, suddenly very unsure of agreeing to join her.

"What are you talking about, hun?"

Panic sets in. Fuck. My mind fumbles through possible excuses I could give for my out-of-character response, but I don't have any ideas. I wish Everett was here.

"Wine night is becoming our little tradition. If anyone is imposing, it's me. I'm just happy you young girls let this old bird join in."

"Where have you been?" Lolly asks when she and Aster meet us at the door of Citrine Brews.

"Busy," I lie.

"So busy you can't respond to any of our texts?" Lolly asks.

"For real. I was starting to think we had upset you or something," Aster says. "We've missed you."

Blush crawls up my neck. "Yeah, sorry. Stella's been extra about me and Everett getting special treatment ahead of the Extravaganza. Didn't want her thinking you three are influencing the outcome."

"What Stella doesn't know won't hurt her," Cami says, winking.

"I can't believe you and Everett agreed to judge this year's competition. It sounds miserable," Aster says.

"It's not like they had a choice," Cami says, unlocking the door of the shop and gesturing for us to follow her inside. "You know Stella. Once she gets an idea, the whole town has to go along with it."

"God, I know," Lolly says, as she, Aster, and I make our way over to one of the couches. "I still can't believe she made Chip and me the co-chairs of the decoration committee and then somehow convinced him to let me use his freezer to make my peppermint bark today."

"What happened?" I ask.

"Did you remember a bottle opener?" Cami asks, walking behind the counter.

"I did," Aster replies, pulling it from her bag and opening the bottle.

"The freezer went out, and you guys know how long it takes to get parts for that kind of thing delivered here, so I have no way to set the peppermint bark. Stella's grand idea was for me to use Chip's freezer, and for some reason I will never understand, he agreed."

"Are you worried he's going to sabotage it?"

"No," Lolly says, rolling her eyes. "He's harmless. Infuriating, but harmless. I don't know what Stella is thinking."

"I do," Cami says, approaching us with four wine glasses in her hands. "She's trying to push you two together because she thinks you'd make a cute couple."

Aster collects the glasses one by one, filling each with a heavy pour of red wine.

"You know how she works," Cami continues, and Aster hands me the first glass. I take a sip. A mix of oak and spices run over my tongue and warm my body, putting me at ease. "I mean, she did the same thing to Everett and Claire."

I choke on my sip, coughing and sputtering.

"You good?" Lolly asks.

"Yeah, fine," I say, clearing my throat. "What do you mean she did the same thing to Everett and me?"

All three burst out laughing. "Please, Claire, you may be

obsessed with the man now, but you hated him when he first moved here," Lolly says. "Don't act like you don't remember."

"Well, she hated him until she slept with him," Aster teases.

"Maybe that's what you need to do," Cami adds, looking in Lolly's direction.

"I'm not sleeping with Chip," she deadpans. "He wears grandpa sweaters and reads the newspaper like he's a ninety-year-old man. I doubt sex with him would be anything other than mediocre."

"It's always the quiet ones that surprise you." Cami shrugs. "Take Joe for example. Just last night—"

"Stop," Lolly and Aster yell.

"Please don't ruin Joe for us," Lolly says. "He's like the town dad."

"Cami's right about the quiet ones, though," Aster agrees. "I remember Claire thinking the same thing about Everett, and look at them now. Heard you two took quite the dip in the hot tub yesterday. Gave the whole block a show."

"Who told you that?" I ask, my eyes going wide.

"Ruth." Aster laughs.

"Of course she did," I say, forcing a laugh and pretending like I understand anything they're talking about.

"The hot tub?" Lolly questions over the rim of her glass, wiggling her eyebrows in my direction. "What happened?"

"Nothing," I say.

"Oh, come on," she says. "It's us. Give us the dirty details of your slutty little marriage so we can live vicariously through you."

"On the way to our house, he started a snowball fight, and that led to us freezing our asses off in the snow, so when we got back to the house, we took a dip in the tub and made out a little. It really wasn't anything scandalous. We are married after all." I fidget with the ring on my left hand.

"You two are really the sweetest things ever," Aster says. "I wish I could find my person."

"You will, honey," Cami says.

"Well, last time I checked, there were no other single women in this town interested in me, so I doubt that will happen anytime soon."

"If it makes you feel any better, the pool of single men is severely lacking too," Lolly says.

"That's not true," Aster says. "You have your pick with Chip and Reid."

Lolly gags. "Reid!" She gasps, gagging again and making all three of us laugh at her reaction. "You did not just insinuate that Reid is a viable option."

Aster shrugs. "I'm just saying, you have two, and I have zero."

"Claire, will you please explain to our friend why Reid wouldn't be an option even if he was the last man on the planet."

I giggle, trying to come up with reasons why a man that I know nothing about is a bad choice.

"He does give me a strange vibe."

"A strange vibe?" Lolly laughs. "He's the neighborhood recluse! When he showed up to the town meeting the other day, I couldn't believe it."

"Fine, so you have one choice," Aster says. "But that's still better than zero."

All four of us burst out laughing.

"You know you girls are always welcome to my crystals," Cami says. "I was just telling Claire the other day that that's how I nabbed Joe."

"I might have to take you up on that," Lolly says.

I find myself relaxing back on the couch, sipping my wine, and enjoying their company. I don't know these women, but something about being surrounded by them and hearing them talk makes me feel more included in their friend group than I ever have before.

What a sick joke.

After another hour, both bottles are empty, and I make my way to the front of the coffee shop with the girls. Each one offers me a hug, and I try to push away the feelings that tonight brought about friendships and my life back in New York. The things that I wish I had but am missing.

Opening the door, I leave them, walking onto the street. The sun is low in the sky, and in the distance you can see the first signs of the moon. I check the time and find it's a little before six.

Lamp posts and strung twinkle lights glitter above the snow-covered street, ready for whatever tonight will bring.

Pulling my jacket tight across my chest, I turn to head toward the ice rink. Everett is standing tall on skates and holding a hockey stick. Four young kids are in the middle of a circle of cones, playing keep away while their teammates, Joe, and Everett watch.

The boy in the middle steals the puck, and Everett blows his whistle. "Nice!" he calls out. "Alright, last group, you're up."

The four children skate to meet their team, and four new kids move into the middle of the cones. The whistle blows, and the three on the outside begin pushing the puck across the ice to one another, keeping it away from a little girl in the middle.

Everett moves around the ice with such ease, and it's clear every child there looks up to him. The four practicing keep looking in his direction for approval, and the others watch his every move. He's incredible with the kids, and my heart swells as I watch him.

The girl catches the puck as it passes by her, ending the game, and Everett claps his hands. "Good job," he calls, blowing his whistle again. "Alright, that's practice. Everyone help pick up the equipment."

The team does as they're told, and when everything is put away, they all meet him in the middle of the ice.

Huddled around Everett and Joe, each one puts a small hand outward. "Polar bears on three," Everett shouts. "One, two, three."

"Polar bears!" they all yell together, breaking away toward the entrance to the ice where their parents wait for them.

I wait patiently for Everett to finish gathering his things, and I can't take my eyes off of him. He greets a few of the parents as he steps off the ice and walks over to a bench. Sitting, he begins to change his shoes, and I walk over to meet him.

His whole face lights up, and his eyes seem to twinkle when he sees me. "Hey, Sugar."

"You looked good out there."

"You were watching me?"

"Not for very long."

He stands then bends down, kissing me.

"You hungry?" he asks.

"Starving and a little drunk," I say as the effects of the wine swirl around my head.

"You had fun with the girls then?"

"I did."

He throws me a reassuring smile as he stands, swinging his bag over his shoulder and taking my hand.

We begin to walk back down the street toward the house. The sun has dropped even lower in the sky, and a dusting of snow falls around us. The streetlights are casting a soft glow on the snow beneath. It's quiet, with most of the people dispersing to other ends of town away from the main square. The cool air burns my nose, filling it with the scent of fresh snow.

We walk in silence for a while before I hear him clear his throat.

"Tonight was strange," he says as we pass by The Chocolate Bar.

"What do you mean?"

"Coaching felt natural, like I've done it forever, and Joe kept talking to me like he was one of my oldest friends."

"My night was similar."

"Yeah?"

"It was weird. I felt more included in that group of women, who should be strangers, than I've ever felt with anyone else. I don't have a friend group like that back home, and it was nice to pretend like it did."

"Does it make you want to stay?" he asks.

"God, no," I say, shaking my head. "My family is in New York, and so is my career. It was just nice for tonight, that's all."

Everett hums to himself. He stops walking and pulls me into him, his mouth finding mine.

"What was that for?" I ask, pulling away slightly.

He shrugs. "I've been thinking about kissing you since you walked away earlier, and I couldn't wait any longer."

Pushing up on my toes, my lips find him again. He kisses me hard as the snow falls around us, and I allow myself to dream about what a life with Everett in New York could be like.

CHAPTER 35:
ONLY FOR YOU
EVERETT

DECEMBER TWENTY-THIRD

Claire seemed lighter after last night with Lolly, Aster, and Cami. While I know those women could never take the place of her sister, it was nice to see her enjoy herself with people who think of her as a friend.

"I was thinking we skip Stella's today and just grab some coffee from Citrine Brews," Claire says, walking out of her closet. She's wearing black leggings, fur lined boots with white socks, and a pink and white checked jacket. Her hair is pulled up out of her face, and a thick, light pink headband covers her ears.

"Sounds good to me."

We walk toward the front door to grab our coats and then begin the short trek to the coffee shop, and I instinctively take her hand in mine. Her eyes find where we connect, and a soft smile breaks across her face.

"I like holding your hand," she admits.

"Me too," I say, trying to play it cool, but on the inside, a full on celebration is happening. *She's starting to fall for me. She likes to hold my hand.* Fuck, that feels so good to hear.

"I also like kissing you," she says, glancing in my direction.

"Oh yeah?"

"Yeah," she says, tipping the corners of her mouth upward.

Pulling her into me, she pushes up on her toes. My hands caress her face, and our lips meet. She giggles against me as her arms find my back, and I kiss her like no one else in this world or any other world exists.

"Ewwwww," a little voice calls, interrupting us. Stopping, we both turn to find Fen, Ginger's son, standing behind us.

"Hey, Fen," I say, chuckling as Claire's cheeks turn a rosy pink.

"What happened?" Cori, his brother, asks, running to meet us with both of their sisters close behind.

"Coach and Mrs. Claire were kissing," Fen explains to them.

Cori gags. "Yuck. That's so gross."

"So gross," Fen agrees, causing Claire to giggle.

"Kids, get back here," Rusty calls from the front porch of their house. "You know you aren't supposed to be outside without your coats."

"Hey, Rusty," I wave.

"Sorry about them," he says.

"Don't be," Claire assures him.

"Tag, you're it!" Fen yells, slapping his brother across the back and then taking off through the snow-covered yard.

"You're dead!" Cori yells, running after him.

The two girls follow after their brothers, giggling and singing some nursery rhyme about me and Claire kissing and it leading to a baby in a carriage.

"If we were staying in this town longer, I'd make them skate sprints at practice for interrupting that kiss."

"No, they were cute," she says. "Plus, I promise we can pick up where we left off later."

"Oh yeah?"

"Yeah," she says, her eyes twinkling with something that makes my cock strain against the inside of my pants. "Now come on. I need coffee, and then I'd like to get back to the house. I have plans for you."

"Oh, do you?"

She flashes me a flirty smile, and we begin walking again. This time she grabs my hand first, and my heart leaps in my chest as we continue down the street.

"Do you want kids?" she asks when we make it to town.

"Kids?"

"Yeah, I don't know. The girls' song made me think about it. Not right now obviously…or even with me…shit…"

"Have I ever told you you're cute when you get flustered?"

She shoves me playfully with her shoulder.

"I've honestly not given it much thought," I say. "What about you?"

"When I'm done with ballet, I think it would be nice to have a couple. I could never have six like Ginger, but the idea of creating a family like the one I grew up with sounds nice."

"I don't have what you have with your family, but the idea of creating that, with the right person…"

With you.

"…does sound nice."

Silence stretches between us.

"I think I'd want a dog too," I add.

"A dog?"

"Yeah, I can't have one with hockey, but when I do finally settle down, I think I'd want a dog."

"What kind of dog?"

"Something that looks tough but secretly isn't. Like a rottweiler that really just wants to cuddle."

"You want the dog version of yourself?"

"What's that supposed to mean?" I laugh.

"Oh come on! You walk around like you're this big, tough hockey player who starts and finishes fights on the ice." She drops her voice to whisper. "I mean you have a leg sleeve and dick piercing." She giggles. "But then, you start snowball fights and have my favorite flower tattooed on your thigh and you give me forehead kisses and apparently you really like to cuddle."

"So?"

"I'm just saying you're actually a really big softy."

Only for you.

"Maybe I am."

We make it to the door of Citrine Brews. I begin to pull the door open, but she stops me.

"For the record," she says, "I really like the soft side of you."

"And I really like you," I return. Leaning down, I kiss her forehead, then pull the door open so we can step inside.

"Good morning." Joe waves from behind the counter. "I'll get your usuals made right away."

"Thanks, man."

Claire and I make our way over to one of the couches and sit while we wait.

"You excited for our date tonight?" I ask.

"I am, but are you sure you can't give me any hints as to what we're doing?"

"No." I chuckle.

"Just one little itty bitty small hint?" She pinches her fingers together.

"You really hate surprises don't you?"

"I'm just excited. You've been talking such a big game about your plans, so now I'm dying to know if the date's going to live up to all of the hype."

"It will. I promise."

She pulls her phone out of her pocket and smiles.

"Aster and Lolly?" I ask.

"Yeah." She continues smirking as she reads the texts.

"You guys have been texting?"

"After last night, I unmuted the group text," she explains.

"So what's going on with the girls?"

"Lolly is freaking out because she and Chip almost kissed this morning."

"Is that so?" I ask, raising an eyebrow.

"I know. Something about him coming over to borrow something, and they got stuck in the candy shop stock room together."

Her phone buzzes again, and she taps against the screen.

"You know, it kind of feels like a sick joke that I found people who really seem like they could be my friends and we're only going to be here for a couple of more nights."

"I know. I've been thinking about that too."

"Part of me wishes we could take them all back with us."

Leaning over, I kiss her forehead and wish there was a way I could give her everything she deserves—family she's close with, friends who care about her, her dreams coming true, and a love that would rival the best fairytales—but we can't take the people here back to New York with us, and I fear that reality will hit us both harder than we think it will when it comes to fruition.

"Drinks are ready," Joe calls. I stand, leaving Claire alone to walk over and pay for and retrieve our drinks.

"We still on for later?" Joe asks.

I glance over my shoulder to see that Claire is distracted by

Cami. "Yeah, thanks again for your help and for coordinating with the girls. I really appreciate it."

"Anything for you two." He smiles.

Cami walks away as I start to head back to where the girls were chatting, and Claire stands to meet me. "Here you go," I say, handing off her latte.

"So, apparently, Aster is closing her shop to go debrief with Lolly about this almost kiss situation, and they really want me to come, but I don't want to go if you had other plans."

"That's fine. I have some errands to run around here before tonight."

"Errands? What do you have planned?"

"That's for me to know and you to find out, Sugar." Leaning down, our mouths meet in a quick kiss.

"Text me when you're done, and we'll meet up," I assure her. "Tell Lolly and Aster I said hi."

She turns without another word, and I watch her until she disappears out of the shop. Then I get started on prepping for a night Claire will—hopefully—never forget.

Chapter 36:
Traditions

Claire

The kiss debriefing turned into a long lunch, and it's now somehow after three in the afternoon. I'm incredibly suspicious that Everett had something to do with Lolly and Aster taking up my whole day because every time I texted him to check in, he just kept telling me to have fun and take my time. Aster also took an extremely long trip to the bathroom, and I could swear I saw her walking outside the restaurant as Lolly tried to keep my attention on her instead.

Everett texted twenty minutes ago telling me to meet him at the house, so that's where I am. Walking up the small staircase to the front door, I do my best to fix my hair.

The door swings open, and I look up to find Everett standing there. He's holding a bouquet full of anemones, eucalyptus, thistles, and a few other plants I can't identify. It's stunning and also explains why Aster was gone so long.

"What's that?" I ask.

"Flowers for you," he says, his face warming as his eyes take me in. "I figured I couldn't take you on a proper date without bringing you flowers."

"Thank you," I say, taking them from him. He leans down and places a soft kiss against my lips, then guides me inside to reveal the most perfectly shaped fraser fir sitting in the living room.

"Is that a Christmas tree?" I beam, setting the flowers down on the table and removing my coat.

"We didn't have one, and so I thought it might be fun to cook some fettuccine alfredo, light a fire, turn on a Christmas movie, and decorate the tree together."

"You planned a Christmas-themed date?" I ask, turning to face him.

He shrugs. "I know how much you love it, and I figured the next couple of days might be a little hectic with the Extravaganza and getting back to the city, so I thought we could have our own little Christmas together here before we go."

Closing the space between us, I pop up on my toes and kiss him. "It sounds like the perfect night."

"Oh, I almost forgot," he says, moving across the house and into our bedroom.

"Forgot what?" I ask, following behind him.

"I got us matching Christmas pajamas."

"You got us matching Christmas pajamas?"

"Well…kinda."

"What do you mean?"

"There weren't a ton of options, but I managed to find a men's flannel pajama set and figured you could take the top and I could wear the bottoms."

I burst out laughing.

"So we're sharing pajamas?"

"Technically, but I figured the over-sized sleep shirt would look better on you than me, and you wouldn't mind if I only wore the pants."

"No, I don't think I would mind that at all," I say, taking the red and green plaid sleep shirt off the dresser where it's folded.

"Why don't you put that on, and I'll go get dinner started?"

I nod, and he places a kiss on my forehead before walking out to begin dinner.

A few minutes later, I join him, wearing the shirt.

"How'd you manage to get a Christmas tree in here without me knowing?" I ask.

"Chip and Joe helped me sneak it in while Lolly and Aster distracted you."

"Did they?"

"Yep!"

"Did you have the whole town in on this date?"

"Well, Aster helped with the flowers of course, and the guys moved in the tree. Cami helped me find some ornaments and lights for us to use, and Lolly made some dessert for later." He grins. "So, yeah, I guess you could say it was a team effort."

"I wish they were all real," I say, grabbing the bouquet off the table and bringing it to my nose.

"I do too, but let's not think about that tonight."

We both begin to move around the kitchen. I put the flowers in water and pour us each a glass of wine while he cooks. I bask in the normalcy of it all. How easily this could be a night in New York after a long day.

"I really like this," I say, sitting on the counter and sipping my wine.

"The wine?" he asks, stirring the sauce and turning the knob to simmer.

"Well yes, but I like doing this," I explain. "I like doing normal things with you. Like watching you cook dinner and talking about our days."

"Are you reading my mind now?"

"Were you thinking that too?"

He nods.

"It's strange," I begin. "Because I've always known that you and I had the sex part down, but I wondered if this part would be just as good. Like if the quiet moments would feel just as intense and wonderful."

"And?" he asks.

"They do," I admit. "I find myself wanting these moments with you just as much as I want the other ones."

Walking over, he wraps his arms around me, and I press my forehead to his. "Me too, Sugar. This past week has meant every-thing to me."

He lays a gentle kiss across my lips, then moves to finish making the food. I watch as he carefully makes us each a bowl.

We move into the living room, and he lights a fire before disap-pearing to change into his pajamas.

He walks out of the bedroom wearing just the pants. "I have a feeling you had an ulterior motive when you decided to go shirtless tonight," I tease.

"It did feel like a win-win," he jests.

"What made you want to make this? I've never had pasta as part of a Christmas celebration. Is this what your family does when you're together?"

"No, we don't really have traditions, but I thought, if you liked it, we could start some of our own."

"Our own traditions?"

"Yeah, like every year I cook us some fettuccine and then we decorate our tree."

My heart jumps in my chest, and my stomach swoops with butterflies.

"Is that what this is? A night of new traditions?" I ask, a little breathless.

"Only if you want it to be."

"Is that what you want?"

He nods, and his eyes find mine. "Sugar, I want it all, and I want it with you."

"With me?"

He moves closer and cups my cheek with his hand. "For a while now, I've been scared of what my future would look like. I was afraid of giving up the one thing I thought would make me happy because of who I'd be without it, but I'm realizing none of that matters if you aren't a part of it."

I smile, and pressure builds behind my eyes. Every time I think he can't blow me away, he does.

"So yeah, I want the traditions."

"I want them too."

My heart expands in my chest. Each leaning forward, our mouths meet in a kiss.

Chapter 37: A Christmas Travesty

Everett

Our empty wine glasses and dirty dishes litter the coffee table. Empty boxes that once held ornaments are spread across the floor. Christmas music is playing in the background, and the warmth from the fire fills the space.

"I think we need a few more over here," Claire says, eyeing some bare branches. "Here, pass me a few of the silver balls."

I collect the items and walk over to meet her.

"You're really good at this," I say.

"I've had a lot of practice," she says, taking the first ball and hanging it on one of the limbs. The smell of pine engulfs my senses.

"Do you usually do a real or a fake tree back home?"

"I always had a real one growing up, and my parents still do, but because of dance it's easier to have a fake one," she explains, taking the second and third ball from me and placing them on the tree.

"I like the real one. It smells good."

"Doesn't it." She smiles, stepping back as she studies our work. "I think we're almost done, but it could use a couple more."

Walking over, she digs in one of the boxes and laughs as she pulls out two ornaments.

"These are cute," she says, holding up two small nutcracker ornaments. One is dressed like a hockey player and the other is dressed like a ballerina.

"They kind of look like us," she muses. "Here."

Reaching out her hand, she gives me the hockey player and then moves to the center of the tree. She carefully places the ballerina on a branch, and I move forward, hanging my ornament right next to hers.

"I know you said not to crowd them, but I think these two need to be together."

"I agree. Where did you find those?"

"Cami helped with the ornaments, so she must've snuck them in there. I like them though."

"Me too," she agrees.

She walks over toward the overhead light switch and pauses. "Okay, on three, I'm going to flip the switch, and you plug in the lights."

"Okay."

"One…two…three…" The room goes dark for a split second before the tree comes to life. The white lights twinkle, creating a magical glow.

She gasps. "It's beautiful."

"Very," I say, my eyes finding her instead of the tree. She glides towards me, and I wrap her up in my arms. The soft glow from the fire and twinkling lights dance across her skin, and I take her mouth with mine.

Pulling away, I push my hand into my pocket and pull out a small velvet box. "I got you something."

"A present?"

"Yeah, I saw it, and it reminded me of you."

"But Christmas isn't for a couple of days," she says. "I didn't get you—"

"I don't need a present," I say. "Open it."

She takes it from me, her fingers gently grazing mine and sending a shock through my body. She flips it open, revealing a white gold necklace. A dainty, diamond-encrusted snowflake pendant sits at the center.

"I love it," she says. "You didn't have to get me…"

"I wanted you to have something to remember our time here by."

"But what if we wake up on Christmas and the necklace is lost with this town?"

I laugh. "I guess that's a possibility, but it was a risk I was willing to take."

She runs her thumb over the small snowflake.

"Here, turn around."

She gathers her hair to the side, and I carefully remove the silver chain she always wears from her neck, replacing it with the gift from me. Dipping forward, I wrap my arms around her and press my lips to her delicate skin. She tilts her head to the side, and I trail soft kisses up toward her ear, making her hum in return.

"Stop…" She giggles as my facial hair tickles her skin. "There is one more thing we haven't done yet." She flips around, taking the necklace from me. "Lie down," she says as she places it on the coffee table.

"Lie down?"

"Just do it," she scolds.

Walking over, she takes my hand and guides me down to the floor so that we're lying shoulder to shoulder under the tree. "Now, look up," she says.

The lights twinkling above cast a romantic glow over us. She reaches over to take my hand, intertwining her fingers with mine, and my heart leaps in my chest. Turning my head, I'm surprised to find she's looking at me.

Without another word, our mouths crash together, and I feel the happiest I think I've ever felt.

She pulls away, smiling.

"So, what's the next part of this date?"

"A movie."

"Do I get to pick?"

I nod.

She pops up and moves to the couch, so I follow. Grabbing the remote off the coffee table, she flips until she finds *The Grinch.*

"Have you ever seen this one?" she asks, settling down on the couch and into the crook of my arm.

"Nope."

She gasps. "You've never seen your biopic? What a Christmas travesty."

"Hilarious," I deadpan, tickling her sides.

"Stop," she whines. "The movie is starting."

Settling into one another, I hold her close, knowing without a doubt that she is it for me.

Chapter 38:
Gimme Three
Claire

Tonight has been everything I could have ever imagined. I feel myself falling hard for Everett, and I know there's no going back. The kiss we shared under the tree lit something within me, and I know he wants me like that too. I can feel it.

"Thank you for making tonight so magical," I say, crawling under the covers next to him.

"I'd do anything for you," he assures me, pulling me back into him tightly and causing my ass to brush up against his crotch.

"Claire," he warns, his voice dripping with desire. I love that I have this effect on him. That all it takes to turn him on is an innocent, or not so innocent, graze of my ass against his cock.

"What?" I feign, need already rippling through me as I anticipate what he'll do next.

"Didn't you just turn off that Christmas movie because you were tired. You move like that again, and you won't be falling asleep anytime soon."

"Promise?" I purr, pushing my hips back again. In one swift movement, he tangles my legs with his, completely restricting my movement and giving him access to all of me.

He presses his lips to my neck, and his hand trails down my abdomen toward the top of my underwear.

"You have no idea what you just started," he teases.

"Oh, I think I do."

His fingers toy with the silky fabric, and I push back again, finding his erection. Tilting my head, I expose more of my neck to him. His mouth sucks gently on my sensitive skin, and I guide his hand lower.

"Touch me," I beg.

He chuckles against me and spreads my legs a little further apart using his. My breaths grow heavy as I anticipate his touch. Gliding his hand down, his fingers tease my wet slit, and I let out a moan as he finds my clit. Circling it gently, I writhe my hips back again.

"Fuck, you're wet," he says.

I begin to pant under his touch as he continues to apply the perfect pressure, sliding two fingers deep inside me, curling them at the perfect angle.

"Is this what you want?" he asks, his voice firm and low. "Want me to play with your perfect pussy until you soak my hand."

Fuck, I like when he talks like this. I like when he takes control and makes me beg.

"No," I breathe out.

"No?" he questions, pushing deeper inside me.

"I want more than…" His thumb presses against my clit, and my head lolls back. "I want more than just your hand."

"Patience," he says. "I'm just getting started."

He curls his fingers inside me, and pressure begins to build between my legs.

"Everett," I moan, as he removes his hand, stopping my climax in its tracks, and leaving me desperate and frustrated. Slowly, he runs his hand up and under my sleep shirt and grinds his hips forward.

"Don't stop," I beg, desperate for more. "Touch me again."

Running his thumb and finger over my peaked nipple, he pinches gently, and his warm breath tickles the back of my neck, causing me to shudder underneath him.

"I don't want you to let go until I tell you to," he commands.

"Okay," I pant, as his hand starts to trail down my body again. "I can listen."

He groans behind me, and his hand dips below the fabric of my thong once more.

"I want to fuck you with my hand," he says, pushing one finger inside of me.

"Then, I'm going to fuck you with my tongue." He adds a second finger, curling them upwards, and my breath hitches.

"And then, when you don't think you have anything left to give me, I'm going to fuck your perfect cunt with my cock." He adds a third finger, stretching me wide. My hips buck, and he stills me with his strong legs.

Holy fuck, I think he could honestly make me come with the shit he says to me.

"Yesss," I breathe.

He continues to pump his fingers inside me, and his thumb applies the perfect amount of pressure to my sensitive bud. I do my best to hold on, trying not to fall until he tells me to, but with every movement, pressure begins to build low in my belly.

My body heats at the thought that I'm at his complete disposal. I'm his to play with, and fuck I like it.

"Come for me," he says.

My legs shake as I fall, my body naturally wanting to squeeze my thighs together around his hand, but he doesn't allow it. Instead, he uses his legs to hold mine slightly apart, adding to the intensity of my release. He continues to finger me through the waves of my orgasm, and when I'm done, he rolls to his back.

"Fuck," I say, trying to catch my breath.

"Get up here," he says.

"What?" I ask, breathless and not entirely sure how he just made something as simple as fingering me that hot. Or how I just came that hard.

"Sugar, I told you I wanted to fuck you with my tongue, so I'm going to need you to take off those panties you just soaked and sit on my face."

My breath hitches, and I remove my thong, then turn to face him. His eyes are dark, and his pupils are blown.

I run my hand under the waistband of his boxer briefs, but his hand grips my wrist gently, stopping me.

"I don't think you understand how badly I need to taste you," he says, shaking his head.

"What if I want your cock first," I quip.

"Soon," he says. "Now. Come. Here."

Crawling up his body, I straddle his head and grasp the top of the headboard. His hands trail up my thighs, bunching the shirt around my hips. Gripping them firmly, he pulls me down, taking my entire pussy into his mouth. His tongue works up my center, and I grind my hips against the rough hair that covers his face.

Pressure immediately starts to coil low in my spine as he devours me, gripping my ass tighter with every lick of his tongue. My hips buck against him as he toys with my clit, and I grow more and more desperate for his cock.

"Fuck me," I beg as he works me with his mouth. "Fuck, I need you."

He groans into me, vibrating my core, but doesn't give in to my plea. All it takes is a few more flicks of his tongue against my clit for me to fall again. Liquid pools between my legs, and he drinks in every drop I give him.

I roll off the top of him, attempting to catch my breath again. He turns to meet me, taking my mouth into a filthy kiss of clashing tongues and teeth, and I frantically attempt to pull his boxers away and free his cock. I manage to get them over his hips, and he kicks them the rest of the way off, and then he pulls the shirt over my head.

"Condom," he says. "We need a condom."

"I can't wait," I say. "I need you bare."

"You sure."

I nod my head eagerly.

"Please," I beg again. "I have an IUD, and you can pull out for all I care, but I want you bare."

Rolling to my back, he moves over me, lining up his shaft between my legs. In one movement, he pushes his hips forward so that we're flush against each other.

"Oh my, Everett…" I moan as his thick cock stretches me.

"Shit," he says, "you feel too good."

Pushing my hips upward, we begin to move against each other. The metal balls of his piercing make contact with my most sensitive spot, and I scream out his name again.

His mouth finds mine as we continue to match each other's pace. Tonight feels more intense than ever before. It's rough, but gentle. Naughty, but nice. It's everything I've ever wanted with him, but nothing like we've ever had before.

"I need you to let go again," he says, pulling his mouth away from mine. "I'm so fucking close, but I need to feel you come undone one more time."

"I don't know if I can."

"Gimme three," he says, rotating his hips perfectly. He pumps into me a few more times, and I'm gone. Falling again over the edge. His mouth meets mine, and he swallows my screams as my orgasm rips through me. Liquid floods between my legs as he continues to chase his own release and carries me through mine.

He groans into me, pulling out and painting my stomach and chest with his cum. The look on his face is feral as he comes down from his high.

"Fuck, I wish you could see yourself." His eyes rake down my body, following the trail he left. My chest rises and falls, and I've never felt sexier than I do right now painted in him.

Without warning, he slowly moves down my body. His tongue glides up my center in a long, languid stroke before trailing across my stomach, through his own release.

My breath becomes more rapid as I watch in awe of him. His mouth finds mine, and the mix of our releases dance across my tongue, causing me to moan into him. The kiss is erotic. Our tongues tangle and our teeth clash. I can't get enough.

He pulls away, and his mouth grazes just below my ear. "Did you taste that, Sugar?"

Swallowing hard, a small moan escapes me.

"Did you taste how good we are together?"

"Yes," I breathe out.

Rolling off the bed, he goes into the bathroom and returns a moment later with a warm towel. Gently, he cleans me up, something he's never done before. There's a tenderness to his gaze, and my heart flutters as I watch him.

"I've never come that hard," I admit.

"I knew I could make you squirt," he says, trailing the towel down my abdomen and over my thighs. "Fuck, you look beautiful."

Bending down, he kisses me gently. He helps me out of bed, and I disappear into the bathroom to finish getting cleaned up while he remakes the bed.

I crawl back under the freshly changed sheets and melt into his embrace, certain in this moment that no matter what happens, I never want to know a world where he and I don't exist together.

Chapter 39: The Devil's Tango

CHRISTMAS EVE

Last night meant everything to me. I shouldn't be surprised. She and I have had sex more times than I can count, and it's always been incredible, but last night was transcendent.

Something felt different. It felt more intense. It felt like the words that neither of us have ever said.

Our bodies reacted to each other like they never have before, and seeing her covered in my release changed something in my chemistry. She looked like mine, and seeing her laying there like that with her chest heaving, her pupils blown, her skin flushed—it made me feel feral, like I would go to the ends of this world and the next for her and no one could stop me.

Those three little words were on the tip of my tongue the entire evening, but I didn't say them for fear it would freak her out again and ruin our night, but I know I'm not going to be able to wait much longer.

My gut's telling me that she isn't just beginning to fall for me, that after last night, maybe like me, she's already there.

"You know, I was thinking…" Claire says, walking into the living room dressed for The Christmas Extravaganza wearing a thick pink sweater, a silk skirt that hits her mid-shin, and ankle boots. Her hair is down.

When she looks up at me, she must see what's written in my face. "What?" she asks.

"You look beautiful."

She smiles and walks over to where I stand. Pushing up on her toes, she plants a chaste kiss against my lips.

"I like your turtleneck." She smirks.

"Are you going to be cold in that skirt? It's freezing out."

She lifts the bottom hem, showing off her legs that are covered in opaque tights. "Fleeced-lined tights," she says. "They look like I'm just wearing tights, but I'm very cozy. They're like magic."

"Ha! So what were you thinking?" I ask.

"Oh, right. In the ballet, after "Waltz of the Flowers," which will be Aster's entry, the Sugar Plum Fairy and her Cavalier dance, and then all of the Kingdom of Sweets characters return for the finale before sending Clara and the Nutcracker Prince home."

"Okay, so what does that mean?"

"I don't think the ballet will be finished once we judge Aster's cocktail. I think we have to see it through all the way to the end."

"So, you think Stella needs to dance?"

"Maybe, but it depends on the version. In some of them, when Clara isn't played by a child, she and the Nutcracker Prince share the final dance."

"So which one do you think we're living in?"

"Well I'm not a child, so I think maybe we need to dance tonight just to be sure."

"Dance?"

She nods her head. "Yeah. Dance."

"What kind of dance are we talking about? Like the devil's tango?" I tip my chin toward the bedroom and wiggle my eyebrows.

"No, like a proper dance." She swats my chest and begins walking toward the coat closet.

"I don't know," I say, following her. "Maybe we should try it just to be sure. Don't you think so?"

I wrap my arms around her waist, flipping her around to face me.

"You can never be too careful with these kinds of things," I whisper against her neck, and her whole body shudders against me.

"You're ridiculous. We've already had sex twice since we woke up."

"We could do it again. We have time…"

She shakes her head, letting out a giggle.

"We actually have no time. Stella said to be there at one, and that's in less than ten minutes."

I let out a groan.

"Stella might be my least favorite person ever."

"Come on," she says, grabbing my hand and pulling me towards the door. "We have a ballet to finish."

Claire and I walk into town with our crowns and sashes in hand. Nerves ripple through me. If this doesn't work, and we don't wake up in New York City tomorrow, I don't know what Claire will do.

"This looks magical," she says as we walk down the street. "Do you hate it?"

Small booths are set up around the skating rink. Each one is decked out for the holiday. More lights have been strung above us for when it gets dark. A tree that rivals Rockefeller Center is waiting to be lit. Christmas music is being filtered in to add to the ambiance. The whole town seems to be here laughing and visiting with one another. Children dart in and out of the crowd, and a few people are skating. The sense of community wraps me in a warm hug, and the thought of leaving forever makes my chest ache.

"No," I say, chuckling. "I actually kinda like it."

She gasps. "Have I converted you to a Christmas lover?"

"I wouldn't go that far," I jest.

"Oh, come on and admit it."

"Fine," I grumble. "I *like* Christmas."

She claps her hands together. "I'll take it, and I knew you would if you gave it a chance."

"There you two are," Stella says, hurrying towards us. "I expected you to be here ten minutes ago."

Claire cuts her eyes at me.

"Sorry," I say. "We got caught up at the house."

"Well, quick, put on your crowns and sashes. You two have a competition to judge!"

We follow to the first booth, adjusting the sashes and crowns as we walk.

Chip is standing behind it with a warm smile.

"Chip has been kind enough to set up a tasting tray for you both," Stella explains. "Remember to take note of overall appearance, taste, and Christmas cheer."

She hands us two clipboards with score cards attached. "Put your scores here, and then I'll tally them."

There's an antique silver tray sitting on the small counter. On top is a stack of peppermint bark. Layers of dark, milk, and white chocolate are layered evenly and topped with crushed peppermint. Every piece is cut into a perfect triangle. Chip's lips are pressed together, and his fingers tap against the side of his leg.

"This looks delicious," Claire says, and Chip attempts a smile. He watches us closely as we each pick up a piece and take a bite.

"Holy shit!" I let out, taking a second bite of my piece.

Each layer of chocolate is creamy and perfectly balanced. It honestly might be the best chocolate I've ever tasted, and the peppermint adds a little festive kick.

I knew this would be fucking delicious, and it is. I can't imagine anyone else is gonna come close.

Chip watches us, and the nerves seem to melt off him as we both react to his creation.

"The recipe was my grandfather's," he explains, proudly.

I pick up two more before I'm finished with the first piece. "Just making sure it's consistent," I say as I begin to eat again.

Playfully shoving me, Claire shakes her head. "We have seven of these. Pace yourself."

"What, it's good," I say around a mouth full of chocolate.

"Great, now let's get a photo of all three of you together," Stella says.

The SDN photographer moves in front of us as we pose, and my mouth falls open when I see who she is—the reporter from the press conference.

"You," I say, pointing at her and causing Claire to whip her head in my direction.

"You're looking more settled since the last time I saw you." The reporter smiles.

"I'm s—"

"Now, Everett," Stella chimes. "Please smile, we have a busy day. You and Starla can catch up another time."

Starla brings her camera to her eye.

"Thank you," Claire says to Chip after we jot down our scores.

More settled? I look over at Claire, who's smiling and laughing with Stella. Taking a deep breath, I decide it doesn't matter. I am more settled. I don't need to analyze what she meant.

"Good afternoon," Joe says from behind his booth. "Ready for me to blow your minds?"

"You know my husband. He's convinced he's going to win this thing and you haven't even tried his drink yet." Cami calls from the booth next to his, laughing.

"She's just afraid I'm going to beat her," he whispers to the two of us. He slides two mugs to the edge of the counter.

One is bright green and covered with little, three dimensional Christmas lights, and the other is blue with a snowman. Each is topped with a healthy dollop of whipped cream and a dash of nutmeg. Both sit on top of a matching saucer and are accompanied by some sort of long, brown cookie.

"Yes, I'm dying for some caffeine," Claire says, picking up one of the mugs.

"What's this?" I ask, pointing to the accompaniment.

"Homemade gingerbread biscotti," Joe explains. "I think it tastes delicious when dipped into the latte."

"Thank you," Claire adds, lifting her mug and tapping it against the edge of mine. "Cheers!"

"Cheers," I repeat.

We both take a sip, savoring the warm, creamy drink. It's heavy on the nutmeg and cinnamon, but I don't hate it. Picking up the biscotti, I dip it in, trying what Joe suggested, and he's right—it does taste good.

Finishing our drinks, we mark our scores and pose for another photo before moving on along.

"How many more of these desserts do we have to try?" I groan.

"Five."

"I'm not used to this much sugar."

"Then maybe don't eat and drink everything they give us." She giggles.

"But it's so good."

Claire shakes her head.

"Hiya, you two," Cami sings. "I made a Christmas chai latte."

Sitting in front of us are two antique Christmas tea cups and saucers. Each one is topped with a simple star anise.

Claire reaches for her cup, and I do the same.

"Cheers!" I say, and we tap our cups together and take a sip. It's delicious, but not what I would usually drink. The spices overpower my mouth, and I smile through a few more sips before setting the cup down.

"The latte was delicious," Claire says to Cami.

"Blink twice if it was better than Joe's," she says playfully, looking back at her husband.

"Hey, no canoodling with the judges," Joe calls.

"Don't worry," I say. "We won't be giving anything away until the end."

"Thanks for stopping by you two," Cami says, after we've taken yet another photo.

Claire begins to write down her scores as we walk away, and I peek over her shoulder.

"Hey," she scolds. "You can't copy me. Pick your own scores."

"Come on," I whisper. "Let me see what you gave her."

"That's not how it works."

"I'll trade a kiss to see your scores."

"No."

I bend down close to her ear. "I'll do that thing with my tongue that you like if you—"

She shoves me away, a blush covering her face. "Tempting, but no. We have to do it right."

"Fine," I grumble as I do my best to judge Cami's latte.

Three Down. Five to go.

CHAPTER 40:
SAY, COOKIE

CLAIRE

"The decorations look good," I say as we approach Lolly's booth.

"I'm just glad they didn't kill me," Lolly says, cutting a look toward Stella.

"I told you, you and Chip were the right people for the job," Stella sings. "Now what did you make our king and queen?"

"Oh, I like that necklace," Lolly says, ignoring her.

My hands find the small snowflake, and I run it along the chain. "Everett gave it to me last night."

"It's really—"

"Ladies, please focus. We do not have all day. Lolly, what did you make?" Stella cuts in.

"Peppermint bark, of course." She smiles, tilting her head to the side.

On top of a Christmas plate covered with colorful lights and ornaments sits a stack of peppermint bark. Unlike Chip's, Lolly's has only two layers of chocolate—milk and white—and on top is a mix of peppermint, red and green chocolate candies, and festive sprinkles. A white chocolate drizzle zigzags across the tops of each piece. It's not cut perfectly, but instead broken into different sized pieces.

"This looks great," I say, reaching for a piece at the same time Everett does.

"I want that one," he says, our hands colliding. A spark shoots up my arm at the feel of his touch.

Popping up on my toes, I whisper into his ear, "I'll do that thing with my tongue you like if I can have it."

He swallows hard. "It's all yours, babe." I let out a snicker, and Lolly's eyes crease as she studies me.

The candy is scrumptious, and the added texture from the sprinkles and chocolate candies make it even more delicious.

We pause for a photo, and then we move on to the next booth.

"We'll catch up in a bit when this is all over," I say, marking my scores.

"We better. I want all the details about last night," she teases. "Good luck."

Reid doesn't offer a smile or greeting as we approach. His booth isn't decorated like the others, and he has a small, white tray covered in marzipan fruits.

Everett's eyes find mine, and he lifts a brow.

"Hi, Reid," I try.

"Hello."

"These look good," Everett says, reaching out and taking one shaped like a lemon. He pops it in his mouth and wrinkles his nose. I watch as he does his best to pretend like he's enjoying the candy as he slowly chews it and then swallows hard.

Picking up one shaped like a pear, I take a bite of the side of it, plastering on as much of a fake smile as I can as I chew.

It's not the worst thing I've ever eaten, but it's definitely not the best.

"Thank you," I say, and we quickly score his entry. We all pose for a photo then move to the next booth.

"Please tell me whatever is next is going to be better than that," Everett whispers.

"Stella?"

"Yes, dear?"

"Could we get a couple bottles of water?"

"Oh, of course. I'll be right back." She turns to leave as we approach Ginger's booth.

"Hello, Nuttalls," she trills.

"Did the kids help you make these?" I ask, eyeing the dessert. Messy icing and lots of sprinkles cover a plate full of sugar cookies

—they look like Christmases past, and nostalgia hits me right in the chest.

Ginger's children maze around us, playing in the snow. One of her girls stops and watches as Everett and I reach forward for a cookie.

"I helped make the green angel," she says, flashing a toothy grin. "Try mine, Mrs. Claire."

"Okay, sweetheart," I say, taking an angel shaped cookie covered in green icing and pink sprinkles.

Reaching forward, Everett takes a red Christmas bell covered in green sprinkles.

It's soft and chewy, and it unlocks a memory of making cookies with my grandmother as a little girl.

"Do you like my cookie," the little girl asks.

"It's very good," I assure her.

Stella returns and hands both of us water. Sipping it, I do my best to judge the entry, but it feels harder than it should be.

"Let's get a photo with The Nuttalls, Ginger, and all the kids," Stella says, directing the photographer.

"Kids," Ginger calls. "Ms. Stella wants a picture with Coach Everett and Mrs. Claire. Come on now."

Everett and I move together in front of the counter. Ginger and her kids circle around us.

"Say *cookie*," Ginger chimes.

We begin to move toward the last booth, and Everett's hand finds mine.

"Judging some of these is harder than I thought it would be," I admit. "I just feel like we've gotten to know these people, and I don't want to hurt their feelings."

He squeezes my hand. "They know we were given a job and it's not personal, but I agree—I'm going to really miss everyone."

"Me too."

"Hey, lady," Aster says, waving at us. "Ready to get your drink on?"

In front of her are two stemless wine glasses full of red liquid. Each one is topped with a sugared rosemary, a cinnamon stick, and pomegranate seeds.

"Finally, something that isn't super sweet," I say, taking one of the glasses. "What is it called?"

"A Mistletoe Kiss."

"It looks so good."

"It was super easy," she says. "I'll text you the recipe."

"Please," I say. Turning to face Everett, I lift my glass to toast with his.

"To whatever tomorrow brings," he says.

"To tomorrow," I repeat, clinking my glass against his. We both take a sip of the drink. The tart citrus flavors dance across my tongue, and the hint of vodka burns my throat.

"Damn," Everett says, "That's great."

Aster smiles and shrugs her shoulders.

"It really is good," I agree, taking another sip.

"Fantastic," Stella bursts, clapping her hands. "Now you two pose with Aster, and then we'll be all done with this part of the day. Feel free to enjoy the festivities, and I'll meet you in front of the tree at"—she checks her watch—"seven sharp to announce the winner."

I jot down my final scores and hand her back the clipboard, and Everett does the same. My heart sinks a little at how bittersweet it all feels.

"Enjoy your evening," Stella says, walking away. "I hope it's everything you ever wanted it to be."

Seven dances down. One to go.

CHAPTER 41: DOES SHE KNOW YOU LOVE HER?

EVERETT

Today has made my heart feel fuller than ever. After the competition, Claire and I spent the afternoon with the people who we've grown to care about, and I can see why she loves this time of year so much. There's something special about spending time with people who fill you up and make you feel good, and I think that it's something I want to do more of when I get back to New York. Just not with Claire, but with my friends and family too.

We make our way to the front of the Christmas tree where a podium with a microphone is set up. The sun is gone, and stars fill the night sky. The lights strung between the buildings are glowing and casting warm light along the snow covered street.

A crowd is gathering in front, and I look around, spotting all the people we're going to miss when this is over. A light dusting of snow begins to fall around everyone.

Stella taps the mic, and the thuds send a hush over the town. "Welcome to the Sugarplum Park Annual Christmas Extravaganza," she chimes. Applause erupts, and she gestures for everyone to settle down. "Thank you to everyone who helped make today possible. I thought we'd kick things off by announcing the winner of the competition."

She gestures for me and Claire to walk forward.

"Our king and queen have scored all of the entries, and I tallied the results. So without further ado…" She hands Claire an envelope, and we both step up to the microphone. Claire's eyes find mine, and I nod, encouraging her to open it.

"The winner of this year's Christmas Cup goes to..." Claire begins, her eyes going wide as she flashes the card towards me.

"Lolly from The Gum Drop Sugar Shop," I announce.

The crowd erupts in applause, and Lolly wraps Aster in a hug before making her way toward us. Claire throws her arms around her friend and squeezes her tight. Both of their faces are pure joy, and my chest tightens at the thought that going home means Claire will lose her.

"I can't believe it," Lolly says.

"Congratualtions," I offer, moving backwards so Stella can take my place. Lolly takes the silver Christmas Cup trophy and holds it into the air. More applause and cheers come from the town, and Stella steps up to mic, thumping it once more to quiet everyone down.

"And now the moment you've all been waiting for," she says, lifting her arms and then dropping them at the same moment the tree behind us bursts with light.

Everyone's eyes are glued to its magnificence except for Lolly's. Hers are locked on Chip, and his are locked on hers. Shaking his head, I watch as he leaves the crowd and walks away.

"Shit," Lolly mutters under her breath.

"I'll go," I offer, catching Claire's eyes and handing her my crown before I move off the stage and after him.

"Chip, wait up man," I call as I approach him on the outskirts of the party. "You aren't heading in? The night's still young."

"She's so fucking infuriating," he says, turning to face me.

"Who?" I ask, trying not to chuckle.

"Lolly."

"I don't know. Claire seems to like her, and I think she's pretty cool."

He throws back his head and exhales, causing a white puff of smoke to appear in front of his face.

"You don't get it. You don't know what it's like to have a woman get under your skin like this." He starts to pace in the street. "She's maddening the way she walks around the town looking like some type of goddess. She makes me feel insane, and then she had to go and make the exact thing I made and do it better. Because of course she would because she has to be so fucking perfect all of the time."

"Does she know you love her?"

"What? I don't love her."

I shrug. "Kind of sounds like you might."

"No." He shakes his head. "Impossible. She drives me nuts. I'm just pissed she beat me."

I chuckle. "Claire drives me nuts sometimes, but it's part of the reason why I love her so much. She tests me and pushes me like no one else has before."

"I don't love Lolly."

Exhaling, I hesitate before I say the next part because I realize I have to choose my words carefully.

"You know Claire has an opportunity in a different city."

"What?"

"Yeah, uh…we haven't said anything to anyone, but I think we might be…uh…*moving*."

"Moving?" His mouth falls open.

"Yeah, and for a while I've found myself considering not *moving* because life feels really easy here, and going to this other place would bring back some…um… *feelings* I never fully dealt with." I roll my shoulder and swallow hard.

"Seems like a really weird time to tell me this, Everett."

"I have a point. I promise."

He nods.

"The thing is, I realized that even if *moving* makes me uncomfortable, I'm willing to feel that way if it means Claire will be happy."

"Well, yeah, because you love her. Everyone knows you'd do anything for her."

"Exactly, so I say all of this because I think you aren't actually mad that Lolly beat you. I think you're freaking out because you're realizing you'd gladly lose the competition that meant a lot to you, if it meant she was happy."

He stops moving and stares at me, his eyes blinking like he's realizing his feelings for her for the first time.

"I could be completely off base, and by all means you're welcome to go wallow about losing somewhere else, but if I were you, I'd go get the girl." I nod back in the direction of the festival.

He nods and looks behind me. "I want to talk more about this move, but—"

"Go get her," I say. He takes off jogging to find her, and I turn to find Claire standing a few feet away from me.

"Was all that true?" she asks.

"How much did you hear?"

"Just the part where apparently we're moving." Her face breaks into a grin. "Have you really considered not going back?"

"Not really. I don't know," I say, walking toward her. "I mean, I don't really want to face the reality about my shoulder and what it means for my career, and not being in pain everyday has been nice, but I'm not going to let my fear get in the way of your dreams."

"I don't want you to be in pain though," she says.

I shake my head. "No. I told you I'd get you home, and that's what I plan to do. Whatever is waiting for me back in New York, I'll be able to handle it if you're next to me."

She pops up on her toes and kisses me.

"Ready to go share our final dance?" she asks.

We turn, walking back to the party and onto the make-shift dance floor. The crowd seems to part as I take Claire's hand and begin to spin her around as the music plays.

"You know how to dance?" she asks.

"What, like it's hard," I tease, spinning her out and then back into me.

"Seems like your pep talk worked," Claire says as Chip and Lolly join us.

She smiles towards her friend, and Lolly grins as Chip spins her into his chest.

One by one, the rest of the town begins to join us. Cami and Joe and then Ginger and Rusty. Their kids grab Aster by the hand, pulling her on to the dance floor, and the little girls giggle as she spins them in circles over and over.

Stella floats by us, heading straight for a very uncomfortable looking Reid.

"Oh no!" Claire laughs. "He's not going to like this."

"Now, come on," Stella sing-songs as she moves. "Everyone must dance, and that includes you, Reid." She takes his hands, and a blush covers his face as she begins to drag him around to the music.

"I'm surprised Lolly won," Claire says as we sway to the music. "She was my third highest score. I voted for Ginger."

"Really?"

"Yeah. You voted for her?" she asks.

"No, she was like fourth on my scorecard."

We both turn to find Stella and begin to laugh.

"She rigged it," Claire says.

"Sounds about right."

Pulling her close to me, I breathe her in. "You know," I whisper. "There's a real chance that tomorrow we'll wake up here."

"I know," she says, laying her head against my chest.

"How does that make you feel?"

"Honestly," she says, peering up at me. "I think if that happens, then I'll know we tried, and I'd be more than content to live out the rest of my days married to you here. I'm realizing that home for me is wherever you are. You?"

She thinks *I* feel like home. My heart leaps in my chest and then dips down into my stomach.

"Yeah, Sugar, I think I'd be good with that too."

My heart rate begins to build, and my mouth goes dry.

"What's wrong?" she asks, sensing my shift and slowing our dance.

"I don't know what tomorrow is going to bring, but I do need you to know that I love you."

Her breath hitches.

"I've been wanting to say it, and I don't expect for you to say—"

"I love you too," she says, smiling.

"You do?"

"Yeah. I love you so much," she repeats.

My mouth finds hers in a passionate kiss, the snow continuing to fall, and the whole world blurs into swirls of pink around us.

CHAPTER 42: COULD IT BE?

CLAIRE

DECEMBER EIGHTEENTH

Laying in bed, I try to ignore all the sounds coming from outside my window—dogs barking, people shouting, horns honking, and an ambulance siren blaring. The sunlight pouring through the blinds causes me to squint as I fumble to grab my phone off the nightstand and check the time. It's not even eight in the morning.

Groaning, I shut my eyes tightly and shift backward in the bed, expecting to nuzzle against my sleeping husband, but I don't feel him behind me. Flipping over, confusion overtakes me. Instead of Everett, I'm met with a pile of cream and olive blankets and pillows gathered into a messy pile.

Cream and olive. Not pink.

Sitting up, my pulse begins to race as I take in the room I'm in. I'm on a large king-sized bed with a rattan headboard and black trim. The neutral colored bedding is gathered around me. The bed is framed by two large, black, wooden bedside tables. Each is adorned with a large ceramic lamp. My alarm clock and a photo of me with my sister sit on the nightstand to my left.

"Everett!" I yell.

Nothing.

This is my apartment in New York, and Everett isn't here. He's gone.

Reaching for my phone, I frantically search for his phone number, but it's not there. My chest aches as I try to think through the night before, and nothing makes sense. Why would he leave?

Swiping through my contacts, I click on my sister's name. It begins to ring, and a mix of emotions washes over me when I hear her voice.

"Hello," she says, groggily.

"Andi?"

There's a pause, and the sound of her moving in bed to sit up to talk to me comes through the phone.

"Uh, yeah, who else would it be?" She ends her question with a yawn.

"I just…I wasn't expecting you to answer… I've missed you so much." The words spill out frantically as I try to deduce what's happened.

I should be happy that I woke up in my own bed. I should be relieved to finally talk to my sister, but I'm none of those things. If I can't have him in this world too, then I don't want to be here.

"We were literally together less than twelve hours ago. At the hockey game, remember? What are you talking about?"

Pulling the phone away from my ear, I check the date—December eighteenth.

"Oh."

"You okay, Sis?"

Looking over at the empty side of the bed, reality hits me like a bolt of lightning to the heart. It was all a dream, and he left without saying goodbye because, in this reality, last night was a one-night stand.

He doesn't love me. He never did.

"Claire? You there?"

Pressure builds behind my eyes, and I do my best to hold it together. It seems so silly to cry about a dream, even if that dream was maybe the best one I've ever had.

"Yeah…um…I just had a crazy dream last night. Everett and I hooked up, and I dreamt that we woke up in this…uh, it doesn't matter."

"You hooked up in your dream?"

"No, he came home with me last night after the game."

"What do you mean Everett came home with you last night?"

she practically yells through the phone, excitement covering every word.

"Geez, Andi."

"Forgive me, but I'm trying to wrap my head around this very new information you're telling me because when I left you last night, you were dating Raph, and now you're telling me that you hooked up with your hottie ex from back in the day."

"He's not my ex."

He's my husband. Or, he was my husband.

Sugarplum Park never happened.

"Well you used to sleep with him, and now you're sleeping with him again. So can you please explain what happened?"

My gaze drops to my hand. There's no ring on my finger, and my heart aches at the thought that none of it was real.

We aren't married.

I do my best to recall the night with my sister, but it feels like a lifetime has passed, and I don't know what to make of this feeling.

"Raph was cheating. I ran into Everett at a bar and brought him home," I say, holding back tears.

"And? Is he still there? Did he stay over?"

Pinching my eyes shut, I run my hands over my face and then through my hair. "Yeah, with the power out, he stayed, but he's already gone." My voice cracks.

"Power out?"

"There wasn't a blackout last night because of the weather?"

"No."

A sob bubbles out of my throat.

"Are you okay? You sound so upset and aren't making sense. I knew I didn't like Raph. What an asshole. If I ever come face to face with him, he's going to get a piece of my mind."

But he's not the reason I sound like this. Everett is, but how do I explain that to her without sounding crazy?

More tears begin to fall, and I wipe them away with the back of my hand. I try to explain myself but instead just end up sobbing into the phone. Incoherent jumbles of nonsense is all I can form, and once I start, I can't stop.

"Oh Claire Bear, I'm coming over."

"No...no...um..." I try to take some calming breaths and swallow down the sadness that's flooding my head.

This is ridiculous. It was a fantasy concocted by me, not a break up. It's impossible to lose the love of your life when he only existed inside your head. "I need to get up and get to the studio anyway. I'm okay. Just tired and emotional," I manage.

A male's voice says something in the background of the call.

"Who's that?" I ask.

"Isaac. I went to see him after the game. Remember?" She moves the phone away from her mouth, and her voice becomes muffled as she tells him something I can't quite make out.

"Right. Well, I'll let you go."

"Are you sure you don't want me to come over?"

"Yeah." I look down at the time. "If I don't get up, I'll be late."

"I thought you didn't have rehearsals until ten?"

"Yeah, I just want to grab a shower and get some coffee. Don't want to rush."

"Okay. Call me if you want to hang out tonight. I can bring over all the breakup snacks, and you can wallow about Raph while we gorge ourselves on wine and ice cream."

"Yeah, okay."

"I love you."

"I love you too."

The call drops, and I force myself to crawl out of bed. Shuffling across the floor, I move to my dresser and open the bottom drawer. Digging wildly, I don't stop until I find the old, worn Crowns T-shirt Everett left with me four and a half years ago. Pulling it on, I breathe it in, but it doesn't smell like him anymore. I allow myself to cry for a few moments then inhale deeply, trying to calm down.

Standing, I head to the bathroom, rogue tears continuing to fall. I should pull myself together. Crying over a man from a dream surely means I need to be committed, but I can't shake the feeling that it actually happened. That our love for each other was real, and I'm not crazy, but that's impossible. If it had happened, he'd be here.

Bending over the sink, I splash some cold water on my face, patting it away gently with a washcloth, and then stare at my reflection.

I try to remember what happened after our kiss, but it's blurry.

My long black hair is still wavy from the curls I wore last night. Underneath his shirt is the lace bralette and thong that I fell asleep wearing after the game. Did I wear this to bed in Sugarplum Park too? Why can't I remember?

Everything feels the same, except it's not.

I'm in my bathroom in New York, and I wish more than anything in the world I was still Everett Nuttall's wife.

The chain of my necklace is turned, and so I slowly start to flip the clasp to the back, expecting to see my initial move to the front, but I pause when I don't reveal the C charm I usually wear.

No.

Between my fingers is a small, diamond-encrusted snowflake—just like the one Everett gave me for Christmas. I swallow hard as I run my fingers over the small jewels. My heart rate quickens and my breaths become a little more rapid. If I'm wearing this necklace, then that would mean...

The sound of my front door opening echoes through my apartment, interrupting my thoughts, causing my heart to drop into my stomach.

Could it be?

ACT 3:
Home

Chapter 43: Never
Everett

Pushing the door open, I set the food, coffee, and newspaper I found on the doorstep this morning on the table and then close the door. A sharp pain shoots down my arm and catches my breath.

Fuck, it hurts.

Checking the time on my phone, it's a little after eight, and according to the notification from my calendar, I need to be at the training facility by ten. I consider taking some more ibuprofen, but I figure I should wait and ask the doctor.

I remove my shoes by the door, then pick up the breakfast, moving across the apartment. I'm halfway to the kitchen when the door to the bedroom swings open, revealing Claire.

"Morning, Sugar." I smile. "I got us some food and—"

She takes a step toward me but doesn't say anything. Her face is flush, her eyes red and swollen like she's been crying.

"What's wrong?" I ask, setting everything down on the coffee table and moving to where she stands.

"You weren't here," she says, her voice shaking as tears stream down her cheeks. In one more large stride, I make it to her and wrap her up in my arms. She collapses into me, and her whole body begins to shake as she cries. "I thought I'd lost you forever."

"You could never lose me." My hands rub along her spine, trying to soothe her. "I'm sorry I didn't leave a note. I thought I could make it back before you woke up, and then the line at the bagel place was out the door. I tried to call—"

"But you didn't have my number."

"Yeah."

"Is that my shirt?"

"When you weren't here, I dug out and put it on hoping it would smell like you, but it didn't."

"Oh, baby. I'm so sorry."

She takes a few deep breaths and leans back so that she can see me. "How did you know it was real?"

"I just did."

"What do you mean?"

Running my hands through her hair, I gently cup her face. "Claire, I'd love you in every realm. In every world. In every version of our story. It doesn't matter where we are, I will never stop loving you."

"Never?"

"Never."

My mouth finds hers and I pick her up, attempting to swallow down a groan as pain radiates down my arm, but I fail.

"What's wrong?" she says, pulling back.

"It's just my shoulder, but it's okay," I say, trying to kiss her again.

"No, put me down," she protests. "I don't want to hurt you."

She wiggles out of my arms. Gently, she runs her hand over the sore joint.

"We don't have to do this if it's painful."

"But I really want to make love to you," I say, bending forward to kiss her. "I feel like getting back to New York deserves a little celebration."

"Okay," she says, grabbing my hand. "Then I can be gentle."

She leads me back into her bedroom, slowly walking us to the bed.

"Lay down," she says, patting the mattress. "I have an idea."

She turns and walks toward her bathroom, disappearing inside for a few moments. When she returns, she's holding a bottle of lotion.

"Would a massage help it feel better?"

I nod and carefully remove my shirt.

She climbs in next to me and lathers a little of the sweet smelling cream into her hands.

Straddling my waist, the hem of the T-shirt gathers at her hips, revealing her lace thong.

"Look at you," I say, in awe of her, my hands running up her thighs. "You're perfect."

A small smile ghosts her lips, and she places her hands on my bare chest, working them up and over my shoulders and then down my arms.

"Did that hurt?" she asks.

"No."

"Good. If it does, let me know and I'll stop." She repeats the same motion, but this time her hips grind forward against my growing erection.

"Move like that again and I don't think I'm going to be able to wait much longer."

Mischief sparkles behind her blue eyes as she lets out a melodic laugh and repeats the motion, moving her hands across my body and rotating her hips again, but this time with more purpose like it's getting her off too.

My whole body heats as she works me, and I don't think I've ever experienced anything as hot or as tender as this.

Biting her lower lip, she thrusts her hips forward again, and the feeling is agonizing.

"Fuck," I breathe out. "I need you."

Moving off me, she grips the waistband of my sweatpants and boxer briefs, moving them down and over my hips.

My cock springs free, and her hand finds my length. Gently, she runs her palm over the sensitive skin, and my whole body shudders under her touch.

"I need to touch you," I pant.

Her thumb runs over the head, playing with the studs of my piercing.

"Claire," I beg. "I'm so fucking desperate for you. Please let me touch you."

She lets go, and I immediately miss her touch. She quickly removes her underwear, then crawls back up to straddle me again.

With my cock lined at her center, she slowly moves me through her wet slit but doesn't push me inside, moaning as I graze against her clit.

There is nothing chaste or hurried about what we're doing. It's purely intimate. Her eyes find mine for a split second and then dip to where we're touching.

"Do you like this," she asks, breathless and slowly continuing to tease her pussy with my cock.

"You have no idea," I say, not pulling my eyes from where we're joined. She's drenched just from this, and the desire to fill her barrels through me.

"Make love to me," I say.

Lifting her hips slightly, she lines me up again and then slides down my length until she's taken all of me. Her head lolls back, and a loud moan leaves her as she stretches around me.

Tenderly, we begin to move against one another in perfect sync, but she feels too far away.

Sitting up, I move her legs so that they're around my back. Her hands find the back of my head, running through my hair, and my arms hold her close.

We don't even feel like two people anymore, so connected that we might as well be one.

"I love you," she murmurs between kisses.

"I love you too."

Her movements become more rushed as she chases her release. Our mouths continue to tangle as she moves up and down on my shaft. I do my best to match her pace and tilt my hips just right.

"Fuck…I'm going to…ah…" She pants. "Come with me."

Tension coils at the base of my spine, and her pussy flutters around me as we both fall, moaning into each other's kiss.

The feeling is euphoric, and I know at this moment that whatever happens now that we're back, with my shoulder or my career, it doesn't matter. The only thing that matters is how much we love one another, and nothing can go wrong as long as we have each other.

Rolling out of bed, we both move to get cleaned up, and I accidentally knock my phone on to the floor and under the bed.

"Dammit," I call out, dropping to the floor to pick it up.

"What happened?" she asks, walking to meet me.

"My phone slid under the bed," I explain, pushing my good arm under the frame, but the space between it and the floor is small. My face is scrunched up against the hard surface of the bed, and my bare ass is pushed up into the air while I continue to search. I can't see what I'm reaching for. "Fuck."

She begins to giggle. "That's quite the position you're in." She cocks her head to the side as I look up toward her. "Do you need help?"

"No, I think…"

My fingers brush up against something hard, and I shove my arm forward as far as I can, gripping the object and pulling it out.

"Shit," I say, staring at the little blue rock I'm holding. "This isn't even my phone."

"What is that?" Claire asks from above me. Handing it to her, I shove the same arm back under the bed. My hand finds something hard again, and I grip it.

"Got it!" I pull my phone out and pop up to meet Claire, but her eyes are locked on the blue stone. "You good?"

"This is apatite," she says, running her hands over it.

"Huh?" I say, standing to meet her.

"How long do you think it's been under there?" she asks.

"No idea," I say, taking it from her and placing it on the nightstand. "I thought we decided those stones were bullshit."

"Hmm…yeah…maybe."

We both get cleaned up and walk into the living room. Sitting on the couch, her eyes land on the newspaper. "What's that?"

"Oh, it was on the doormat when I got back this morning. Figured I'd bring it in."

"Like right outside my door?"

"Mmhmm," I say, unwrapping my bagel.

"That's weird," she says, grabbing it. "I don't get the paper." She slowly unfolds it, and a smile erupts across her face.

"What is it?" I ask around a bite of food.

"Just the Sugarplum Daily News," she says, turning it to face me. On the front page is a photo of me, her, and Lolly, and the headline reads "Lolly Levine Takes The Christmas Cup."

Moving to sit next to her, we scan each page of the paper and find every photo we took at the Extravaganza.

Tears form in Claire's eyes. "I'm really glad it was real."

"Me too, Sugar."

Bending over, I place a kiss on her forehead, happy to be back in New York with the girl of my dreams.

CHAPTER 44: GOODBYE, FOR NOW

EVERETT

DECEMBER TWENTY-SECOND

The past few days have been full of ups and downs, the only consistent thing being Claire and me. She's been so patient while I talked with my doctors and navigated my decision about what I should do about my shoulder—and ultimately, my career. I couldn't have done it without her.

The front of Madison Square Garden looks like we're here for my celebration of life, and fuck it's depressing. My photo is on every screen with the words: Thank you Everett Nuttall. I'm sitting at a long table with the Crowns' general manager, Grant Ackerly, and our head coach, Rob Zillman. Behind us is a backdrop covered in the Crowns' insignia, and off to the side is Sally overseeing it all. The crowd is a mix of my teammates and reporters, all poised to hear what I have to say.

Scanning the crowd, I exhale when I see Claire sitting in the back row. Her eyes are locked on mine, and she gives me a reassuring smile. I know that this is the right move, but it doesn't make it easier.

"We want to thank everyone for being here this morning," my coach begins. "I think instead of hearing from me, I'm going to go ahead and turn it over to the man of the hour."

Everyone's eyes land on me, and I nervously shuffle the notecards in front of me that are covered with the speech Claire helped me write.

"First, I want to thank everyone for coming out. I realize it's a busy week with the holiday right around the corner, so this means a lot."

My eyes find Claire, and she nods, encouraging me to keep going.

"As you all know, I'm no longer healthy enough to continue to play. This decision to retire did not come lightly, since hockey has been my life for as long as I can remember, but after talking with the team doctors, I decided that it was best that I go out on my own terms, and I can't think of a better team to end my career with."

A few flashes from cameras light-up, and I clear my throat, swallowing down the tears threatening to break free.

"As a kid, I dreamed of playing for the New York Crowns, and I'll never forget the opportunity they gave me at the start of my career. No where else has felt like home, like this arena and the people associated with this organization have. When the opportunity presented itself to come back at the start of the season, I was thrilled, and while I didn't foresee my career ending this early, it does feel right to finish out my career with this team."

Lifting my head, I see Claire smile and give me a thumbs up.

"Recent events in my personal life have shown me that life is too short to live in pain, and so I hope the fans can understand this decision. We have some of the best fans in the league, and I am looking forward to joining them and forever cheering on the Crowns."

Taking a deep breath, I shift the cards in front of me.

"There are so many people I want to take this opportunity to thank, so please bear with me while I try to get through the list." A few chuckles echo through the crowd. "Coach Rob, it's been an honor getting to play for you again. You believed in me when I was a rookie, and I will be forever grateful to have played for you. To the rest of the coaching staff, thank you for your support and your guidance."

I shift in my seat, trying to hold it together.

"Mr. Ackerly, thank you for believing in this team and me. To the team medical staff, thank you for your honest guidance while I navigated this decision. I'd like to thank my team. It's been the honor of my career to be your captain. I truly believe you all have what it takes to go all the way, and I look forward to watching it happen."

Clearing my throat, I find Claire again, and she nods her head, calming my nerves.

"I know my family, especially my nieces will be watching this, so I need to give them a shout out." I chuckle. "Elsie and Iris, thank you for keeping my locker decorated with your drawings and for being my biggest fans. I can't think of two more special kids. To the rest of my family, thank you for making it possible for me to live out my dream. If it hadn't been for my parents supporting this passion from a very young age, none of us would be here today. And lastly..." I find Claire one more time, and my eyes become glossy. "I'd like to thank my girlfriend, Claire Silverman."

Gasps roll through the crowd, and a smile breaks across my face.

"I guess you all can consider this our hard launch." I chuckle, earning some laughs from the crowd. "Claire, I love you, and I could've never come to this decision without your unwavering support and understanding."

Her eyes fill with tears as she mouths "I love you too." Sitting back, I rub my eyes, wiping away the tears that are now falling.

"I'm just grateful," I say. "And I hope that this isn't the last you see of me."

The crowd stands and erupts into applause. I allow myself a moment to take it all in and feel every feeling I'm having about the end of my career as I've known it. The applause settles down, and a highlight video of my career begins playing on the large screen, catching everyone's attention but Claire's. Her eyes stay locked on me, reassuring me from across the room that it's all going to be okay.

"The girls keep making me replay the part where you say their names," Maren, my sister, says over FaceTime.

"Hi, Uncle Everett!" Elsie sing-songs, popping into view over my sister's shoulder. "Is Claire there?"

"Hey, Els! Yeah, she's right here." I turn the phone so that Claire comes into view.

"Hi, Elsie," she says, waving, but my niece has already disappeared.

"Sorry, the TV is on," Maren explains.

"It's okay," Claire says, laughing, and I flip the phone back to me.

"So, anyway," Maren continues, "how are you feeling now that you're officially done?"

"Exhausted. I knew it would be hard to announce, but it's just been a whirlwind all day. Looking forward to relaxing over the holidays before my surgery."

"That's part of the reason I was calling; I wanted to go over the plan for this weekend. Our flight lands around three forty-five on the twenty-sixth, so we'll probably head straight to the hotel and let the girls rest and chill out. And then we'll see you on the twenty-seventh."

"Yeah," I agree, smiling to myself. "I'm really happy you're coming in town. It's been a long time."

"I'm really happy you called and asked us to. It's been too long," she says. "The girls are so excited to get to see the city and have already picked out their dresses for *The Nutcracker*. Please, thank Claire for the tickets to the show."

"It was nothing," Claire says. "I can't wait to meet you all."

"Alright, well it's getting late here, and I need to get these two into bed, but I'm really proud of you."

"Thanks, Sis. See you soon."

"Love you," she says.

"I love you guys too."

The call ends, and I set my phone down on the table. Claire moves to lay next to me, and I wrap my arms around her.

"Thank you for coming today," I say. "I couldn't have gotten through that speech without you being there. It meant a lot to me."

"I wouldn't have missed it. How are you feeling about it all?"

"Good," I admit. "I mean, it wasn't easy, and I'd be lying if I said I wasn't going to miss playing, but I know I made the right decision, and I'm looking forward to what the future might bring."

"I understand. When I finally hang up my pointe shoes, I know it'll be a really bittersweet day."

"How are you feeling about the show? It's just a couple of days away."

"Nervous," she says. "I've been dreaming about this my entire life, and I just really want to do it justice, you know?"

"You will."

"Rehearsals have been going good, so I feel confident."

I kiss the top of her head and run my hand up and down her back. "I'm really looking forward to seeing you dance and meeting your family in person."

"They're really excited. You know it's weird—when I realized Sugarplum Park actually happened, I was a little worried everyone in our lives would question us. Like be suspicious of us claiming to love one another, but no one has. Not even my sister."

"I like to think some residual magic is responsible." I chuckle. "I don't know. I think it has Stella's name written all over it."

"You're probably right. I've been finding myself missing the town," she admits. "Don't get me wrong, I'm glad we're back, and I'll never be able to thank you enough for helping us get here despite everything returning meant for you, but I wish we could've brought the people with us."

"I feel the same way."

"Do you think they still exist out there?"

"What do you mean?"

"Like do you think they're still living their lives without us, or when we left, did they disappear too?"

"I like to think they still exist."

"So do I."

She nestles into my chest, and I breathe in her sweet perfume.

"So, what do you want to do the rest of the day?" she asks after a few quiet moments have passed.

"I was thinking maybe we could put on a Christmas movie and order some take-out?" I suggest.

A wide grin spreads across her face.

"Sounds perfect."

CHAPTER 45:
ABSOLUTELY MAGICAL

CLAIRE

The live orchestra plays the final notes of Tchaikovsky's "Waltz of the Flowers," and the Dewdrop Fairy and the corps dancers take their final bows on stage as the crowd erupts in applause.

Adrenaline courses through me as my partner takes my hand in his, and I ready myself for my final dance of the night.

The crowd quiets, and I close my eyes, inhaling deeply and calming my nerves.

I can do this.

My eyes open as the beginning notes of Tchaikovsky's "Grand Pas De Deux" begin to play, and he leads me on stage.

The slow tempo of the music is beautiful, and I move, on pointe, with each soft rise and fall, doing my best to settle my racing heart and control my breathing as I hold each pose and extension perfectly. The audience claps softly with each impressive movement, and pride swells in my chest that I'm not only living out my dream, but I'm doing it well.

The bright stage lights warm my body, and with every twirl and dip, I grow more confident in my ability to perform the dance I've worked my whole career for.

The music shifts, and with the rising crescendo, I float across the stage, leaping into my partner's arms. He brings me to his shoulder, and I maintain my composure, breathing out a sigh of relief that the first of many lifts is done.

He slowly spins us around, and despite the bright lights, my eyes land on Everett in the front row of the audience. His eyes are locked on me, and pure amazement covers his entire face.

We finish the first part of the dance, each taking our bows as the crowd erupts. He guides me off stage, and the minute I'm out of view, I start inhaling deeply, trying to catch my breath, knowing I don't have long until I'm required to be back in the spotlight.

From off-stage, I watch as the music begins again, and my partner shows off a series of leaps, wowing the crowd.

On my cue, I replace him. It's only twenty seconds, but the series of turns and leaps make my head spin, and I do my best to push through the feeling, holding my form until it's time to disappear off stage once more.

He returns, and I work to calm my equilibrium as I prepare myself for our grand finale.

Rejoining him, I perform spins and leaps that are perfectly timed to the music. Moving away from him, we take each side of the stage, and I spin toward him as the music builds before ending at the same time he dips me.

The audience erupts, and we stand, taking a bow and then moving off the stage to make room for the encore.

The orchestra strikes up the final song, and one by one, each group of dancers performs their final dance—Chocolate, Coffee, Tea, Candy Canes, Marzipan, Mother Ginger and her polichinelles, and the Dewdrop and her flowers—and then pose around the perimeter. As I watch each perform, I'm reminded of the friends I was lucky enough to get the chance to know even if it was just for a little while.

On our cue, my partner and I return to the stage and complete a series of lifts at center stage before joining our fellow dancers in the last dance of the night.

Adrenaline pours through me as I near the end. Making my way to the front, I perform my final pirouette and hit my final pose.

The music shifts and the lights dim as Clara and the Nutcracker Prince make their way off stage. My chest rises and falls as I do my best to control my breathing and maintain the perfect pose until the curtain is completely closed and the ballet is officially over.

Walking out from backstage, I'm met by my parents and Andi. All three of them wrap me in a hug before stepping back, revealing Everett behind them.

A large bouquet of anemones is in his hand, and his body crashes into mine as we wrap each other in an embrace.

"You were stunning, Sugar," he says, pulling back but not letting me go. He bends down, his lips finding mine, and from behind us, I hear my sister let out a dramatic "Awwwww."

"Could you not ruin our moment?" I quip, looking over to where she stands.

"What kind of little sister would I be if I didn't?" she retorts, smirking.

"How are you feeling?" Everett asks.

"Tired, but really proud of myself," I say, letting him go and taking the bouquet of flowers.

"You should be, Claire Bear," my dad boasts.

I offer them a smile. "Thank you all for coming. It means the world."

"We wouldn't have missed it," Andi says.

"No place I'd rather be," Everett adds.

He pulls me against him again, kissing the top of my head.

"What do you say we get out of here and go have some Christmas dinner?" my mom says.

"Yes, carbs sound like exactly what I need."

We walk outside with my family. My feet and body ache in ways I didn't know they could. Exhaustion covers my every move as I pull my coat tight around me.

"We'll see you at your apartment?" my dad asks as a cab pulls up next to the sidewalk.

"Yep, we will be right behind you," I reply.

We watch as they climb in, and then Everett lifts his arm, hailing one for us. The yellow car whips in and out of the passing traffic, coming to a sudden halt next to the curb. Everett opens the door, and I slide in. He follows me, and I give the driver my address.

Leaning against him, I try to relax on the short drive, already dreaming about the warm bath I'm going to take once the Christmas celebrations are over.

"Having a good Christmas?" the cab driver asks when we're a few blocks away from my building.

"Maybe the best ever," I say, nestling against Everett. "You?"

She pulls the cab to the curb and flips around. Everett's breath catches next to me, as we both spot her pink strands poking out from beneath her winter hat.

"It's been absolutely magical," she beams, winking one of her violet eyes in our direction. "Merry Christmas, you two."

"Merry Christmas," I say, and both Everett and I move from the car, hand-in-hand. We join my family, who's waiting at the bottom of my steps, and my whole body warms at the thought that the people I love the most are all together on my favorite day of the year—absolutely magical indeed.

Epilogue
Claire

One Year Later - Early December

The snow falls all around us as Everett and I maze down the street with our goldendoodle, Mac, exploring West Village together. The store window displays are decorated for Christmas, and the neighborhood is busy with people coming and going. Their hands are full of shopping bags, and everyone, but us, seems to be in a hurry.

"Mom and Dad said they are excited to see you perform," he says as we move around a couple of tourists staring at their phones in the middle of the sidewalk.

"I'm really excited they get to come this year," I say, squeezing his hand. "I think it's going to be a lot of fun to have everyone together."

"I think so too. They mentioned dinner with your family to celebrate our engagement since everyone will be in town."

"Like a mini engagement party?"

"Yeah."

"That sounds perfect."

My heart expands in my chest, and happiness settles over me. The past year with Everett has been pure magic. Everything in life feels more settled with him by my side, and while I have everything I could ever want with him, Mac, and our families, I still find myself missing the people we left behind in Sugarplum Park.

"I'm really happy I get to marry you again," I say, glancing in his direction.

"You have no idea, Sugar."

He bends down, placing a kiss on the top of my head at the same time someone bumps into my shoulder. Turning my head, I catch a flash of pink in my periphery, but when I look behind me, there's no one around.

"You okay?" he asks.

"Oh…yeah. I could've sworn I just saw…"

"Saw what?"

"Stella." I laugh.

Whipping his head around, his eyebrows raise. "Really? Where?"

"I think sometimes I want to see her, but I haven't since we got back. It was nothing, probably just my eyes playing tricks on me or something. I'm tired."

"Want to get some cof—"

"Mac!" I yell, tightening my grip as he jolts forward, straining on the leash and almost pulling me over. He continues to tug, causing me to lunge forward again and the leash to fly out of my hand.

"Fuck!" Everett shouts as we both break into a sprint to chase him.

"Mac! Stop, boy!" My heart rate climbs and the cold air burns my lungs as we zigzag around the holiday shoppers.

"Where the hell is he going?" Everett asks.

"You're guess is as good as mine."

We all weave in and out of the people passing by, none of them attempting to help us catch him despite our calls for help.

"This is why I wanted the rottweiler," Everett shouts, breathing heavy.

"Don't start. You love him," I say.

"Mac!" Everett yells, but he continues to move. "I tolerate him. Love is a very strong word."

I look over at him and roll my eyes.

"Says the man who was curled up on the couch with him last night watching *Home Alone*."

"Ha!"

"Fuck, where did he go?" I ask, my eyes shifting back in front of us, but I can't find Mac—just a large group of people. My stomach knots, and my heart pounds faster. If we lose this dog, I'll never forgive myself.

Shit! Shit! Shit!

"He was just up ahead," Everett says, his voice sounding a little more panicked as his eyes scan the street.

The crowd parts, and we both stop and exhale. Sitting outside the door of a shop a few feet away, unbothered, is Mac. His tongue hangs out of his mouth as he pants, and his tail is wagging like he didn't just make us run after him.

"We should've known this dog was going to be a problem when we were seventh in line to adopt him, and we still got him." Everett laughs as we walk up to where Mac sits.

Bending down, I ruffle the white curls on top of his head and grab his leash. "You're such a troublemaker."

He paws at my coat and licks my face.

"Ahhh, Mac. Not my mouth," I say, wiping the sleeve of my jacket across my face and standing.

"Umm…Claire."

"Yeah?"

I look over to find Everett peering up at the sign hanging above the shop. It's orange and *The Book Rack* is written in a whimsical font.

My mouth parts, and I blink reading the sign a few more times.

It couldn't be. Could it?

"That was the name of…"

"Ginger's store," I finish. "But, that doesn't make sense." I shake my head, and my calming pulse starts to rise again.

The building is painted orange, and large windows are painted with a mural of a candy-colored town covered in snow. A flower arch with multi-color blooms frames the door. It stands out among all of the neutral colored brick and stone. It's impossible to miss, yet we live just a few blocks away, and I've never seen it before.

Well, I've never seen it *here* before.

"Should we go inside?" Everett asks.

"We have the dog."

"It says animals are welcome." He points to a small sign hanging in the window.

"I don't know. Do you think she's in there…Ginger?"

"There's only one way to find out." He shrugs, and the corner of his mouth tips up.

"Okay."

I nod, and he pulls open the door.

"Welcome in," a voice says once we're fully inside, causing us both to turn. Behind the counter is a woman who looks just like Ginger. Full figure. Red curls. Freckles. They could be twins.

"Hello," Everett says.

"Come in. Come in," she encourages, walking over to where we stand by the front door. "Today is our grand opening, so we have some refreshments in the back of the store, and everything is twenty-five percent off for Christmas."

I glance at Everett and then around the shop. It's a carbon copy of The Book Rack from Sugarplum Park, but instead of being there, it's here.

Mac jumps up and licks the woman's face. "I'm sorry," I say, pulling him off of her. "He's still learning his manners. Mac, sit," I grit out.

He obeys, and his tongue falls back out of his mouth.

"Oh, I don't mind," she says, scratching his ears. "I'm Ginger, by the way. Do you two live in the neighborhood?"

Ginger.

My eyes cut up to Everett, and my stomach bottoms out.

"We do," he says. "I'm Everett. This is my fiancée, Claire, and our dog, Mac."

"It's so nice to meet you. Please check out the refreshments and make yourselves at home." She walks away, and we make our way around the store. It's semi-busy, and I look at each person we pass expecting to see Stella, but no one has pink hair or violet eyes.

"Holy fuck," Everett whispers as we continue to explore.

"Do you think that means the others are…"

We both freeze as we arrive at the back where the refreshments are set up.

"You're Everett Nuttall!" a man who looks just like Chip exclaims.

My head whips toward Everett. He's standing there stunned, and my eyes widen. How does he know who Everett is? Could Ginger not know who we are, but Chip does? Why would that happen?

"You…you know who I am?" Everett stammers.

"Yeah, you're an assistant coach for the Crowns, right? I'm a huge fan."

Oh.

"Oh, right." Everett chuckles, grabbing a piece of peppermint bark off the table in front of Chip and taking a bite. Mac moves toward the chocolate, but I grab him by the collar, holding him back.

"Hey, honey," Chip calls. "Get over here. There's someone I want you to meet."

Turning my head to where he's looking, I see Lolly and Cami walking up to where we all stand. A wide grin is spread across both of their faces. The urge to hug them overcomes me, and I have to force myself to keep my feet planted on the ground.

Reaching out, Everett must sense the way I'm feeling because he grabs my hand and squeezes it gently, instantly helping me to relax.

"This is my girlfriend, Lolly, and our friend, Cami. This is Everett Nuttall and…" He looks at me.

"Claire. I'm Claire. His fiancée." I let go of Everett and put my hand out in her direction.

"It's nice to meet you," Lolly adds, shaking my hand and then turning toward Everett to do the same, but his hands and mouth are now full of the peppermint bark.

"Oh, sorry," he says over a bite of the candy, fumbling to try to empty one of his hands.

"Quite alright." She laughs. "How do you know Chip?"

"We don't," Chip explains. "Everett coaches for the Crowns and used to play for them too."

"That's cool," she says. "Chip's a huge hockey fan."

Mac jumps up on Cami and wags his tail.

"Mac!" I tug the leash, pulling him down. "Sorry."

"Oh, don't worry about it. You're just a big softie. Aren't you," Cami says, scratching between his ears.

"The peppermint bark is delicious," Everett notes. "Is it a family recipe?"

"My grandfather's," Chip boasts. "The real show stopper is Joe's hot chocolate." He gestures over to another table where a man stands from the floor.

"Sorry, I was looking for my stash of marshmallows," he says, offering us both a warm smile. "Cami, do you know where we put them?"

"Hmmm? Should be in the plastic bin under the table." She walks past us and begins to search.

"Care to try some?" Joe asks.

"Thank you," I say, grabbing a cup.

"Found them," Cami says, standing. "Joe, I swear you need to get glasses. They were right on top." She looks toward me. "Sorry about that. Would you like some marshmallows?"

"Um…sure." I hand her back the cup, and she tops it with a few.

My eyes scan the four people in front of us.

Chip. Lolly. Joe. Cami.

They all seemed unfazed by seeing us. It's a strange feeling knowing who they are and them not knowing who we are. It doesn't make sense, but nonetheless my heart expands at the thought that we might actually have a chance to have them back in our life. That they actually exist.

"Can we get you something else?" Lolly asks, tilting her head to the side.

"Oh…um, no. It's all delicious."

"Should we keep shopping?" Everett asks, nodding away from where they stand.

"Yeah. Let's."

He grabs another piece of candy, and we continue to snake through the aisles, leaving the four of them behind.

"Do you think it's really them," I whisper when we are out of their earshot.

He shrugs. "It looks like them, and they all have the same names."

"But how are they all here?" I keep my voice hushed as we step behind a shelf. Mac lays down at my feet with a loud thump. My heart aches for the friends I once knew, and my brain swirls, trying to come up with a way to befriend them that's not completely creepy and weird.

"I don't know. You did say you thought you saw—"

"You don't think?"

"You two good over here?" Ginger says, popping around the corner and causing Mac and me to jump. "Can I help you find something?"

"Actually, we're out looking for our nieces' Christmas gifts," Everett says.

No, we aren't. We finished shopping for them last week.

"Oh yes, but you're in the wrong section." She begins to walk back to the front of the store, and I cut my eyes at Everett, who shrugs as we follow after her.

What is he up to?

"How old are they?" she asks when we get to the children's section.

"Seven and five," he says.

"Anything in this section should do the trick," she says. "And then on that shelf over there"—she points—"are some easier chapter books the seven-year-old may enjoy."

The bell above the door chimes, and she moves away to greet the incoming customers.

"What are you doing?" I ask.

"I don't know. I figured we should probably support her store, and maybe if we're loyal customers we'll get to see everyone more often." He shrugs.

"And then what?"

"Not sure."

"Excuse me," a voice says behind us, causing us to flip around. Standing before us is Aster.

"Hi," I say, not fully believing who is standing a couple feet from me.

She smiles warmly. "Hi, I'm Aster."

"Claire. And this is my Everett...I mean, this is Everett, my fiancé."

"It's nice to meet you both. I'm starting a monthly bookclub," she says, reaching out her hand with the small flyer she's holding. "Lolly and Cami, who are in the back passing out the refreshments, are both a part of it, and Ginger, the owner of the store, of course. We'd love for you to join if you like to read."

My mouth parts, and my eyes blink as I stand there, unmoving. She gestures her hand again.

"She loves to read," Everett says, nudging me with his elbow. "Right, babe?"

"Oh...yeah," I say, taking the flyer from her outstretched hand.

"Amazing," she chimes. "Our first meeting will be in January, and we're reading *A New Leaf* by Samm Wilde. It was my pick, but if you join you can bring suggestions for the next one. Anyway, all the information is on the flyer."

"Okay. Yeah, I should be able to make it."

"Good. See you around," she says, smiling as she moves away from us and over to another woman around our age perusing the game shelves.

"See ya." Pressure begins to build behind my eyes, and I do my best to swallow down the emotions flooding my brain.

"Well, would you look at that?" Everett smirks as his eyes find mine. "Wait, what's wrong?"

"I just didn't think we'd ever see them again, and I've been trying to rack my brain since we walked in on how I could befriend any of them and it not be weird, and then she just appeared with a book club, and I don't know…it feels a little too good to be true."

He chuckles and pulls me into a hug. "Don't overthink it. I have a feeling this is a good thing. Maybe you did see Stella, and this is her engagement gift to us."

I smile. "Does that mean we have to invite her to the wedding?"

His whole chest moves as he laughs. "I hope not. The last thing we need is her meeting Andi."

"Oh, my god. Could you imagine? She'd have a hey day."

He presses his lips to the top of my head, and I take a deep breath.

"I love you," I say.

"I love you too, Sugar."

"So, now that there is a book club, do you still want to get the girls a gift?"

"Of course I do. I was thinking they each need at least three more."

Pulling away, I watch as he begins to search the shelves for more presents for my soon-to-be nieces. I don't think I'll ever tire of him wanting to spoil those two little girls who mean so much to both of us.

His hazel eyes find mine. "You two coming?" he asks.

I nod and smile, joining him near one of the shelves. Mac falls to the floor at our feet, and my whole body relaxes as his arm wraps around my back, and I settle against him.

It's amazing how wonderful life can be when you give into the magic and find someone who feels like home. Someone who knocks you off your feet when you least expect it. Someone who likes the things you like simply because you like them. Someone who would go to the depths of every realm just to be with you.

And being loved by Everett, and loving him, feels like all of those things. It's warm and all encompassing and wonderful. And how lucky am I to have found this kind of love—with the help of a little magic.

ACKNOWLEDGMENTS

To my readers new and old: thank you for reading *A Dance Of Sugarplums And Power Plays.* I think I say this with every book, but I will never get over you choosing to pick up something I wrote. It means so much to me, and I couldn't do this without you.

To my husband, I will love you in every realm and every world. Thank you for your unwavering support! You're the best booth babe, cheerleader, and rock I could've asked for!

To my children, never settle for people who dim your light. You both shine so bright, and I hope you always remember that.

Kalie, four books. FOUR! Thank you for pushing me to keep going and for believing in me. Your friendship is everything to me, and I truly could not do this author thing or life without you.

Kim, thank you for making the cover of my dreams. It's beautiful!

Tina, thank you for putting up with me and always easing my fears. Thank you for adding commas where I forgot them and rereading the parts I wasn't sure about. I feel so fortunate to have you on my team.

Andrea, thank you for reading every version of this book and for giving me your honest feedback. Your support means so much to me. I feel so lucky to have you on my team!

My wonderful beta team, thank you for taking the time out of your busy schedules to read this book and give me feedback. You all were so patient and flexible with me, and I really appreciate it.

Mr. Wilde, thank you for all of your hockey wisdom! I'm so pucking thankful for you and all the time you spent helping me. You're the real MVP!

Samm and Jordana, thank you for never dimming my light. In a world where it's hard to find your people, I'm so glad I found you two!

About the Author

Jess Christine is a speech therapist turned contemporary romance author who writes cotton candy smut: sweet, fluffy, and utterly irresistible. With low angst and high swoon, Jess crafts stories that feel like the perfect indulgence. Readers will quickly be lost in the warmth of unforgettable characters, light-hearted humor, delicious spice, and feel-good romance.

Jess resides in Georgia with her husband and two children. When she's not writing, she enjoys binge-watching her favorite TV shows, spending time with her friends and family, and getting lost in love stories.

If you would like to stay in the know about Jess' upcoming books, join her reader group: The Cotton Candy Collective, or subscribe to her newsletter at https://jesschristine.substack.com/subscribe

Also By Jess Christine

Romance Rehab Series

When You Left Me Speechless - Poppy and Logan's Story

When You Had Me Adapting - Lacey and Jace's Story

When You Rec'd My Plans - Wren and Tanner's Story

Book 4 - Coming 2026

Fairytale Season Series

A Dance of Sugarplums and Power Plays- A Nutcracker Retelling